CW01551401

MADNESS & MAYHEM

HELLCREST HEIGHTS BOOK TWO

USA TODAY BESTSELLING AUTHOR

A.R. BRECK

No part of this book may be reproduced in any form or by any electronic or mechanical means, including information storage and retrieval systems, without permission in writing from the publisher, except by reviewers, who may quote brief passages in a review. The characters and events in this book are fictitious. Any similarity to real persons, living or dead, is coincidental and not intended by the author.

Copyright © 2023 by A.R. Breck. All rights reserved.
Cover design by Pretty Little Design Co
Editing by Rumi Khan
Formatting by AJ Wolf Graphics

Madness & Mayhem contains mature themes that might make some readers uncomfortable. Foul language, criminal activity, drug use, explicit scenes, and various kinks are included in this book. People with triggers should read with caution.

PLAYLIST

After Dark Mr.Kitty
Dark Beach by Pastel Ghost
Deceptacon bu Le Tigre
Call Me by Blondie
Atomic by Blondie
Psycho Killer by Talking Heads
Rhiannon by Fleetwood Mac
Gallowdance by Lebanon Hanover
Girls on Film by Duran Duran
Little Dark Age by MGMT
Final Girl by Electric Youth
I See Red by Everybody Loves an Outlaw
There Will Be Blood by Kim Petras
Tag, You're It by Melanie Martinez
Polly by Gem Club
Mat Hatter by Melanie Martinez
Dedicated To The One I Love by The Mamas & The Papas
Always Forever by Cults
Mr. Sandman by The Chordettes
Wires by The Neighourhood
Daddy Issues The Neighbourhood
Guys My Age by Hey Violet
Freak by Sub Urban, REI AMI
Sociopath by StayLoose, Bryce Fox
Heaven by Julia Michaels
Crazy in Love by Sofia Karlberg
Pillowtalk by Zayn
Sweater Weather by The Neighbourhood
Do I Wanna Know? by Arctic Monkeys
I don't think I love you anymore by Alaina Castillo
Like That by Bea Miller
Formula by Labrinth
Bang by AJR
Darkside by Neoni
Smells Like Teen Spirit by Nirvana

Should I Stay or Should I Go by The Clash
Holding Out for a Hero by Nothing but Thieves
Survivor by 2WEI
Stand by Me by Mona
You Are My Sunshine by Jamey Johnson, Twiggy Ramirez
One Way or Another by Until The Ribbon Breaks
I Want You to Want Me by Children of Paradise, Chantal Claret
Every Breath You Take by Chase Holfelder
Love is a Battlefield by Wrongchilde, White Sea
Be My Baby by Snow Hills
Survivor by Tim Halperin
Umbrella by J2, JVZEL
Bang Bang by 2Cellos, Sky Ferreira
Wrecking Ball by Walk Off the Earth
Creep by Radiohead
Happy Together by Spin
Paint It, Black by Ciara
California Dreamin' by Sia
What a Wonderful World by Joseph William Morgan, Shadow Royale
I Want You to Want Me by Chase Holfelder
Under Pressure by Chase Holfelder
I Will Always Love You by Chase Holfelder
In the Air Tonight by Kelly Sweet
Tainted Love by Hannah Peel
Don't Stand so Close to Me by Denmark and Winter
Sweet Dreams by Emily Browning
Creep by Ember Island
What is Love by Kiesza
Love You Like a Love Song by Cats on Trees
I Wanna Dance With Somebody by Scott Matthew
I Will Survive by J2, Blu Holliday

Everybody Wants to Rule the World by Lorde

CHAPTER ONE

LAKYN

Tears flow endlessly down my cheeks, cooling as they kiss the night air. They create a river through my makeup, clinging to my skin as they race toward the edge of my chin. My jaw grinds, and the tears wobble back and forth before plummeting toward my wrist.

I can feel the splash as each drop rolls down my palm and the handle of the knife clutched in my grip. My fingers squeeze tightly, and I watch as my tears mix with blood as they slide down the blade, soaking into the bloody wound against the man in front of me.

The slasher.

My lover.

My enemy.

Blood seeps between the blade and my palm, and I choke out a sob as it sinks in a little deeper.

My masked man chokes, letting out a groan as he curls over slightly.

"Please," he wheezes.

Screams ensue around us, and all I can hear is, "*Police, police, police.*"

He looks up at me, his brow furrowed, dark, sharp shadows cutting down his face, becoming pale as every drop of blood flows from his body.

"You have to let me go, or there won't be a tomorrow for us."

My heart leaps in my chest, and I let out a hiccup as more tears fall.

I never want to see you again.

I blink.

I can't live without you.

"Please, Lakyn," he pleads, his voice a pained groan that rips from his chest.

I can hear the blood squish between my fingers, and on a gasp, I pull the knife free, my fingers coated in warm, thick blood. A sob rips from my chest as the knife drops from my fingers, falling to the rocky sand beneath me.

His breaths are labored as he hunches forward, his hand pressed firmly against his wound. He looks as if he's barely able to stand, so much pain ripping through his body his eyes are slits, his lips cracked and bleeding, a sheen of red covering them.

He's going to die.

Panic rolls through me, and I can't find the words to explain. Pain, regret, anger, betrayal… it all runs through my blood at a rapid pace and I can't find it in me to let out anything besides a tortured whimper.

He looks up at me, his eyes blank, though I can see the emotion that's deep inside, all the way at the bottom, buried beneath all the death.

Love.

So much love.

He steps up to me, and I can feel the blood on his shirt smear across my costume. His body falls into me, and I can barely hold him up as his lips press against mine. The taste of his blood is powerful against my lips. His free hand lifts, and he buries it into my hair, his fingers curling around the strands as he pulls my head to the side.

Dragging his fingers up my head, his fingers swirl through the messy strands of my hair.

"You can hide from the world, Lakyn, but you'll never be able to hide from me," he whispers, his fingers sliding over my chin. "We're the same. Your madness is the same as mine. Don't hide, because I'll be back, and we'll create the most beautiful mayhem."

My chest shakes as I inhale, confused at his words, at the cryptic message that spills from his lips in the face of death. Nothing makes sense, though he's the only thing I can focus on. The pain is too great, as if I have my own knife plunged into my gut.

I want him to leave. I never want to let him go.

My mind, heart, and soul are torn, yet he chooses for me, giving me one sad, pained look before he slides his own mask over his face, straightening his body the best he can before running off.

The moment he's in the woods, people flood out, surrounding me, screaming and shouting at my best friend, who has drowned in a pool of his own blood.

Some random girl looks at me. "What happened to him?" she screams. "*What did you do?*" Tears flow down her cheeks, as if she has a close relationship to him or something.

Like they mean anything to each other.

As if their hearts have been connected for years.

My chest blooms with anger, until my ribs feel as if they're shredding apart, opening and allowing the torment and pain of my best friend's death to seep inside.

"Shut the fuck up!" I snarl, feeling like a rabid dog as spit flies from my mouth. "Get the fuck away from him."

"You murdered him, didn't you?" another girl asks, fear in her tone. Her mouth twists in horror. "You killed your own friend, just liked you killed everyone else in this town!" She points at me as everyone floods around her, like some fucked-up, cultish clan. "Murderer!"

"Murderer!"

"*Murderer!*"

People start chanting it, staring at me in hatred and fear, as if I'm a witch on her way to the gallows.

"Murderer!" a girl screeches, throwing her red cup at me. Dark liquid flies through the air, splashing across the front of my dress.

My anger rises, building in my veins until my skin throbs with rage.

I'm not the murderer.

I could never kill my best friend.

Tears spring to my eyes, my fingers burrowing into my palms, my nails piercing the skin. Blood covers blood, until it drips from my palms. I'm covered in it, tainted with it.

Mine.

Creeds.

His.

An angry sob breaks free, and I swipe my palm against my face, no doubt covering my skin with a swipe of blood.

"You're going to jail for this one, you fucking psycho. I hope you rot in prison! Creed was a good guy! How could you fucking do this?" The girl who threw her drink at me sobs and makes a disgusting noise in the back of her throat, and spits. A warm, thick glob of saliva lands on my collarbone, dripping down slowly beneath the dress.

She knows nothing about Creed. How *dare* she say a fucking word about him.

I step forward, and everyone freezes as my body snaps, my fist swinging back before shooting forward, my fist landing straight into the girl's face. Her head swings back, and I can feel the bones of her nose break underneath my knuckles.

A gush of blood flies through the air, the droplets thick and, in slow motion, they land on the people standing nearby, fear rolling through their faces as they think me, *the slasher*, is going to take her next victim, right in front of everyone.

They're fucking fools, because I'm worse than he could ever be. He's calculated, planned, and purposeful.

I'm wild, untamed, and short-tempered.

The masked man will plan his attack, and I'll attack before they even take a breath.

I chuck my shoulder into her side as everyone starts screaming, and the girl falls to the ground in a heap of limbs. I'm covered in blood, spit, and liquor. I don't care about my costume or my appearance anymore.

The only thing I'm out for is revenge. I want to dole the pain I'm feeling inside myself out on anyone who I can reach. This girl, this fucking slut of a being, pours her drink on me, spits on me, and thinks I'd kill my own fucking best friend.

My fists can't stop, and I feel like the monster that's always lived in my soul finally breaks free, heartbreak, death, destruction, and every painful emotion I'm feeling ripping through me like a wave I can't swim against, and I allow the tide to take me. To overcome me. To swallow me until I'm no longer myself but the beast everyone makes me out to be.

The girl below me tries to fight back, attempting to get me in any way she can, but I'm too far gone, my anger too high, and I can do nothing but continue to pin her against the sand, my bloody, cracked knuckles dripping across her pale skin.

She stops fighting.

She stops moving.

And *I. Can't. Stop.*

My head tilts toward the starry sky, darkness above me, darkness inside me, and I inhale the tangy scent of blood and death as it fills the air around me.

A scream rips through my throat the same moment I'm lifted off of the girl. Strong arms wrap around my waist, and I'm pulled away from the crowd. I arch my back, feeling possessed by death, a sob breaking from my chest as I see my best friend, my fucking *Creed,* lying face down in the sand.

Dead.

Dead.

Dead.

I scream rips from my throat, and I'm sure I look like a monster, a savage animal with blood and sweat across her face and body.

"Shut the fuck up, Lakyn. The police are here," Kyler growls, gripping me tightly.

My body locks up, my spine arched against his hard muscles, and that's when I hear it.

The sirens.

The ambulance.

Shit, it even sounds like a damn firetruck is here.

The groaning of a door opens, and my body grows limp with each step as Kyler's feet pound quickly through the empty lighthouse. It's smells like liquor and mistakes as he pulls me across the first level, through a door behind the stairs, which I realize is a small bathroom.

He slaps the light on and sets me roughly on the small counter. The cool tiles are a shock to the back of my thighs, my skin on fire, though quickly turning to ice in the room that feels like a damn morgue.

"What the fuck!" he roars in my face, his eyes red, cold, and tormented.

Glossy with tears.

My chest opens a new slew of pain to see the agony filling his face, and I can't help but reach forward, my fingers curling into the flesh of his chest. His pec twitches under my grip, and I want to bury into his warmth, though the look on his face has me shuddering in place. He's vibrating with an energy that could shake the world.

His heart pounds, erratic, thumping heavily against his suit coat.

"I didn't kill him," I croak, pain bleeding from my pores. A sob breaks from my chest, and I want to crawl on my hands and knees back there until I'm in front of Creed and I can weep for him.

Mourn for him.

Kyler growls, his fingers gripping my jaw so tightly, I'm sure I'll have bruises on my cheeks tomorrow. He tilts my gaze to his, and all I can do is breathe in the rage emanating from him.

"You didn't kill him, but you may have killed her. In front of everyone, Lakyn. I think you just committed murderer in front of over a hundred fucking people!" he roars, his fist flying out. I flinch, afraid of Kyler for the first time ever.

But he's not coming for me.

The glass behind me shatters, loud, noisy shards cracking like a spiderweb and falling into the sink behind me. They fall over my shoulder, scraping against my bare shoulders.

"I'm sorry," I weep, sobs racking my spine. I feel broken, lost, unsure where to turn or who I can even turn to.

Everyone thinks I murdered my best friend.

I was just exiled from the one place I call home.

Hellcrest Heights is no longer a place I feel safe in.

"You should be fucking sorry, Lakyn." Kyler narrows his eyes, his gaze traveling from the top of my hair, down my rumpled dress, to my thighs, which have cuts on them, slices against my skin with dried blood. His palm flattens over my thighs, his fingers clenching, squeezing my blemished skin.

There's no way to cover them, no excuse up my sleeve.

I've made my bed. There's no hiding from this.

"Who the fuck is he? Who the fuck is he, and what the fuck did he do?" he growls, his fingers pinching my skin. "I swear to fucking God, if you lie to me again, you'll regret it, Lakyn."

I stare at him a moment, my heart pounding in my chest as I stare into his ruthless eyes. I can't lie to him. I can't keep this secret anymore. It's destroying us.

My lips pop open, my tongue sticking to the roof of my mouth as I get ready to tell him everything.

Since the beginning.

"Where is she? *Where the fuck is she*!"

The voice.

Chills run up my spine, and my eyes widen, my hand moving backward in an attempt to shimmy myself away from the door. Provide more distance, more of a barrier between us.

Because I'm terrified of the wrath I'm bound to encounter.

"Where the fuck did she go!"

He's close.

He's so fucking close.

The door suddenly flies open, banging against the wall directly next to Kyler.

Archer stands there, pale, the skull painted on his face half wiped from his skin. He looks haunted as he stares at me, his eyes a bit lost, but there's also a rage there.

An absolute fury, and it's directed *at me.*

He says nothing as he stands in the doorway, his chest heaving, his eyes spitting fire that could burn me alive.

"Archer," I whimper. I readjust my shaky hand, losing my grip and slipping into the bowl sink. A shard of glass mirror cuts into my palm, but I barely notice among all the other cuts and wounds covering my hands.

He shakes his head at me as he storms up to me, getting right in my face. "What the fuck happened, Lakyn?"

I exhale a shaky breath, bringing my hands forward. I wipe them against my bare knees, smearing more blood across my skin.

"I… I…" I don't know what to say, or where he wants me to start, or even what he intends for me to confess.

He steps into the bathroom, kicking the door shut behind him. Raising his hand, he points toward the door. "You realize there's police out there right now, right? Picking up the body of my best friend. Have you seen V? She's fucking hysterical, Lakyn," he growls.

I glare up at him with watery, angered eyes, squeezing the blood between my fingers. "I didn't kill him, Archer. Is that what you're fucking accusing me of?"

His eyes narrow. "I know you didn't kill Creed, Lakyn."

His unspoken words are loud, painfully clear.

His head tilts to the side slowly. "Where's Reign?"

I swallow, dread pooling in the pit of my stomach.

Tears slip past my cheeks, and I let out a groaning sob as I glance up at him.

He's gone.

I stabbed him.

He might be dead.

I love him.

I hate him for what he's done.

Reign is him.

My masked man.

A sob breaks free, and both Kyler and Archer step up to me, their arms wrapping around me as they hold me closely.

"What the fuck did you do, Lakyn?" Archer groans, his voice thick with emotion.

I shake my head against his chest. Leaning back, I can barely stand to look him in the eyes. "Reign is gone," I whisper quietly.

Archer freezes against me, his fingers tightening slowly before peeling away from me, finger by finger.

He leans back, staring at me blankly, as if everyone is coming to realization, bit by bit.

I can feel the dread soak me like a downpour, chilling me until goosebumps break across my flesh.

This is the moment.

The moment of truth, and I'm not ready for it.

Slowly, Archer's eyes narrow, until he's glaring at me with hatred.

He straightens, taking a step back until his spine hits the door. He looks angry, hateful as he glares at me. Taking a deep, shaky breath, he exhales, though his body never loosens.

He's *so* angry.

"Reign is the fucking slasher, isn't he?" Archer's voice is *lethal.*

I lick at my lips, not ready to admit the truth, but knowing I can't lie anymore.

"He killed those people? He killed your fucking father, and you didn't say anything?" he roars.

My eyes widen. "I didn't know! I didn't—" A sob works its way through my chest. "I had no idea," I whisper. "Not until tonight…" My voice breaks off at the end, withering away in my chest. A match that loses its flame.

"Fucking son of a bitch!" Kyler roars as his hand slaps the wall right next to my face. I flinch, tears and snot rolling down my face as my body trembles with a sob.

Archer steps up to me, a growl ripping between his teeth as he grips my hair. He pulls me off the counter. I can feel the threads of my hair pop from my scalp, and I let out a yelp as I grab his arm for leverage, stumbling after him.

"Archer," I cry out.

He growls, slamming me against the door. His fingers span across my neck, his jaw clenching as he rolls his knuckles down my body. I shiver as they slide past my ribs, into the dip of my waist, and around my hips. He stops at the hem of my dress, shoving it up slightly, revealing my multiple cuts and the blood stains on my thighs.

His eyes lift to mine, burning fiercely into me. My palms lay flush against the wooden door. "I'm sorry, Archer," I croak.

His upper lip curls, showing vicious, sharp teeth. "I don't even know who the fuck you are anymore, Lakyn."

Kyler nods, and it feels like an agreement.

I've broken it. I've broken everything to them.

His fist flies out, plowing through the door behind me. I listen as the shards of wood splinter beside me, falling across my body and to the ground at my feet. I let out a scream, curling my head forward and folding my arms around my neck.

"You're fucking lucky you're one of us. You're lucky you're *you*," he snarls. Grabbing onto my shoulder, he pulls me away from the door. Swinging what remains of it open, I shiver as I stare at the empty lighthouse.

Though it's not empty outside. I can hear the chaos. The screaming, the sirens, the people losing their absolute minds.

"I suggest you get out of here, baby Lake. Everyone saw you out there. There's only so much we can do to protect you in here," Archer says quietly, almost like it's a threat.

I swallow, my arms and legs and chest shaking in terror. I look up at my two friends, the people who mean so much to me growing smaller by the day. "What are you guys going to do?" I whisper.

He pushes me out the door, stepping out with me.

"We're going to try and clean up your fucking mess." He shakes his head at me. "I could kill you right now, Lakyn, but if you're going down, you're going down by our hands, not the hands of the fucking police," he growls, and my eyes widen in fear.

"Get the fuck out of here, Lakyn. Disappear for a while. It's for your own good," Kyler snaps, stepping out and stopping alongside Archer. They stare at me, a wall of their own, refusing to crack.

They are emotionless. They are brutal.

"Fucking go, Lakyn!" Archer snaps under his breath, and my gaze drops to my hands, covered in dried blood, bruised and swollen around my knuckles. I realize my body has gone numb, to the point I don't know whether I'm standing or floating.

Nothing feels real.

I spin on my feet, running toward the back door of the lighthouse. Police are setting up the yellow tape. The yellow tape that seems to be following my life lately. It's everywhere I look, and I'm unable to escape it.

CHAPTER TWO

REIGN

Fuck.

I let out a hiss between my teeth as I pull my hand away from my stomach, feeling the stickiness against my leather glove. The leather is warm against my skin, the overwhelming flood of blood seeping down my wrist.

"Ughhh," I groan, pressing my hand back against my stomach as I stumble through the woods. My entire stomach throbs, radiating through my arms and down my legs. Even my head pounds, and the need to fall to my knees and give up, let my body sink into the dirt or wash away in the ocean, only intensifies by the second..

I can't, though. I can't give up. One stab in the fucking stomach won't break me.

Though, the betrayal on Lakyn's face very well might.

My free hand flies out, and I wrap my fingers around the roughness of the bark of a tree, my nails digging into the sharp wood and as I pull myself forward, my feet stumble over a loose root.

"Fuck!" I roar at the top of my lungs.

I refuse to get caught. The police won't get me. I won't allow them to. They'll have to drag me through the woods and the dirt, across the pile of dead bodies I've created.

Everything I've ever done is for her, and what happened tonight won't stop me.

Even the aching in my gut of murdering my best friend. It was never supposed to happen. I never wanted him to fall from the window. I never wanted him to die. It was an accident, something that should've never transpired, though it did.

And I can't take it back.

I can't put air in his lungs. I can't make his heart beat.

What's done is done, and my best friend is dead.

I'll have to live with his death. I'll take the pain for what I've done.

Because it is all for her.

It started off because of her.

And now it's for her.

I love her.

And if I survive this shit, I'm going to tell her.

I growl, my hand shoving off the tree as I continue to stumble through the woods, the bark brushing against my gloved palm. Sweat drips down my back beneath my clothes, my body rinsing itself of my sins.

My mask is no longer on my face, but on top of my head. Breathing is now difficult, my lungs quenching in pain, and I need all the air I can get to make it through this.

Sticks break under my boot, stones rolling across the ground as I finally make it through the woods, the trees breaking and leaving me with a clearing. I gasp in a breath, looking at the small town over the hill, most everything closed this late at night, mostly with the curfew from all the murders.

Though a few remain open, and I stumble down the hill as Walgreens stays in my view. My legs grow tired, and I feel like I'm running on barely any fumes as I stumble into the parking lot, my feet dragging behind me.

I'm full of blood, and sweat, and the scent of sex remains, but I ignore it all as the automatic doors roll open, and I slip my mask over my face as I walk inside.

The lady sits behind the cash register, bent at the waist, her arms planted on the counter as she works on a sudoku book in front of her. She stands and barely glances at me as I quickly walk down the aisles.

"Can I help you with anything?" she shouts at my quickly retreating back.

"No," I bark, my eyes scanning the rows until I find the medical aisle. My hand falls onto the shelf, blood smearing on the gray metal. Cough medicine spills to the ground, and I kick it aside as a travel medical kit comes into view.

Perfect.

I let out a groan as I bend over, because of course that shit is on the bottom shelf.

I keep my hand to my stomach, feeling my skin scream beneath my clothes. My head whooshes, and I grow light-headed, my vision fading as my fingers grasp around the white-and-red kit. I'm losing too much blood. I need to fix this shit, fast.

With a sigh, I pull myself upright and grip the pack tightly as I drag myself down the aisle. My shoulder knocks against one of the shelves, and supplements scatter over my shoulders and rattle to the ground.

"Sir, are you all right?" a woman asks from the pharmacy.

I nod, not sparing her a glance as I make my way to the register. I head down the drink aisle, pausing a moment when I see the cases of beer.

I grab one, knowing it won't do much, but I need something. Something to dull the ache. Of both the wound and Lakyn's look.

Fucking devastating.

Once I get close enough to the register, the lady at the counter pushes herself upright, shoving her sudoku book aside and waiting for me to reach the register.

I watch as her eyebrows scrunch together, her body tensing slightly when she gets a good look at me.

And then she turns horrified, stepping back a second.

"What happened to you?" she asks, her eyes wide in fear.

I shake my head at her, slapping the small kit against the counter. "Don't worry about it. Ring me up," I order.

She stares at the bloody kit, then looks up at me, a lick of fear entering her gaze.

She doesn't move.

Fear enters her gaze, and she knows. *She knows.*

"You're the slasher, aren't you?" she asks quietly.

I lean forward, wishing I had my knife, but it's been left at the lighthouse. "Ring me up," I glance down at her name tag, my lips curling beneath my mask. "Sonya. Now."

She lets out a shaky breath as she reaches forward, grabbing the corner of the kit that is unstained. She pulls it across the clear glass, and the beep is like a gunshot between us.

"Uh, that'll be ten thirteen," she whispers.

I let out a wince, reaching back and pulling my wallet from my back pocket. The movement reveals some of the wound on my stomach, and she lets out a gasp as her eyes connect with my blood-stained clothes.

"Are you injured?" she whimpers.

I glare at her through the mask. "No questions."

She bites the inside of her cheek, and I pull out a twenty, slapping it on the counter. When I pull my fingers away, I can see the bloodstains covering the green paper. "Keep the change, Sonya, and don't say a word about my visit, yeah?"

She nods, pulling the bill toward her.

I give her a small nod, grabbing the kit and beer without a bag and stumbling through the automatic doors.

The cool, fresh air slaps across my face, and I stumble through the parking lot, just to the other side where there's a Motel 6. It looks nearly abandoned, with the empty lot, the unlit sign.

It's not abandoned, though, and it's exactly what I need.

Taking a deep breath, I pull the kit around my back, shoving it into the waistband of my pants and lowering my sweatshirt over it. I clench my jaw as I straighten the best I can, holding my breath as I pull the front door open.

The front desk is empty.

I stumble toward the counter, my feet dragging as my hand slaps down on the bell. I can hear a chair groan in the back room before a set of heavy feet slide across the carpet.

An old man comes into view, his white shirt stained with coffee stains and a little too stretched out around the neck.

"Can I help you?" he growls, too many cigars having burnt through his esophagus.

I nod, pulling my wallet back out, attempting to mask my wince without giving away my pain. "I'll take a room for the night."

He nods. "Got a preference?"

I shake my head. "Whatever."

He nods, slow as a fucking turtle as he turns around, his fingers brushing against all the keys for the rooms that are available. When he backtracks, I reach forward, my fingers curling around the counter. The pain is throbbing through my skull, and I grind my teeth together as he grabs the keys for room eleven.

"Here you go," he grunts, turning around and placing them on the counter. "It'll be sixty-seven fifty."

I grab eighty, tossing it onto the counter. "You can keep the change if you don't bother me until checkout tomorrow."

He stares at me a moment, as if he finally realizes a masked man is standing in front of him.

Yes, it's Halloween, but yet it's still a little unusual.

"You in trouble or something?" he grunts.

I stare at him blankly through my mask.

His eyes narrow. "Or are you causing the trouble?"

I sigh. "I can take my money elsewhere." I reach forward, ready to grab the money, when his hand slaps down on bills.

"No need. No one will be botherin' you until checkout. Which is at eleven tomorrow morning." He snorts, clearing the phlegm from his throat before audibly swallowing it.

My stomach lurches, and I hold back the bile.

I slip my gloved pinkie through the ring of the keys. "Wonderful."

He stays where he is, watching me, as I turn around and walk toward the door.

"Oh, and, room eleven?"

I don't turn around, though I stop, waiting for him to say whatever it is he'd like to say to me.

"I don't like trouble here at my motel. Keep it to yourself, yeah? I don't want any police here or anything."

"Noted," I grunt, before shoving my hands against the door. The case of beer knocks against the glass as the bell rings above my head.

I stumble out into the night, slipping my mask off my face as I hobble my way toward my room for the night.

The sound of tires rolling slowly through the parking lot has me turning toward Walgreens. My eyes widen a moment when I see a police car. The officer has his window down, his flashlight pointing throughout the dark lot.

Shit.

I shuffle back until my spine connects with room number five. My back goes flush with the door, and I hold my breath as the officer shines the light around the motel parking lot.

Fuck. Fucking fuck.

He pauses for a second, his light shining through one of the nearby windows.

My eyes fall closed, my veins working their hardest to pump whatever

17

blood remains through my body. I'm weak, I'm tired, and I'm in so much fucking pain.

Eventually, the car starts moving again, the light turning off as the police officer drives away.

I wait a moment, then continue shuffling toward my room. It feels like it takes forever, and by the time the rusted number eleven comes into view, my feet are no longer lifting off the ground, but dragging. My wound no longer hurts, though my entire body is ice cold, and I wonder how much blood I honestly have left in me.

With shaky fingers, I shove the key into the lock, turning it and knocking my shoulder against the sticky door. It budges after a few pushes, swinging open with a loud groan.

The scent of stale fries and old cigarettes permeate the room, and I don't even have the strength to wrinkle my nose as I walk inside. I close the door, locking the bolt and the chain before I stumble my way to the bed.

The beer drops to the mattress, and then I fall beside it, rolling to my side.

Thump, thump. Thump, thump.

My heart pounds heavily, the blood in my veins rushing through me at the adrenaline from the night.

Reaching behind me, I grab the kit from the back of my jeans, ripping the plastic off with my teeth. I tear into it, placing it onto the mattress beside me and opening it up.

I can't even get the strength to lift myself off the bed.

I unzip the package, my eyes landing on the antibiotics, gauze, needle and thread, Band-Aids, and wraps.

I flop onto my back, arching my back slightly as I pull my sweatshirt up to my chest.

I hiss out a breath as the raw air hits my skin, an almost burning sensation tearing through me. The fabric from my shirt attempts to stick to the open wound, and I rip it away with a painful groan.

My hand moves to the gauze pads, and I grab a few of them. Taking a deep breath, I press the gauze against my wound, letting out a groan as the open wound grazes against the rough material.

My head turns, and I pull on the cardboard from the case of beer, tearing it open and grabbing a can. It's room temperature, and will surely taste like shit, but anything is better than nothing at this point.

I push myself up until I'm sitting, my head spinning to the point my vision starts to darken.

I crack open the beer, bringing it to my lips and swallowing down the entire contents. It's warm as it rolls down my throat. Once empty, I crush the aluminum in my hands and drop it to the ground, letting out a belch as I turn my gaze back to the first aid kit.

Now or never, I guess.

I clean the wound quickly with the antibiotic ointment. Grabbing the wrap from the kit, I tear the plastic off and shove it between my teeth as I bite down and grab the needle and thread. The needle is long but thin, and I easily thread the thick stitching through the top hole, even with my shaky fingers.

With a deep breath, I glance down at my bloodied wound, now completely numb, though I'm sure I'll be able to feel the needle work its way through my skin.

I move, my fingers growing steady as I pierce the first layer of skin. I bite down on the wrap firmly, letting my teeth sink into the soft material as I pierce through fully, digging through the wound and out the other end.

A groan rips through my throat, my eyes watering as I pull the thread tightly, then move back to do it again.

I can't help the moisture that tracks down my cheeks as I let out another groan. The needle goes through, and blood oozes from my skin, tracking down my abdomen and soaking into the waistband of my briefs.

Fuck, this hurts.

I pull the thread again, until my skin pinches together. Saliva collects around the wrap, and my face is soaked in sweat and tears as I let out another groan, the needle going in once again, only for it to be pulled out the other end.

I continue doing this, until the wound is closed, and my hands are once again shaky. The wrap between my teeth is soaked in saliva, pooling from the corners of my mouth as the pain becomes overbearing. I pull the needle one more time, tightening the thread just as a ringing starts in my ears, and the edges of my vision grow cloudy.

And quickly, everything fades to black.

I gasp in a breath, shooting upright in bed.

Holy shit.

Pain rolls through me in tremendous waves, and I let out a groan as I look down, seeing the needle and thread dangling from my suture wound.

Fuck.

I knot it tightly and reaching over, I grab the scissors from the pack on the mattress and snip the needle off. I toss it into the kit and reach over, grabbing another beer.

Fuck my life.

Cracking it open, I take a sip, using all my strength to shove myself off the mattress. My legs feel slightly weak, but better than earlier. Walking to the window, I pull the heavy curtains aside, glancing out at the morning sun. It's barely risen over the horizon, and I've got to guess it's somewhere around five in the morning.

I drop the curtain, taking a sip of my beer as I hobble back toward the bed. Sitting down on the mattress, I scoot back until my spine hits the headboard. My body aches, all the way to my chest, and I know it goes deeper than just the physical pain.

The reality of what happened last night hits me.

I killed my friend.

Lakyn knows it's me.

A part of me wonders if I should just flee. Disappear like I did three years ago, so no one can find me. It was easier then, like I never existed. Or maybe I did, but I just hid well enough that no one could find me. I could do that again, easily, maybe even more so.

But I can't.

Because leaving Lakyn before was torture.

I won't leave her again. Even if she doesn't want me, or is repulsed by the fact that I've fucking killed people left and right, including her best friend and her father, I still won't let her go.

I can't, my soul won't fucking allow it.

She's the other half. The one half that we all wander around the world looking for. We don't live to go to school, or get a job, to get a college education.

That's not what we, as humans, are made for.

We're made to find our mate.

Lakyn Ashford is mine, and I won't let her go.

Even if I have to kill everyone around me to get to her.

I'll tear down everyone in Hellcrest Heights if I have to.

She'll hate me for killing Creed. Shit, a part of me hates myself for killing Creed. He's a part of us. Part of the crew. Creed was a good man, and his death was unneeded, but it happened anyway, and I can't restart his heart, no matter what I do.

I'll live with the consequences of Lakyn's wrath. I anticipate it. I'm waiting for it.

With a grunt, I roll over, grabbing the remote from the end table and turning on the TV. It switches on to the news, and I instantly swallow when I see the lighthouse in front of the camera.

And that dumb bitch newscaster.

"From Fox 7 News, this is Bridget Bofield, and I'm reporting here from Hellcrest Heights. Another death from a local resident of this sleepy town, and this time it has come on Halloween night. We all have to wonder, when will these brutal slayings end? Tonight's death comes from Creed Lennon. A local boy who was attending college here. His father is the secretary of state here in Maine, and we expect him to make a statement later this morning. As for now, police have barricaded off the area. The curfew is still in effect, and we suggest all residents stay in their homes until law enforcement can detain the serial killer."

My hand lifts, and I turn the TV off, tossing the remote against the wall. The plastic back breaks off the body, and they clamor to the ground noisily.

I take another sip of my beer before setting it on the nightstand, and I slouch down, my head hitting the pillow.

I need to talk to her. I need to explain, but it's impossible with the streets so hot right now. I need to let shit cool off, and when I do, I'll make things right.

With Lakyn, it'll happen.

I just doubt any of my other friends will ever forgive me.

If I'm being honest, I think they'll try to kill me.

I'll do whatever I have to do to get Lakyn back, even if it means more death to get to her. There isn't anything I wouldn't do.

CHAPTER THREE

LAKYN

My chin slips from my palm, and I jerk awake, gasping in a quick breath before I settle my chin back into my palm and glance beyond the tree line.

Where is he?

I can't let him die.

I don't know how long I've been sitting here. Long enough that the sun is now up, and what was impossible to see into the trees is now clear. It's no longer Halloween. Creed's body no longer lays at the bottom of the lighthouse. It's cleared now, only a red stain of blood painting the rocky sand.

I've long past left there, then gone back after some time.

Whether I'd hoped it had all been a dream, or maybe I was hoping Reign would have gone back there, looking for me.

Neither wish came true.

I'd unfortunately gone back to a depressing and sad lighthouse which has now been the home to multiple deaths. Footprints and blood and police tape litter the premises, along with broken Halloween decorations which make it end up looking like the aftermath of a horror movie.

I wanted it to be a lie. A nightmare I would wake up from. But it wasn't. Somehow, Halloween has become its own nightmare.

A place where only death rises and life falls.

I should hate him. I should fucking despise him for what he's done for me. And I do.

I don't regret putting the knife in his stomach.

He deserved the pain he caused me, our friends, and everyone around us. Out of all the people in our group, Creed was the most loyal, the most genuine and nicest person, yet he's the one that picks the shortest stick.

He never deserved his ending to be this way.

Though, where do I go now? What does life entail for the rest of my days? Do I walk away from my heart that beats in my chest, or do I take the pain and rub it into my veins, and allow myself true love, knowing the pain may always be existent?

There will always be pain in my heart when it comes to Reign.

But without him, it's agony.

They both hurt yet walking away from him seems impossible.

He should rot in jail, yet I'd take his place if I had the chance.

I don't understand his reasoning, and I deserve to understand. I want to know everything, yet as I stare into the woods, I wonder if my chance is gone, and all that's left is a trail of blood and a broken heart.

With a sigh, I turn my car off, leaving my Halloween mask on the passenger seat as I hop out of the car.

After running from the party, I made it home, where I got my car and left right away. I couldn't wait around for anyone or anything. I had to leave, the only thought in my mind finding the man who owns my heart. I've been hiding near the woods all night, hoping Reign found a place to hide out for the night, and he'd come stumbling out this morning, but no such luck. I haven't seen him anywhere, and panic is beginning to set in.

I'm cold, still bloody, and a part of me is waiting for the police to get here, to haul me in for murder.

I have no clue if that girl died, or if she's alive. I don't regret my actions. Not even a little bit. The only thing I wish I would've changed is me not having done it around a group of people.

Because now the finger is pointed at me, and I already had the red flag painted on my back.

Now the flag is black, and I'm essentially fucked.

I'll have to deal with this eventually, but my first course of action is to find Reign.

I step up to the woods, the air cold, my body shivering as I walk through the crisp, dry air. The trees have a glaze of dew on the tips of the green, and every so often, I listen as the squirrels and small critters race through the forest.

The beginnings of sunlight shine through the trees, bringing with it a shimmer through the forest. I glance around, hoping to see a dark body hiding in the shadows, though all I can see is dark green, orange, and red trees. The ground is littered with dried leaves, every step creating a crunch that fills the air.

If anyone were here, I'd be able to hear them.

My eyes follow the pathway of leaves, hoping to see a stirring, boot crunched leaves, or a trail of breadcrumbs for me to follow—anything, honestly.

Though, there is nothing.

Until there is.

I pause, the toe of my boot hitting a larger rock that knocks against my foot.

I hiss through my teeth, letting out a curse under my breath as I stare at the ground.

"Shit," I whisper, crouching down.

Reaching forward, I pick up a bright yellow leaf. Stained with a drop of blood right in the center, I bring it toward my face, my finger dropping right in the center.

It smears, turning a lighter pink as it spreads to the edges. I rub it between my fingers, and I can tell instantly.

I don't need to taste or smell it. It's Reign.

He was here.

I keep the leaf in my grip as I step forward, my eyes locked to the ground. *There.*

I bend down, grabbing another leaf, this one a dark orange. Though there is no mistaking the crimson blood painted on the tips of the leaf.

I keep going, picking up leaves along the way, until I'm at the other edge of the forest, my hands filled with a collection enough to build my own tree. Enough blood that it's concerning, and I know this isn't even all the blood he's lost.

He's lost a lot more than this.

I step out of the woods, glancing around at the busy end of town. In front of me is a small strip mall, filled with a Wendy's, a few stores, a Walgreens, and across the lot is a Motel 6. I head toward the back, wondering how many people are looking for me.

I wonder if my face is painted across the media just as the slasher's was.

Moving up the hill, I keep my gaze in the distance, watching for cars, the press, anyone that would get me running in the opposite direction.

Once I make it to the top of the hill, my eyes fall to the parking lot, and all I can see is a small dribble of blood which leads straight into Walgreens.

Which has a police car sitting in front of it.

Fuck.

I back up, stumbling slightly as I make my way back down the hill. I frown, my chest aching as I slide back into the woods.

I'm so close.

I can feel how close he is.

He's within reach, yet I can't get him.

Has he been caught? Or are the police following the trail just as I am?

Feeling mentally and physically depleted, and on barely any sleep, I walk back the way I came, letting leaf by leaf flutter from my arms.

I feel useless, like I can't do a thing.

Is he even alive?

Does he miss me?

Will he forgive me for putting a knife in his stomach?

My throat swells, and I clear it as tears spring to my eyes. I don't want him to hate me. I don't want to be at the end of his wrath.

I want him.

But I also hate him.

And I don't know if I can ever forgive him.

Yet I don't know if I can live without him.

With my heart and head torn, I walk back to my car, feeling like my head is tucked between my legs.

With no other options on what to do, I realize, it's time to go home.

Pulling up in front of my house, I know I'm about to deal with hell from the people closest to me.

My insides already clench with stress, and I'm worried about how they will react to me.

I wonder if they know who he is. Who it is that killed Creed.

With a deep breath, I turn off my car and slip out, making my way up our Halloween-decorated pathway, wishing Halloween would disappear altogether. This holiday has been ruined for life.

My foot presses against the wooden stair of the porch, and the moment the groan hits my ears of the aged wood, the front door swings open, and Posie stands there, looking angry, shocked, hurt, relieved.

All emotions. Every single one.

"Posie," I whisper, my voice raspy. I don't know when the last time was that I drank or ate. Too long.

She shakes her head at me, disappointment in her gaze.

"You should probably get inside. The town isn't too happy with you right now," she mumbles, stepping away from the door, giving me her back.

I grind my teeth as I make my way up the steps and head inside. Shutting the door, I wince when I hear it.

The sobs.

The gut-wrenching, painful sobs that echo through the house.

My brow furrows, and I glance over at Posie, who stares at me blankly. "She's been crying all night. Hasn't stopped once. We haven't slept at all, Lakyn."

I swallow, my jaw clenching as I stare up the stairs. "Maybe I should go talk to her."

She shakes her head. "Not a good idea. She doesn't want to talk to anyone. Eloise has barely been able to talk to her."

I nod, my nose burning as I toe off my shoes and head toward the kitchen.

Posie is silent as she follows behind me, not saying a word. I walk to the coffee maker, making myself a cup. I keep my eyes averted, though I can feel Posie's heavy gaze on me as I pour my cup.

My eyes raise, and I find her already staring at me.

"What?" I whisper.

She blinks. "How long have you known Reign was the masked man?"

I frown, shaking my head. "I didn't know. Not at all. Not until last night."

She doesn't look convinced. "And you have been sleeping with him? The masked man?"

I bite my lip. How the hell would she know?

She rolls her eyes. "I spoke to Archer and Kyler. They told me it's Reign." Her eyes drop to my thighs. "It doesn't take a genius to know what's been going on."

Shame hits me, and I can feel the heat creep up my skin, coloring my neck and cheeks. I don't know what to say, so I say nothing at all.

How did I not know the love of my life was the masked man? Have I been that oblivious?

"We've been scared of him, and you've been fucking him, Lakyn?" she asks quietly, though there's an edge to her voice that has my body stiffening.

Her face twists, anger growing ever so slowly. "We had to throw a body into the ocean because he brought one *into our house*." She takes a deep breath, exhaling heavily through her nose. "He *killed* your father, Lakyn," she growls.

My body tenses, and I grow cold, as if my body is being submerged, limb by limb, into the frigid ocean water.

Posie narrows her eyes at me. "We're supposed to be best friends, Lakyn," she whispers.

I step forward, ready to grab her, though she steps back, out of my reach.

"We are best friends, Posie. We've always been best friends. That's not going to change."

She huffs, shaking her head. "There's nothing you can say. This is some fucked-up shit." Her eyes drift toward the ceiling when Vienna lets out another gut-wrenching cry. "Your secrets ended with Creed dead, and your best friend mourning the love of her life."

I move around the corner, and Posie steps in my way, blocking my path. "No. There isn't anything you can say that'll make anything better. Stay away from Vienna, I'm serious."

My brows dip, and my lips pop open, hurt and a slight edge of irritation bubbles in my chest. I don't know whether to cry or scream.

They don't understand. None of them do.

I never wanted this.

I didn't search for the masked man. He sought me out. He stalked me. He kept me as his prey, and I couldn't fight it.

Because I've never been able to.

And I tried to kill the masked man. I did.

"She's right, Lakyn. Vienna wants nothing to do with you right now. Not after what you've done."

I glance toward the stairs, seeing Eloise there, in baggy sweats in a t-shirt, her hair a mess, her makeup still smeared from the night before. Her hand is on the railing of the stairway, and she grips it tightly, her body tense as she glares at me.

I grow angry, because my very best friends are painting me like I was the one that held the knife and slayed all those people. As if I'm the one who caused Creed to fall to his death.

I'm not at fault, though they make it feel like it is.

"I stabbed him, you know." I lift my hands, the stains of red still lingering against my skin. "I took his knife from him and turned it around, sinking it into his gut. Do you realize this? That I was going to kill him for Creed's death? Even after I found out it was him, there was a part of me that wanted to end his life. Because I love Creed." My eyes water, and I bat angrily at the tear that attempts to escape. "I loved him."

I listen as the sound of heavy feet pound down the stairs. Vienna turns the corner, looking horrible with her puffy, red face, her blonde hair a mass of tangles on top of her head. She is wearing Creed's clothes, and they flood her body as she makes her way toward me, hurt, vengeful.

She rushes me, and before I have a chance to react, she stands before me, her body trembling as her hand swings back, then forward, her palm connecting roughly against my cheek. I don't move, don't react as the rush of burning pain slips across my skin.

"You allowed your love to become more important than mine," she whispers. "He stuck up for you, Lakyn, even when he didn't need to, he had your back. Always. He didn't think you were sleeping around, even when everyone else did." She shakes her head, disappointment and rage in her gaze. "I guess he was wrong about you. We all were."

She turns away, getting ready to walk back to her room, her eyes filling with another set of tears. The moment her foot hits the first set of stairs, she turns back at me, her cheeks damp. "I get it, Lakyn. We're all fucked up. Our crew is sort of twisted. But you've crossed the line. You and Reign are on another level. You obviously belong together," she snaps, and I let her insult hit my chest and bounce off.

She's grieving.

Vienna is my best friend. Her words could hurt, but they don't. I won't allow them to. She can be cruel and petty, because if Reign died, I would feel the exact same. Revengeful on anyone who was involved.

"The wounds are raw right now, Lakyn. It's going to take time for them to heal. And even then, I'm almost certain they'll leave scars," Posie mumbles under her breath.

She follows after Vienna, and I'm left alone in the kitchen, feeling off-kilter, my heart slightly empty and a little raw, as if it's gotten carpet burn against the surface.

Reign is fucked up. I've always known he was. But I never would've guessed he was the masked man. The darkness has revealed itself, and my eyes have opened to see how depraved he really is.

Maybe both of us are fucked up. Maybe we do belong with each other.

Perhaps I'm so sick and twisted, the poison fills my blood.

If Reign is twisted, I want to be just as twisted as he is.

I want our knot to be so entwined, we'll never find our way apart.

My breathing comes out heavily. I can feel a panic attack coming, and I don't know how to stop it. With feet like lead, I start moving toward the front door, when it opens, and two men who look like they want to rip my head off stand in front of me.

"Lakyn," Archer sneers, looking so fucking betrayed.

My brow creases, and I take a step back. "Archer."

"Where the fuck do you think you're going?" Kyler asks, stepping through the doorway.

I glance over my shoulder, wondering if I can make a run for it. I can't deal with any more of their wrath.

"Ah, ah, ah," Archer tsks. "Don't for a second think you're leaving this house."

I glance over at Eloise, who's gripping her phone in her hand. "You called them here?"

She shrugs. "My loyalty has always been with you, Lakyn. But at this fucking moment, it lies with them. They wanted to know when you showed up, and here you are."

I bare my teeth at her. Turning my gaze to Archer, I growl, "I'm leaving."

He shakes his head, taking a step toward me. "Where're you going to go? The entire town is looking for you, Lakyn."

My heart double thumps in my chest, and I wonder how the fuck I'm ever going to get out of this alive. I can feel my phone inside my bra, but I know it's been dead for hours.

Does my mom know what's happened?

"You can't go looking for him, Lakyn. Let him die." Kyler steps toward me, and I take another step back, knocking into the table behind me. A glass pumpkin rattles on top of the table, and I reach back, righting it.

"I can't leave him out there to die or get caught. We need to help him. We've always fucking stuck up for each other, and I'm not stopping now."

"He fucking betrayed us!" Archer roars, his hand flying in the air. He points at me, his finger tense, looking lethal as it juts in front of my face. "We stick up for one another when we're against others. He betrayed all of us. He killed one of us! *Fuck him,*" he seethes.

Tears spring to my eyes, and I feel nothing but my insides clawing into shreds. "I'm not giving up on him," I gasp, pain ripping through me. "I'll never give up on him."

"You're fucking stupid then," Kyler snaps, taking one more step until he's toe to toe with me. His hand reaches out, and he brushes his fingers along my lower lip. "He'll never be with you again, Lakyn. Hopefully he's dead. Hopefully you drained him of his blood," he rasps, an evil smile taking over his face.

I bring my hand out, shoving my palms against his chest. He barely budges, barely moves an inch. "I hate you." I glance at them, everyone who looks at me in pity, in fucking anger. "I hate all of you right now. I don't even know who you are anymore. He is one of us! It was a fucking accident."

"He lost that fucking right when he killed Creed. When he tried to kill *me!*" Eloise snaps.

I shove myself past Kyler. Archer snaps forward, grabbing me around the chest. Kyler grabs my waist, lifting me in the air by my thighs. I kick and thrash, desperate to get free, but their grip is tight as they walk toward the stairs.

"Where the fuck are you taking me?" I scream.

"You're going to go do some reckless-ass shit and get yourself in trouble. You're blind right now, but we're not going to let you ruin your life. Go the fuck to sleep, because you look like shit," Archer growls as they carry me up the stairs.

"I'm not going to sleep!" I scream, arching backward. It doesn't do a thing, they only hold me tighter.

"You're going to sleep, because you aren't leaving your room. You aren't going anywhere besides your bed."

They make it to the top of the stairs, turning right down the hall and into my room. Their hands release around me, and I tumble to my mattress in a heap of limbs.

Archer points at me. "You aren't leaving this room, Lakyn. So don't even fucking try it," he snaps, his eyes narrowed in rage. He's about to leave, when he turns around at the last moment, walking up to the bed. He leans down, his fingers curling in the back of my hair, pulling my head up toward his. My forehead knocks against his, and he grips my hair tightly, until I feel a pinch of pain. "The only way you're leaving me is death, Lakyn. Remember that. Remember who the fuck it is you belong to."

He presses his lips roughly against mine, so briefly I have no time to react, before he shoves me against the bed. "All of us. Every single fucking one of us."

Kyler grips my fingers, turning my hand over and glancing at the blood, at my bruised knuckles.

"You've always been wild, Lakyn, but I'm starting to wonder how deep the madness runs."

He gives me a look before he spins around, walking out of the room, closing the door behind him.

And I lay there, wondering how I will ever survive this.

How any of us will survive this.

CHAPTER FOUR

REIGN

With one more glance, I see the coast is clear, and I dart across the street, toward the house I know where my baby Lake lay. Is she asleep, in pain, or is she awake, waiting? *For me?*

Archer's car is out front, and for all I know, they're all waiting for me, weapons in hand and ready to wield them at my throat. I wouldn't be surprised. Actually, I expect it.

I can't stop, though. I can't not reach for her, search the world left and right until I find her.

My side aches as I walk around the house, and my hand goes to my blood-stained shirt, the stitches beneath haphazard and painful.

Only after another day and into the night have I gained the power to leave the motel. When the cops stopped scoping the area and I felt safe enough to stumble out. I know they're searching for me, their eyes scanning the faces of everyone in town as they look for mine.

They will never find me. Not even one of them.

Making my way to the side of the house, my hand reaches up, my stitches stretching as I grab the lowest branch. I pull myself up, gritting my teeth in pain as my entire being clenches in agony. My leg swings over the thick branch, and I grip it with my hands as I bend over, hissing through my teeth. My strength isn't there. I've lost too much blood in the last few days and need rest to gain my strength.

I don't have time, though. I'm on borrowed time before the police close in on me. But before they do, I need Lakyn.

My Lakyn. My dark Lakyn, who may deny it, but she's become just as dark as I am.

The energy around her drips with an energy that matches mine. It's why we are so good, yet so bad for each other. We may create chaos, but it's a fucking magnificent chaos.

I can see it in the way she walks, the way she carries herself. Long gone is the girl who was aloof to the world.

Three years ago, Lakyn walked around without noticing anyone. I noticed them. How the guys wanted her. How the girls envied her. How there wasn't a person she would walk past without them giving her a double take, with wonder in their eyes and jealousy twisting their lips.

She had a confidence about her. She didn't care about her family's wealth or the fact that she herself dressed like she belonged at a fucking rock concert half her life. She was uncaring, but still effortlessly beautiful.

It was the confidence and the way she didn't give a shit about anyone around her which drew everyone in. It's what drew me in.

Though, when she came home last month, there was an awareness in the way she watched everyone. As if her eyes were finally opened to the world around her. Maybe it was Zane's death that woke her up. Maybe it was the way her freedom hung in the balance, and she had to earn the trust of those around her.

She came home, and she still didn't care what people thought, though I could see the open wound being picked every time someone called her a murderer. She pretended it wasn't a direct hit to the pain, but it was. She was becoming human.

It's what made my love for her turn into an obsession. And I'd never let her go.

After a deep breath, I pull myself up, climbing up the next two branches until I'm hanging over the second-story window, staring straight into Lakyn's bedroom.

She's so fucking beautiful.

She lies on her mattress, her knees pressed into her chest as she is curled up in a small ball. Her hands lay in a prayer stance below her cheek, her eyes settled closed as if she's at peace. Though, I know better. The line between her brows gives away her stress. Her messy hair, sprawled across her pillow.

She's a mess, and it's all because of me.

I can see the pain in her face, the misery. I can't imagine what she's going through. The wrath she must have endured from her friends. Archer the most. Though if I'm correct, Posie's hurts the worst. Posie has always been her ride or die, but Posie is also one of the most genuine-hearted people I've ever met.

It's because of me that Lakyn feels this pain.

But there was a purpose in my madness.

I'm not Archer with his slight unhingeness, or Kyler with his charming darkness, or Creed with his wholesome allure when he's a fucking savage beneath it all.

I'm Reign Whitmore, and I've always been insane. When I was a child, when I was a teenager, and now more than ever, as an adult.

My father sent me away with a purpose, and I willingly went to save the girl I loved.

And I came back because I love her, and because I hated her.

I wanted her blood on my hands.

Though the moment I saw her, every emotion I've ever had came roaring to the surface, and not only did I want to draw her blood, but I wanted to hold her heart in my hand and watch it beat. I wanted to protect it and ravage it at the same time.

I wanted to destroy her and watch her flourish, and I couldn't decide which trumped the other.

So I drew it out, toying with her, playing with her mind and watching her fray at the edges.

And as I watch her now, I wonder what it is I plan to do with her.

Do I want to hurt her or do I want to save her?

Possibly, a little of both.

I contemplate leaving, but as I watch the woman I can't be without looking so peaceful and unsettled in the same breath, I can't do anything besides reach forward, my fingers pushing her window up. I swing my leg through, slipping into her bedroom as quietly as possible.

With my mask firmly settled over my face, I step forward, keeping my feet light on the loose boards which I know will groan under my feet. There's only so much time I can be in here until Archer checks on her. I know him, he won't wait long. Someone will always be checking on her, and I know what I have to do. What I hope she agrees to.

I want her with me. Always. And it can never be in Hellcrest Heights.

She needs to come with me, and we need to get as far away from here as possible.

Another step forward, and the floor creaks. Lakyn's eyes snap open, though she doesn't see me. Only the shadow in the corner of her room.

I watch as the fear enters her gaze, a cloudiness that is as heavy as a rainy day. Her body snaps ramrod straight, and she rolls over, crab-walking across the mattress as she attempts to get away from me.

I step toward the bed, and she only grows more fearful.

Leaping forward, I grab her around the ankles, pinning her down as I come into view.

"Lakyn," I rasp. "It's me."

Fear, betrayal, anger, and most of all, love shines through her gaze.

Tears spring to her eyes, and her body loosens as she leans forward. I let go of her ankles and she rolls over, getting to her knees and crawling over to me. Her hands go to my biceps, and she grips me tightly.

"You're alive," she whispers, heartbreak in her tone as her nails dig through my sweatshirt and into my skin. My skin shudders as pain rolls through me.

My finger goes up to her mouth, and I brush ever so slightly against her lower lip. "I'm here. With you."

Her eyes crinkle as pain sinks in, and I know I'm the cause for it.

"Where have you been?" she asks, her eyes dropping to my abdomen.

I brush my hand over the fabric, careful to not press too firmly. "Stitching myself up." Anger fills me, though I can't tell whether it's at her or myself.

"I tried to kill you," she says simply.

Her fingers move to where she stabbed me, and I grab her wrist, pushing her until her back hits the mattress. She fights against me for a moment, but I'm stronger, holding her down as I press my knee on the bed, climbing on top of her.

Her breathing picks up, until she's heaving beneath me. "Please," she whispers, her voice echoing between the trees.

I smirk, reaching out, the tips of my fingers brushing against the fluttering fabric of her sweatshirt.

"Please what, baby Lake? Take what I want? Give you life? Give you death? Take you away from here? Which would you like first, because I will be delivering all of them," I growl, my fingers curling into her shirt. I can hear the threads break from my stretching. She lets out a squeal, and my other arm swings out, curling around her waist. My muscles stretch, and a growl releases from my throat as I pull her against me, her front grinding against my wound.

I sink into the mattress, and our limbs become tangled with each other's. Our bodies collide as we sink into her mattress, and I press into her with a possessiveness, an aggressiveness as I give her a taste of how angry I am.

The skin on my stomach stretches, and I can feel the stitches of my wound pull taut. It's an ache that makes me feel like I'm tearing in two. Her breath whooshes out of her as I grab her wrists, hauling them above her head.

She stares at me with wide eyes, tears slipping past her temples and falling to the mattress. Her chest quakes with each breath, and I move my knees up on either side of her waist, pinning her to her bed.

Her brow furrows and she looks down, her eyes going wide after a moment. "You're bleeding!" she hisses, panic in her voice.

I glance down, seeing the bottom of my shirt soaked in red, a damp circle growing larger by the moment. It starts to drip, too much blood pulling in the fabric.

I reach down, pulling the fabric up, seeing a stitch pulled, torn in the middle. The wound is swollen, red around the edges. Blood seeps between the stitches, dripping down and falling on top of Lakyn's stomach. I reach down, pulling her shirt up, hissing through my teeth as I watch my dark, crimson blood paint her creamy stomach. It quivers when the drops fall to it, tensing lightly as they roll toward her belly button.

"You bleed for me," I grunt, bringing my hand down to her thighs, where I know cuts I've sliced across her skin lay, and then drag it up, to her blood-covered stomach, smearing it into her skin. "I bleed for you."

She whimpers, using her free hand and bringing it down to my cut, hovering below it. A drop of blood falls to her fingertip, and she brings it up, drawing it down my mask. "I thought you were dead," she whispers.

I shove her shirt up, my blood smearing with it. I don't have gloves on. Masking my fingerprints is no longer needed, not unless I take another life.

Which I plan to, but at this moment, it's all about Lakyn.

Her shirt goes up, bunching under her breasts. Her skin ripples with goosebumps, though she remains motionless, watching me with scared eyes.

"You killed Creed," she whispers, hurt weakening her voice. My eyes fall to the side, but not before her face twists in anger. She reaches up, her nails digging into the skin on my neck as she pulls my face toward hers. "You killed your best friend, the least you can do is fucking look at me."

I growl, smooshing my hand into her bloody stomach. Bringing it up, I drag my hand down her face, covering her skin in blood. She lets out a gasp, and I glare down at her.

"You were there, Lakyn," I breathe, pain growing by the moment. I need to fix my stitches, even though the bleeding has slowed. My throat aches with the need for a drink, wishing I could dull the pain that I know will become unbearable soon. "You fucking saw what happened. Don't for one moment think I did it on purpose."

She stares at me, her face covered in red. "You could've stopped it," she snaps.

I snarl, my fingers wrapping around her neck. I pull her up, her back sliding against her sheets, until her back is flush with her headboard. "I tried to fucking stop it." I lean forward, until my nose brushes hers, my upper lip curled back, my teeth bared. "I tried."

She brings her hand to her stomach, wiping away the thick blood there. Bringing her hand up, she pushes on my mask, wiping the blood down the side. "Sometimes trying isn't good enough," she mumbles, her voice detached.

My eyes flare in rage. "You stabbed me!" I quietly lash out. I shove myself up, pulling my shirt up and showing off the irritated wound, begging for fucking ice and TLC. "It would've hurt less if you picked my heart from my chest with your bare fingers. Right?"

Her eyes cloud, shutting down, blink by blink. "I didn't know it was you."

A nasty snarl covers my face. "Right, you thought it was the fucking killer you were fucking behind my back."

Her face pales, and she goes to push me off, but I pin her harder, wanting to smother her into the mattress. Wanting to suffocate her for lying to me. For cheating on me.

Even if she really wasn't, as she didn't have a clue it still feels like a betrayal in some way.

"That's right, baby Lake. What would've happened if I wasn't… me?" I growl in her ear. "I'm almost offended you didn't realize who I was, but that was the entire point. You never touched me. You never got close enough to smell me, or feel me. The only thing that touched you was my gloved fingers and me fucking you into oblivion. You never knew it was me, and it's a fucking knife to the gut, Lakyn."

She lifts her head, her lips painted red. "I always knew… I always… felt something was there."

I smirk, though it's deadly, and I swear if I wasn't in love with this girl, I'd gut her right here. Stab her just as she stabbed me.

"You had no idea who I was. Don't play pretend and try to fool yourself. You were being fucked by a stranger and enjoyed every fucking second of the mystery." I lean closer, seething, angry, every bit of emotion coming out of me. "You were doing all this behind my back. What the fuck, Lakyn?" I growl under my breath.

She squeezes her eyes shut, arching her head back and looking up at the ceiling. She blinks, tears leaking from the corners of her eyes. "I knew it was you."

I open my mouth, ready to interject, but she slaps her palm against my lips.

"Wait. Just… listen."

I grab her wrist, pulling it above her head, holding her steady while she stares at me.

"I knew it was you, Reign. Even if I had no idea, I knew it was the love of my life behind that mask. In the darkest part of my heart, I knew it was you, even if my mind didn't connect the two."

I grind my teeth, wondering how it's possible, not believing it, but wishing I did.

"You didn't fucking know," I snap.

She shakes her head, more tears leaking free, tracking through the bloody marks on her skin. I hate the tears. Reaching forward, I grab onto her jaw, pulling her head to the side. Leaning down, my lips caress her ear.

"You're lucky it was me behind the mask, because if it wasn't, it would've been you flying through that fucking window," I growl, smirking as I feel her shiver.

She reaches forward, grabbing onto my arms, and it's too much, the feel of her, her anger, her relief.

Lakyn is too much.

Leaning off her, I grab her by the hips, flipping her over until her stomach slams against the mattress. She lets out an *oomph*, and I climb back onto her, grabbing onto her hair and pulling it aside.

"How much damage have we caused, baby Lake? What have our actions done to this tiny town? To our own friends?"

She trembles beneath me. "I did nothing. You killed people. Why, Reign? Why are you the slasher?"

She attempts to turn her head and watch me over her shoulder, though I keep hold of her hair, keeping her facing forward.

"It has *everything* to do with you, Lakyn," I growl, growing angry. She's the reason I'm here in the first place, though she has no idea why the real reason is.

She whimpers. "What do I have to do with any of this?"

I laugh, reaching down, pulling at her sweats. They easily slide over her hips and down her legs. I chuck them aside, letting them fall to the floor. Her bruised skin comes into view. The cuts on her inner thighs. She's a beautiful work of art, one I have carved myself. She's been sculpted by my hands, scarred by my soul, and I will mark her skin every day for the rest of my life, paint her with my name so everyone knows who it is she needs. Who she craves.

"Reign, tell me. I deserve to know." She wiggles underneath me, and I know she's desperate to get free. She wants to get all the answers, and I'll give her everything she needs to know. Because it's time. It's time she understands the truth, but first, I take what I want. Because that's exactly what Lakyn does.

My fingers slip between her creamy thighs, the softness brushing across my skin. I press my fingers into the smooth skin, pushing them apart, until she's spread beneath me on her silky sheets, her skin littered in goosebumps but hot to the touch.

Hot from me. For me.

I slip my fingers between her folds, instantly connecting with dripping skin. I clench my jaw, staring at her glistening sex as she shines in the moonlight that slips through her window. Her scent fills the air, toxic, consuming.

That's it, baby Lake, let that pussy drip for me.

She moans, reaching forward, her fingers strangling the fabric of her sheets. She needs something to hold on to, but I want to watch her weep. I want to see her suffer as I tear her apart just as she's done to me.

I want her to feel just as desperate as she made me feel last night.

"Once you're dripping on my wrist, I'll slide my cock between your thighs. You love when the masked man fucks you, don't you? You enjoy being consumed by a murderer, with blood on his hands and a black soul." I growl, tapping on my mask that's stained in blood, marked with scars of its own. "Though just so you know, I'm going to be much more vicious than he could ever be."

She shivers. "What are you going to do to me?"

"I'll show you," I murmur, hissing through my teeth as the burning hits my stomach. It doesn't feel like it's bleeding any longer, at least not consistently. Though the pain is still there, and every movement brings a stretching to my skin which causes excruciating pain.

She mumbles under her breath, and I slip my fingers deep into her pussy, curling them slightly. "What was that, baby Lake?" I murmur.

She turns her face away mine, her eyes full of raw pain and a hint of pleasure. "I said they'll never fucking forgive me," she groans.

I smirk. "Probably not." And it's the truth. One of us is gone. Dead, and it's because of me.

Because of us.

Because I'll forever protect Lakyn, and if that means I need to take the lives of all our friends, I'd do it without blinking an eye.

A silent sob racks her spine, and I bring my fingers to her waist, curling them around her hip. "Don't be sad, baby. You'll always have me."

"I can't be without them. They're my best friends," she moans quietly, tearing out of my hold. She spins around, getting onto her knees as she faces me. Her knees dig into the mattress, pressing against mine. "How could you so easily throw them away?"

I narrow my eyes, bringing my fingers forward and threading them behind her ear. I pull her head toward mine, "You think it feels good to lose my closest friends? I imagine it would feel just the same as a *knife to the gut*." I chuckle, and she shivers in my arms. "Though, I would throw away the world if it meant I was able to keep you," I growl against her cheek.

She whimpers, and I grab onto her hands, pulling them up until she grips her headboard. "Hold on tightly, baby Lake. I'm done talking now."

I shove her shirt up, until it's bunched around her upper ribs, and I watch as a ripple rolls down her spine. I span my fingers around her waist, lining her up against mine.

Her fingernails press against the wooden headboard, the pink flesh turning white a moment before it flushes a dark red.

"Are you mad at me?" she whispers as she holds on tightly.

Squatting down behind her, I inhale deeply, able to smell her fear, her arousal, as is permeates the air. I hum under my breath as I stare at her glistening folds. "Yes, Lakyn, if your heart didn't belong to me, I think I'd have bled you out by now."

My tongue darts out, and I swipe it between her folds, tasting the sweetness of her pussy. She is delicious. Delectable. I dive in more, dipping my tongue deep into her sex, feeling the walls of her pussy clenching around the muscle of my tongue. I swirl my tongue into her, fucking her gently until she lets out a moan, her body tensing around me. I swipe my tongue up, the tip flicking against her clit. It's swollen, pulsing against my tongue, and I let out a moan, flattening my tongue and flicking once, twice, three times.

She lets out a moan, pushing her body toward my mouth. With a shaky breath, she whispers, "Do you want to kill me? Hurt me?" Her words are fearful, terrified.

I smirk. She wants to play this game.

Dragging my hands up her back, I dance the tips of my fingers over her shoulder blades, along the curve of her slender neck, and across her jaw. I pinch her chin a moment, until she lets out a small whimper in pain.

"Yes, baby. I want to hurt you very much. So much so I can feel the tremble in my wrists as I hold myself back from tearing you apart."

Suddenly, it's as if a fire lights underneath her. She tears out of my hold, spinning around until we're face to face. She gets close, so I can see her damp, twisted lips, her burning eyes, her pink cheeks.

"You have no right to be angry with me. You lied to me, you played games with me. You pretended to be someone you weren't." Her eyes grow watery. "Every time I feel like I can get over it, the image of Creed dead on the ground comes back to me. The sound of Vienna crying." She wipes her tears viciously, until all I can focus on is her constant flow of tears that roll down her cheeks. "You killed my father. You tried to kill Eloise."

I open my mouth, ready to tear her apart for the accusation, but she's right.

I *was* going to kill Eloise.

That was in the beginning, when my plan was to kill everyone.

Leaning forward, my fingers curl around her shoulder, and I hold her in place. The tension grows between us, until it's crackling. Anger, viciousness, death popping through the air.

We're angry. We're vengeful.

We've both been wrong. We've both been right. Neither of us want to feel pain but want to give each other it all.

Yet I want to protect her, and I can tell underneath it all, she wants to protect me.

We just don't know how to protect one another without hurting each other in the process.

I push her down, my fingertips bruising her skin. She fights against me, but I fight harder, agony ripping through me as we fall to the mattress. We grapple with each other, both of us squeezing, clawing, ripping at each other's clothes until we're naked, our chests heaving as we stare at one another.

"I hate you sometimes," she whines, tears tracking down her cheeks.

"I hate you, too," I whisper against her lips. My fingers curl under her thighs, and I pull her leg around my hip. She clenches me tight with her thighs. I can feel a trickle of blood seep from the wound, dripping to Lakyn's stomach. She tremors, and I breathe heavily, my eyes slits above her. "But I love you more," I rasp.

Her face scrunches. "Do you really love me, or do you just enjoy the hunt?"

I cup her face, lining the tip of my cock up between her legs, ready to demolish the girl I love to hate, and hate to love. "More than anything in the world, I enjoy hunting the girl I love."

Thrusting forward, I watch as she arches her back, her eyes widening in a mix of pleasure and pain. My wound begins dripping again, wetting her dried red skin, repainting it a dark crimson.

"I love you, Reign, and I fucking hate you so much right now," she whimpers.

I grab onto her wrists, lacing my fingers with hers as I press them against the bed. I get up on my knees, thrusting into her roughly, listening as the bed creaks gently beneath us. The air in the room grows heavy, crackling as if the atmosphere can feel the wild energy we create.

It's love; it's madness.

It's a fucking mayhem that we can't control, but we thrive in it, because it's meant to be.

We're meant to be, no matter how wrong we are together, we're meant to be.

She lets out a moan, her face softening as pleasure takes over, her neck arched, her face painted red. She looks savage, a fucking beautiful wild animal as she revels in the inhibited pleasure she feels.

I grind my hips, circling them as I stare at the slender column of her throat. My marks are there, though they're faint, faded, her creamy skin healing around them.

I slip my mask up slightly as I lean forward, my lips sinking into the dip of her neck. My lips press against the smooth skin, and I curl them, sinking my teeth into the soft flesh, my teeth sinking deep, until I can feel the skin break, her warm blood flowing around my lips.

She lets out a loud moan, echoing through the room, and I pull back as I slide my mask down, watching as a drop of blood sinks down her neck, into the dip of her collarbone.

I speed up my thrusts, watching her creamy and red skin shake with each thrust, listening as her moans pick up volume, until she's screaming, crying out softly, her chest humming against mine.

"Yes, Lakyn, cry for me. I want the tears that track down your cheeks. I want the blood that pumps in your heart. I want to hold your fragile bones in my hands. I will never let you slip between my fingers. You are mine, Lakyn, and you should let the world know it."

I lick my lips, tasting her blood, loving the sweetness as it covers my tongue.

"Fuck me, Reign. Fuck me hard."

I dig my fingers into her wrists, bruising them, straining the bones from the pressure of my grip.

Bending down, my eyes flare as her nipples harden, peaking against the raw air. I shove my mask up from my face and drop my mouth to her chest, securing my lips around them as I suck her nipple into my mouth. Lifting my mouth, I move to the top of her breast, sinking my teeth down.

Bite.

I move my mouth slightly.

Bite.

And again.

Bite.

I continue moving, until her chest is covered in my teeth marks, in her blood, and her body trembles violently in my arms.

I can feel my cock grow inside her as I thrust harder, moving so aggressively our skin slaps. I move us forward slightly, until she's sitting up, her back against her headboard.

Her spine relaxes as I move inside her, and I smirk, watching her flushed cheeks. I drop my hands to her waist, gripping her tightly, embedding my fingertips into her skin as I move.

We both sit up, her legs wrapped around my waist, and I grip her around her hips tightly as I start moving.

I fuck her wildly.

Madly.

Viciously.

She lets out a scream, her eyes clouding with lust as I ravage her, tear her to pieces and put her back together.

We move as one, our bodies connected, our souls, our fucking hearts, a collision. Her eyes are indistinguishable, though she reaches forward, her hand curling around the fabric of my shirt, directly over my heart, and she squeezes, pulling me forward.

"I fucking love you, Reign," she moans, and the walls of her pussy clench around my cock, gripping me tightly. She comes, her entire body electrifying, melting into my grip, I hold her tightly, pulling her close as my own orgasm follows, and I empty myself, my cock twitching against the walls of her pussy.

"Fuck," I grit between my teeth.

She leans forward, crumbling to bits against me as I hold her tightly, coming down from my own high.

"Shit," she groans. She slouches in my arms, and I hold her tightly as I slide down, until we're both laying on her bed, our breathing heavy, our skin damp with sweat.

I'm so wrapped in Lakyn I don't realize her bedroom door has opened.

A shadow comes behind me, and I glance over my shoulder, seeing Archer and Kyler standing there, absolute rage on their faces.

"I knew you'd show up eventually," Archer growls.

Shit.

CHAPTER FIVE

LAKYN

O h, no.

Reign flies off of me so quickly I wouldn't be able to grab for him if I tried. He ends up in the corner of the room, tearing his clothes on with a blank look on his face, his mask lifted to the top of his head.

Kyler sneers. "This a kink for you, Lakyn? Fucking him with his mask on?" he lashes, his eyes narrowed. "And you got blood on your face? What the fuck are you doing!" he roars.

I wince, watching as Reign's body stiffens.

He stands up straight, his pants on, his wound vibrant and swollen against his rippling stomach. His jaw clenches. "Don't fucking talk to her like that, Kyler," he growls. Reaching up, he takes his mask off, dropping it to the ground. "I don't want to kill anyone, but I'll do it for her."

Archer glares over at me, at my naked body. I lift the sheets to cover myself, but the anger is already there. It's so present. "Do you want to be here when I kill him, or do you want to go downstairs? I'll leave it up to you, though you don't deserve the fucking option."

My eyes narrow, and I grab for my hoodie, pulling it over my head.

Embarrassed as his eyes track over the hundred bite marks and the blood that trickles along my skin. "You're not fucking killing anyone, Archer. Quit trying to sound like a fucking hard-ass."

He laughs, his hand going behind his back. When his hand comes forward, he has a knife in his grip.

My body goes cold. My limbs turn to ice. My breath leaves my lungs and I'm left choking for air.

"What the fuck are you doing?" I choke, climbing off the bed toward him. I grab my sweats, pulling them over my hips as I step toward him, my hand raised. "Give me the fucking knife," I snap once I gain my bearings.

He points it toward me, and my eyes widen a second. "Lakyn, back the fuck up." His eyes narrow, and he looks so betrayed. "How can you fuck him? He killed Creed!" he roars in my face.

"He didn't!" I scream, glancing at Kyler. "You guys have to believe us. Reign never meant to kill Creed!"

I can hear the sobs of Vienna start up in the distance, and my heart twists in my chest.

"Fuck this shit," Kyler snaps, stepping around Archer with quick steps and making his way to Reign. Reign is instantly on guard, moving out of the way as Kyler swings at him. Kyler's fast, though, his other fist coming out and knocking Reign right in his jaw.

Reign is barely affected, his own fist swinging out and knocking into Kyler's nose.

Archer steps forward, his knife poised and ready to strike.

I react quickly, leaping onto Archer's back and pulling him away. He attempts to shake me off, but I hold on tightly. We become a mess of swinging limbs, grunts, and shouts as we all wrestle in the room.

"Get off me, Lakyn!" Archer shouts.

"Give me the knife!" I scream.

Archer's hand swings out, and the tip of the blade cuts into Reign's neck. Barely a scrape, but the knife is sharp, and I watch as a beat of blood forms, dripping beneath his sweatshirt.

I see red.

Leaning forward, I sink my teeth into Archer's neck. He lets out a howl as he stumbles back, and all I can feel is the flood of blood as it flows into my mouth. The taste is sharp, and I let it flow around my lips and drip down my chin as I tear my face back, knowing I look absolutely mad right now.

"I'll fucking kill you," Reign growls, stepping toward Archer. He moves toward me, and Archer and him lock into a stare-off that could shatter the world.

"Don't hurt him, Reign! You don't want to hurt him!" I scream.

He sneers, dodging out of the way as Archer shoots his knife forward. "He's hurting you. I'll fucking kill all of them," he clips.

"Stop! Stop!" The voice comes from the doorway, and we turn around at once, our chests heaving as we stare at Posie.

She stands in the doorway, shock and fear in her eyes. "The police just pulled up outside. I think—"

Knock, knock, knock.

Dread sinks into me, my limbs snapping straight as I slide down Archer's body. He lets me, his knife clattering to the ground.

"Fuck," Reign snaps under his breath.

I take a step toward him, my eyes wide. "It'll be fine. They might not even know we're here."

He levels me a blank look. "They know we're here, Lakyn. They have to know we're here."

Archer moves toward the door as another set of knocks sound. Panic fills me quickly, and I can't help the shout that slips past my lips. "Archer!" I whisper-shout.

He stops in the doorway, turning around and glancing at me over his shoulder.

"Please. Please don't say we're here."

His jaw clenches, and his eyes glance to Kyler a moment before he grips the doorframe, giving it a slap before walking off and down the stairs.

"This shit is so fucked up," Kyler whispers as he makes his way out of my bedroom.

Posie stands there, in the hallway, staring at me. Her gaze is a little empty, hurt, betrayed. Worried, for sure. Every emotion I can think of runs through her eyes.

"Posie," I whisper.

She shakes her head instantly, cutting my words off. "Don't say anything right now, Lakyn. It all just… *hurts*."

I open my mouth, but not a word comes out besides a weak breath. I stare at her as she walks up to the door, her hand going to the knob. "Just stay here for a second. Don't… do anything stupid," she mumbles before shutting the door quietly.

I turn to Reign, and he stares at the closed door, his jaw clenched, his body corded tight.

"Reign," I whisper, panic filling me.

He shakes his head as his eyes swing to mine. He says nothing, his jaw clenching. I watch the million thoughts roll through his mind, the different scenarios and options.

I shake my head when I see his gaze go dark. "No, let's go. Let's get the hell out of here."

He takes a deep breath as he turns to the window before backing up quickly. "They're outside, Lakyn. We aren't going anywhere."

I bite at my lip, a whimper seeping out as I sneak to the window. Peeking outside, my eyes widen when I see a police officer walking along the side of the house, one of his flashlights scanning the perimeter of the yard.

"We're fucked," I panic, my palm pressing against my chest. My heart pounds erratically against the hollow cage of my chest. I want to scream, but I swallow it down, my ears thumping, sweat glistening the back of my hairline.

A shadow steps in front of me. Reign grips my jaw, tilting my face toward his. He doesn't look panicked, but instead calm as ever. His eyes are sure, his features smooth if not a little angry as he gazes at me.

"We're going to get through this, Lakyn. I won't let either of us go down," he rasps.

The door suddenly swings open, and both of us jolt as we turn toward the doorway.

Fear lances through me as I stare at Archer, wondering if a horde of SWAT is going to come up behind him.

He nods toward my window. "Kyler's got them preoccupied for a minute. Go out the window."

My brow furrows, and I turn to Reign, seeing his face equally as shocked.

"What?" I whisper.

His eyes narrow. "Don't fucking ask any questions, Lakyn. Get out of here before I change my mind."

I swallow over the emotion, feeling Reign's warm fingers as they wrap through mine. He grips me tightly as he pulls me toward the window. My hand snaps out, and I grab my phone, pulling it along with the charger. The cord snaps loose from the cube, and I tear the cord out of my phone, tossing it aside as I'm hauled to my window.

"We have to go, Lakyn. Now."

I nod, my eyes still locked on Archer's.

"Now, Lakyn," Reign growls.

I bite my lip through my whimper as I make my way toward the window.

"Lakyn," Archer snaps.

I listen as the window slides open softly, my eyes connecting with Archer's possessive ones.

"I'm doing this for you, baby Lake. Not him. Remember that."

My eyes blur with unshed tears, and it feels painful as Reign nearly lifts me off the ground and carries me out of the window.

He climbs into the tree, and I watch as Archer comes to the window. He shuts it, giving me one last look before he turns away from the window and out of my bedroom.

A bedroom I'm not sure I'll ever be going back to.

A silent sob rips through my chest, and I clutch my neck as Reign's weak body shakes as he pulls me down the tree.

"I need you to be very quiet for me, Lakyn. Not a fucking sound," he whispers. All I can see are the police lights in the distance, and I focus on them as they flicker off the shadowed houses. Nearby, a cat lets out a shriek before what sounds like a garbage bin gets knocked around.

The world sounds and looks the same, but everything is so different.

"We'll have about five seconds to get across the street before we get caught. I'm not going to be able to carry you. So I'm going to put you down, and when I say run, you have to move as fast as you ever have in your entire life. Do you understand?"

My breath wheezes from my chest, a shiver working through my body. I didn't even realize my teeth were chattering until Reign snaps at me to quiet down.

I bite my tongue.

"Got it? I need words, Lakyn," he growls under his breath.

"Yeah," I croak, just as Reign sets me down into the grass. My bare toes curl around the dewy green blades. They're cold against my skin, and I glance down at my feet, wondering how far I'll be able to get with no shoes on.

As if just noticing, Reign cringes a bit. "There isn't any time to get shoes, Lakyn. We have to go. Now."

One of the officer's walkie-talkies blares static from nearby, and Reign's eyes widen as he reaches out, grabbing onto me and pulling me to the side of the house.

"All clear," one of the officers says from around the corner.

I can sense another officer farther off in the yard. A few more steps and he'll see us, both of us.

I hold my breath, staring straight ahead as my chest begins screaming for relief.

The blades of grass crunch as the officer grows closer, and I can feel Reign tense up beside me, ready to strike. Ready to kill.

When suddenly, the officer turns around, making his way back toward the front of the house.

Reign lets out a breath, and I follow behind him, my body loosening, only slightly.

"Okay, we need to go." Reign grips my hand, pulling me forward. "Go, Lakyn, now," he clips, giving me a tug.

And *I run.*

I stumble slightly over a root that has grown out of the ground, and lights flash over me.

"There! They're right there!" one of the officers shouts.

"Hey! Stop!" another one says.

"Move, Lakyn, move!" Reign snaps, giving me a harder pull.

I pick up my pace, and we race across the street just as I hear the police car turn on. Sirens come on shortly after, and it lights a fire under my ass.

We run, as quickly as possible between houses and backyards. The woods aren't far away, though it'll be hard with Reign injured, and me with no shoes on.

Every step brings pain, a poke or scratch against the soles of my feet.

"We're almost there, baby. Once we get into the woods, we'll be able to escape them," he wheezes, a pain in his voice. I know he must be in horrible pain, and I feel bad, though I can't take a look at his stitches now, that will have to come later.

"Lakyn Ashford and Reign Whitmore, stop this second!" one of the officers blares through their window.

Reign gives me a tug, and we cross yet another street, the pavement cold, giving away the upcoming winter.

"We're right there, Lakyn. Right there." He points north, to the edge of the woods that seem endless, a place where many people in this world have gotten lost inside.

"You are under arrest! Put your hands up!" The words blare through a megaphone, and chills run up my back as we hop up the curb, the darkness of the woods cloaking us instantly as we broach the tree line.

"Stop right now!" one of them screams from inside their car, louder than the sirens blaring from the car.

"Don't stop, Lakyn. *Don't stop*," Reign breathes, weaving us in and out of the trees. We go farther into the darkness, until I can't see a thing, but somehow, Reign guides us through.

I can hear the officers enter the woods, though we evade them easily in the shadows of the forest. Soon enough, their voices fade, until we can't hear a thing besides branches cracking and our heavy breaths.

My legs grow numb, my body no longer cold, but I feel nothing except the constant brush of air against my cheeks, the occasional branch reaching toward me, attempting to stop me with the sharp twigs as they scrape against my skin.

"I need to stop," I say after a while, starting to feel my lungs clench. I tear my hand from his, bending at the waist as my palms slap against my knees. "I can't breathe," I choke, gasping for air. "Holy shit."

Reign's heavy breaths come beside me, and I glance over at him as he leans against a tree, pain twisting his face. He lifts his shirt, and I can see his stomach painted red. His stitches have loosened, some of them completely missing, others torn.

"Damnit," he snaps under his breath.

I shove off my knees, walking over to him to get a closer look. "We need to go somewhere. These need to be fixed." I go to reach for his stomach, and he bats my hand away as he gives me a look.

"Don't touch it, Lakyn. We can't deal with it right now anyway. Just leave it alone," he barks.

I rear back, my heart aching as I stare at him.

His face softens slightly, and his hand snaps out, his fingers clutching the base of my hair, tangling into the messy threads.

"We're going to find a place to stay, and then you can help, yeah? Don't worry, baby. I told you I'd get us out of there."

I shake my head, worry filtering through me as I see how pale he looks. How tired.

"I won't make it on my own, Reign. I need you to tell me if it's too much."

He shakes his head. "It's not, and it won't be. My only thought is getting you to safety."

He digs in the back of his pocket, pulling his phone out and swiping through it.

"Can't they like… track you or something?" I ask quietly.

He shakes his head, typing something out on his phone. "It's not my phone. I took it from the front desk at the motel I was staying at."

I nod my head. "So, you were staying at the motel."

He gives me a nod before continuing to type.

After a moment, he tucks his phone back into his pocket. "I got us a place a little north of here. It's going to be about an hour walk."

I lick at my lips. "Okay," I whisper, not sure how any of this is going to work but wanting to trust him wholeheartedly.

And I do.

"This looks like it's it," he grunts as we step into a small clearing. To the right, it looks as if there's some small, makeshift driveway. It's overgrown with weeds, as this place looks like it hasn't been lived in for some time.

The cabin is one story, a wooden log home with an old chimney on top. The windows are large, a little dusty with cobwebs on top of the windowsill.

Reign takes a step forward. "Come on. We should go inside."

"Whose house is this?" I ask as I follow after him.

He shrugs. "Don't know, but the electricity works, and there's a fire to heat the place. That's all we need right now until we figure out what our next move is."

He walks up the small front porch, lifting the worn welcome mat which is a shade of brown, though I don't think it was always supposed to be that color.

Reign lifts up the corner, producing a key against the wooden boards. He lifts it up, and a ring of dust leaves a print in its place.

"How did you know that was there?" I ask him, confused on so many levels.

He turns his head toward me. "I know people, Lakyn. Nothing you need to worry about."

I huff behind him as he sticks the key in the door, turning it roughly. The lock doesn't budge for a moment, sticking inside the mechanism until I listen as it slowly turns, unlocking the front door.

He shoves it open with his shoulder, and the wooden door must have warped over the years, scraping against the floor as it slides open. A waft of dust hits me, and I wave my hand in front of my face to rid the stale smell.

The inside is small, with the small living room attached to the kitchen. There's an old couch that looks like it has a pull-out bed in front of an old box TV next to the fireplace. The kitchen is dated from the looks of it, the wood cabinets full of grease and grime. The stove rusted along the edges.

There's an old rug in front of the fireplace that has about an inch of dust on it.

It's not ideal, and nothing like I've ever lived in, or stepped in even, but it's going to have to do. It's either inside here, or outside in the woods.

Reign doesn't say a word as he shuts the door, the groaning against the floor making my ears wince. He locks it before stepping away, his steps suddenly slow and labored as he heads toward the couch.

"Fuck," he groans as he sits down, taking the mask off the top of his head and tossing it onto the ground. He rolls onto his side, going behind his back and pulling out a small first aid kit.

That snaps me into action. I step forward, walking up to the couch and getting to my knees. "Let me help."

He gives me a look. "You aren't going to be able to do stitches, Lakyn, so just let me."

My head shakes. "No, I can do it. Let me help."

He stares at me a moment before he lifts the kit toward me. "Don't fucking kill me."

I narrow my eyes slowly, playfully. "It's not a promise."

He lets out a groan as he leans back on the couch, pulling his shirt up out of the way. His abdomen is revealed, showing off the stitches that are barely holding his wound together at this point.

I drop the kit to the ground, opening it up and seeing the bloody supplies, all tossed inside quickly, without a second thought.

I move the items around with my fingers until I find the needle and thread. I pull them out, along with some gauze, antibiotic cream, and a small bottle of sterile water.

I grab the bottle, unscrewing the top and leaning over Reign, I give him a look as I pour the bottle slightly, dripping some on his wound.

He hisses through his teeth, and I watch as the dark red blood dilutes to a light pink.

"I would say I'm sorry, but I do think you deserve it a little bit," I clip, unwrapping some of the gauze and pressing it against his wound. He lets out a groan, his head turning toward the back of the couch.

The blood soaks through the gauze, instantly filling the white fabric and turning it a red. I pull it back, and he lets out a hiss as I fold the fabric over and press it against his wound a second time. The bleeding lets up, and when I pull it back this time, it looks much better.

I swallow down the sudden knot in my throat as I pick up the needle and thread.

"I can do it, Lakyn," he groans.

I shake my head. With shaky fingers, I weave the thread through the needle as I prepare to stitch him up. "I can do it. You'll do it and botch it like you did last time. Let me do it right."

His brow furrows. "Do you even know how to stitch something up?"

I shrug, inching my knees closer to the edge of the couch. "I mean, I've patched a hole in my pants before. It didn't look really pretty, but neither did your stitch job." I shrug again. "I'll at least get them to stay in place."

He glares at me a moment before he leans back, letting out a sigh. His head tilts toward the ceiling, his Adam's apple bobbing with his swallow. His eyes shutter closed, and I take that as my cue. Pressing against my knees, my spine curls over as I stare at his wound. Only two stitches remain, one on each end of the stab wound.

With a nervous and guilty inhale, I hold my breath as I bring the needle forward. "I'm going now," I whisper as I press the needle against his skin. It twitches and trembles, his muscles tensing beneath my grip.

"Fuck," he growls, his jaw going taut as I move the needle through his skin. I push it through the other end, pulling the needle tight until the thread pulls the wound together.

I wrap the needle around, going into the skin again. I work as quickly as possible, not wanting to delay any longer than needed. Reign's face pales by the second, growing sweaty, though his skin trembles like he has the chills.

When I'm finished, I grab the scissors, snipping the end and dropping the needle on the ground.

"I'm sorry," I whisper, climbing onto the couch and curling up beside him. He's weak, his arm barely lifting to curl around me.

"Fucking hell, Lakyn. You could never be a fucking nurse," he grunts, squeezing me tight, and the next breath, his eyes close, and he passes out.

My eyes crack open to the sound of static. It crackles loudly through the air, and I shoot up off the couch, my breath leaving my lungs in a rush.

My eyes connect with Reign's, and I notice how much better he looks. He's kneeling in front of the TV, messing with the antennas.

"What're you doing?" I ask, rubbing the heel of my palm against my eyes.

"I've almost got it." He moves it around a few more times, and slowly, a picture comes on the screen. It's fully static and not clear in the slightest, the images wobbling and making me dizzy.

But I can see enough.

Reign's picture, along with mine, sits on the screen.

The words slide across the bottom of the screen in large, bold red letters.

Dangerous and on the run. Any leads, please call the local police department.

Reign sits back slightly, staring at his distorted picture on the screen.

"We're dangerous now?" I snap, staring at my picture. "What the fuck?"

Reign shakes his head, an angry look in his eyes. "Don't be fucking surprised, Lakyn. I saw this shit coming from a mile away."

My brow furrows. "So, what are we going to do? They'll find us here eventually, right?"

He takes a deep breath, shoving to a stand. Walking over to the window, he pulls the heavy, dusted curtain back, staring outside. "Well, staying here is only going to be temporary."

"Where will we go?" The thought of leaving everyone behind. My mom, my friends, it leaves a breath of terror in my chest. What does that mean? That we'll be on the run forever? I'll never see Posie again?

Dropping the curtain, he turns toward me. "Staying here will get us killed. You know this."

I swallow, suddenly nervous. Not sure I'm ready to say goodbye to my home.

Reign steps up to me. "You wanted this, Lakyn. You wanted to be with me. There's no going back. No stepping back in time. You decided to walk away from it all." He narrows his eyes, bending over and grabbing my chin. He pulls me toward him, until we're nose to nose. "You want to walk away from me? This?" He waves his hand between us. "Because I'll tell you something." His nose brushes my cheek until his lips caress my ear. "I'm not going to let you. You're with me for good, baby Lake. Forever."

I shiver, my eyes falling closed.

"There isn't anything that will get me to let you go. You're stuck with me, so you better release whatever block is in your mind and get used to it now."

I narrow my eyes as I lean back, glaring into his eyes. "I don't want to leave, Reign. I just don't want to leave everyone behind."

His eyes narrow. "You don't get both, Lakyn. Not after everything we've been through."

My eyes water, and I know he's telling the absolute truth. "I know, Reign."

Squatting down, his fingers curl around my jaw. He pulls me close, giving me a kiss so deeply I can feel it in my bones.

I'm breathless when he pulls back, staring at him with dazed eyes. He runs his thumb across my lower lip, wiping away the moisture.

I stare into his eyes, the darkness that swirls with dark pools that I get lost in every time I glance at him. There is so much unsaid, so many answers that are left unresolved. If he wants me to take a full leap, to go in blindly into whatever future is laid out for us, I need the truth. All of it.

"Tell me everything then," I say simply.

His eyes narrow as his shoulders tense. "Where do you want me to begin, Lakyn?"

My body is trembling, anticipation over the words to come. I've been waiting for so long, for the entire story to be unraveled, yet I'm too worried to even open the cover at this point.

"Why did you leave me?" I whisper.

He stares at me, and I watch him closely. His gaze doesn't waver; if anything, he's never looked surer in his entire life. I don't know why he left, but he doesn't feel guilty about his decision.

He cocks his head to the side. "I already told you, Lakyn. I left to protect you."

I glance up at him through my eyelashes. "Tell me why you left me, Reign. I deserve the truth. No more of this *I did it for you* bullshit. I want the real reason."

His eyes flicker as a wall slowly builds. "You know how our parents are," he starts, and I lean forward, my fingers pressing against his tense jaw. He relaxes a second, watching me until I watch his guard lower.

"Your parents. You killed mine, remember? Well, my father, at least," I snap, pressing a little too hard on his jaw. I release him, dropping my hand to my side.

He growls deep in his chest, and a shiver breaks along my spine. "Watch your fingers and your mouth, Lakyn. Just because I'm injured doesn't make me weak."

I know. I feel as if he's more dangerous than ever.

I blink up at him. "Keep going."

He leans back, relaxing ever so slightly. "Our parents are fucked up, Lakyn. All of them. You know the type of shit they get themselves into."

I nod my head, leaning forward and turning down the small knob that adjusts the volume on the TV. I let the TV go silent, though I can still see our pictures flash across the screen. My insides wince. I'm a fucking *fugitive*.

"My father became wrapped up in something he couldn't handle himself. It wasn't just his career, but his entire life. His family. Me…" He takes a breath. "You."

My gaze shoots to him. "Me?"

He watches me closely before he nods slightly. "Yeah, Lakyn. My father was in some shady shit with some people in New York. Some offshore trading scandal went wrong. They wanted my dad to pay money that he didn't want to give up. So, he didn't. And the guy got pissed, started threatening my father, started putting his people on my father, tailing him, following him to work, and then it came to me. They started watching me, what I was doing, who I was hanging out with…"

My eyes widen as the realization hits me. "And they realized you have a girlfriend."

He gives me one single, slow nod. "They realized there was someone in my life, and they found the wild card they needed. It was enough to set not only my father off, but me off too."

I let out a shaky breath. "And why didn't you tell me? I could've helped. My family… our friends could've helped."

He leans his head back, barking out a laugh. "Are you fucking kidding me? You think a ton of high school teenagers could've helped this shit? You're out of your damn mind. I did what I had to do."

I stare at him, feeling the lump in my throat growing larger and larger with each swallow. "Which was…?"

He blinks at me.

"What did you do, Reign?"

He tilts his head to the side. "What the fuck do you think I did? Someone was after you, so I went and killed them, Lakyn. Gutted them until they we're fucking dry."

I swallow, knowing he's a murderer, but hearing him say it so easily brings a chill across my skin.

"What happened?" I whisper.

"What else happens when you murderer a politician in New York City in his own penthouse? You get fucking caught, because my father is a piece of shit and didn't warn me at eighteen years old what I was supposed to do. It's almost as if he knew I'd end up in jail. He knew I'd take the fall, but at least he'd be saved, and his life wouldn't be at risk. He knew what I was capable of, which is why it was me he handed the loaded gun to."

My nostrils burn, and the urge to cry is strong, but I hold back, because I only know it'll piss him off. "You got caught?"

He nods. "Luckily my father pulled his fucking strings and I only got eighteen months."

Eighteen months.

So he was gone a year and a half. Maybe a little more, maybe a little less.

But he still didn't come back. For over a year.

"If you left to protect me, but you got out of prison over a year ago. Why didn't you come back once the guy was taken care of? The guy was gone. There was no reason for you to stay away."

He watches me, saying nothing. He looks so relaxed and powerful as he lays there, his legs slightly spread on the beanbag, his arms relaxed over the sides. He's full of blood, his hair a mess, his dark clothes rumpled and bloodied.

My insides grow warm, my fingers brushing against the wooden floor as I stare at him.

Brush, brush.

Brush, brush.

I wait for the moment my fingers catch a sliver, but the moment never comes. I almost want it, so it can take away the unease and worry in my chest.

Give me pain in my limbs and relieve it in my heart.

"There was no need for me to come back, Lakyn."

I exhale a shaky breath, staring at him.

Me. I was the reason.

He shakes his head, as if he can read my thoughts. "Coming back was never part of the plan, Lakyn. I was never planning to come back to Hellcrest Heights. Not ever."

"You didn't want to come back? For me?" I whisper.

His eyes darken. "I stayed away for you, Lakyn. After you kill someone, you become a different person. A darker person. I didn't want to infect you." He takes a deep breath. "You were better off without me."

My heart gallops, speeding toward the edge of the cliff. I'm ready to jump off. Ready to meet my fate because I know it would be less painful than listening to Reign rip my heart apart with his bare hands.

"Why did you come back then, huh?" I ask him, unwanted tears springing to my eyes. "If you never planned to come back, why did you? Why become a serial murderer? Why come after me?"

His jaw clenches, his gaze turning cold. It drops the temperature in the room, and I feel frigid from my skin to my veins.

"My father called me, and he had another job for me to do."

My brow furrows. "Why would you continue listening to him? Helping him? He put you in jail, essentially."

He shrugs. "Because my father is as fucked up as I am, and one day, he will die and I will take everything he's ever built."

I let out a shaky breath, knowing Reign is dark on the inside, but never knowing how abysmal he really is. "Tell me, Reign. I can handle it."

His head tilts slightly. "I can assure you, Lakyn, you cannot."

I bite the inside of my cheek, so hard I can feel the skin split, a puncture straight through the skin until the fresh tangy blood reaches my tongue. "Why did you want to hurt me?"

A wave of darkness crackles through his sight. "Because you were fucking Zane."

My mouth pops open. "How would you know that before you even came home?"

His head rocks from side to side. "Does that matter?"

I lean forward, my nails pressing against the wooden planks. "Of course, it fucking matters! Why would you come home because I slept—very briefly, by the way—with some random stranger from school a couple times."

"Zane is my brother, Lakyn," he clips, his eyes darkening.

My eyes widen, my jaw slackening as I stare at him.

It can't be.

No, it's impossible.

Reign doesn't have any siblings. He's always been any only child.

"Zane is *what*? How?" I ask, confused.

"Half," he says easily.

"But... but how?" I cry out. "How is Zane your brother?" I nearly shriek the words, and panic ensues. It's as if my entire world has been flipped on its axis, and I have no clue how to function.

He folds his hands on his upper chest as he watches me, a glint in his eyes as if he enjoys my unease. "My father had an affair with a slutty poker hostess on one of his trips to Chicago when I was two years old. The woman ended up finding my father years later, when Zane was in elementary school. I've never met him. Never cared to. My father moved them to New York and that's where they've lived their entire lives. My father has essentially taken care of them without taking any responsibility. He was their money donor."

My chest ripples with tension, my heart pounding erratically against my rib cage. I feel so confused, processing each piece of this story is adding twenty more questions.

So, Zane is Reign's brother.

It makes sense, even though it doesn't.

They don't even share a last name.

"But... his name is Baswald, and yours is Whitmore."

He rolls his eyes. "It's my father's bastard child. He didn't deserve my father's last name, hence why I've never met him, and why my father didn't really have a relationship with him."

None of this explains why he came home.

"Why'd you come back to Hellcrest Heights, Reign?" I whisper.

His eyes narrow. "I told you, my father had another job for me."

"What was that job?" I ask him, fear causing my voice to shake.

He says nothing.

Goosebumps are like a dance as they pop along my skin.

"Reign... What. Was. The. *Job*?" I grit through my teeth.

He chin tilts up, ever so slightly. "To kill the girl who killed my brother."

A ringing starts in my ears, and I want to scream. Betrayal is like a stab to the chest, and my fingers clutch the fabric of my shirt, squeezing tight, as if it could relieve the pain.

"You would kill me for a brother you didn't know?" I whisper, being able to feel my heart actively shatter. I get we weren't together. I understand we didn't end on good terms. I realize what we had then may have meant nothing to him.

But it meant everything to me, even when we weren't us.

An evil glint enters his eyes, traveling to his lips, quirking up slightly. "I wanted to kill you for sleeping with my blood."

I swallow over the lump in my throat. "You would kill *me*?"

He puffs out a laugh. "I would kill you for many reasons, Lakyn, most of all for sleeping with Zane."

I tremble, and he smirks before it drops, and a blankness washes over his features. "I was going to make you suffer for sleeping with my family. It's what my father wanted. Even though Zane was a bastard and was never considered part of our family, he was still my father's blood, and that was a betrayal in his eyes. You fucking him was a betrayal to me, so the anger was there. The need to kill you. Though, seeing you changed that. It always did, Lakyn. I can't just pull a blade across your throat and think I can call it even. You're Lakyn. My baby Lake."

"Why did you keep going with it?"

He moves his hands from his chest, leaning forward, curling his fingers around the back of my head. His fingers burrow into my hair, and he yanks me forward. His breath is warm against my lips, and he grips me tightly. All I'm able to focus on is him. He is my life. He is my world. No one else exists when it is the two of us together.

"Because you deserved to serve a little penance for letting someone else slide between your legs," he growls, his eyes narrowing. "You know, Zane always fucking hated me and my father. You think he went after you because he liked you? No, he knew exactly what you were to me. He knew you were mine, and he tried using that against me. To get to me." His fingers wrap around my throat, and he squeezes as his upper lip curls, baring his teeth at me. "But you should've known better. You never should've slept with him, Lakyn. You're mine. You've *always* been mine."

I narrow my eyes at him, wanting to dig my nails into his wound.

"You were gone, Reign. I'm not going to stay a fucking nun forever. *You left me.*"

He growls, squeezing me as he pulls me forward, until our foreheads knock together, our skin melding, heat against heat, crackling tension against sharp anger. We're both on edge, both hurt, both of us vengeful.

"You're alive for a reason, Lakyn. I could've killed you, that first night. As you jumped the fence, you wet body sliding against the rods as fear leaked from your pores. How easy it would've been grab you in my grip and plunge my knife into your stomach, watching you paint the cement patio with your delicious, bright red blood. I wanted you dead, Lakyn. At that moment, I wanted you dead."

My breath shudders from my chest, and I realize the truth to his words. I didn't feel a crackling heat between us. I never once felt a lust or connection in that moment. All I felt was hate, an absolute need to spill blood.

"Why am I alive then? Why am I standing here, if I was such an easy death to you?"

He tilts our heads slightly, until our lips are only a breath away from each other's. I can taste the pain on his lips, can feel the way our connection is bone-deep, engrained into each vein and drop of blood in our souls. "Because like I told you the day I came home, baby Lake, you are the fucking diamond that shines brighter than all others. Your love hits a little stronger. Your touch bruises my skin with barely a touch. It's easy to take a life, but it's not easy to take that of the girl you're madly in love with. I tried to take your life, Lakyn. Fate wouldn't let me."

Fate wouldn't let me.

My eyes settle closed, and I lean forward, my lips barely brushing against his. I want to fall into him, into his madness, get lost and be wild with this man who has always held my heart in his clutches, yet I'm worried a step forward would break me completely.

More than I'm already broken.

A shiver works up my spine, and I lean back, my eyes fluttering open. I shake my head slightly, feeling like even as Reign works to repair my heart, you can't repair when the pieces aren't all present.

When he leans back, his body is tense, as if he remembers why he was so angry with me in the first place. "I'm going out to get some firewood. It's only going to get colder, and until we have a plan, this is where we're staying."

He's shut down on me. Completely.

Panic hits me at the thought of the police out there, waiting for him. "What happens if you get caught?"

He smirks, though there is no humor in his gaze, "Not going to happen, Lakyn."

"Can I come with you?" Fear of being here by myself clutches me. I don't know this place. The police could come here at any time and take me away and Reign wouldn't ever know it.

He shakes his head. "No. Stay here. I'll be right back."

"But—" I groan.

He whips his head back and forth. "Stay here, Lakyn. I'm too injured to have to worry about you, too. Stay the fuck here where it's safe, and stay out of trouble."

I swallow down the fear as he walks out the front door. I sit on the floor, my palms against the cool wood, shivering when I realize how cold it is in here.

We do need wood, he's right.

But the fear of being here by myself after he just dropped that bomb on me makes me feel more uneasy than I've ever felt in my entire life.

I shove off the ground, running to the front door and pulling it open with a quick jerk. A burst of cold air flies inside, and I can see a glimpse of

Reign's back as he walks into the thick woods.

"Reign!" I cry out, rushing barefoot into the yard. It's so cold, the weather having quickly moved from fall to winter. I can see Reign's back tense from across the yard, and his shoulders lift to his ears as he stops, turning around to face me. I'm sure I look like a crazy person, barefoot, eyes wild.

"Go inside, Lakyn!" he roars at me.

I shake my head, rushing up to him, feeling like my sanity is slipping from my grip. "I can't. I don't want to be alone in there. Please take me with you."

He shakes his head, gripping onto my shoulders. He spins me around, pushing me back toward the house. "Go the fuck back inside, Lakyn."

I whine, digging my heels into the ground. "If you get caught, how would I know? If I get caught, how would you know? We need to stick together. It's the smartest thing. You're acting like an idiot in a horror movie," I snap.

He wraps his arms around my waist, lifting me in the air and slamming me against a tree. He rolls me around until my back hits the tree, pointing his finger right in my face. "Baby Lake, listen to me and listen good, okay?" he seethes.

I swallow down my fear, nodding slightly.

"I can't fucking do the shit I need to do, stay alive, and watch over you at the same time. Do you understand that? Not when I have a fucking stab wound in my stomach."

I nod, tears flooding my eyes. "I'm scared, Reign," I whisper.

He leans forward, his thumb brushing over my lips. "You don't have to be scared, Lakyn. I'll tear the world down to keep you safe. I can't do that with you out here. So go inside, and I'll be back soon."

My heart thumps, echoing through my hollow chest. "Please come back to me," I whisper, leaning forward until our lips are only a breath away. "Don't leave me."

He leans forward, our lips pressing together in the cold forest. It's only us, and the world fades away as he claims me as what I am—his. Always and forever.

"There's not a thing in this world that will keep me from you, Lakyn. I'll flip heaven and hell just to keep you safe." He kisses me once more before stepping back, wiping away the moisture on my lips. "Now go inside, baby Lake. Wait for me."

I will. Forever.

A gust of cool night air flows inside as I open the door, and I shiver, wishing there was a blanket to keep me warm. I shut the door, walking toward the lumpy couch and settling onto the faded cushion. It's rough, smelling like mildew and cold to the touch. I wish I had my warm sheets, the soft comforter that molded perfectly to my body. Not this lumpy, old piece of furniture.

I stare at the screen, and it feels like it takes ages before our pictures finally leave the screen and a weatherman comes on.

Outside, the wind whistles against the side of the house. The fall branches have lost their leaves, the sharp branches tapping against the side of the house. The insulation is poor, and I can feel a cold draft flow through the air.

"Come on," I whisper, wishing Reign would be here. It's creepy here by myself. This entire situation is creepy and unknown.

I pull my phone from my pocket. Pressing the side button, I swipe to unlock my screen, instantly seeing the messages at the bottom.

Letting out a sigh, I pull up my messages, on the top being my mom.

Mom: Call me right away.

There's about a million more beneath that, but I can barely read them before another one comes up.

Mom: If you see this message, you better call me back right now!

I swallow down my groan as I hit the call button. It only rings once before she picks up.

"Lakyn," she whispers, panicked. "Tell me it isn't true."

My brow furrows, not sure what point she's talking about. "What are you talking about exactly?"

"You tried to kill someone? And you're associated with that serial killer?" she whimpers. "You know who killed your dad?"

I close my eyes, pinching the bridge of my nose as a burning sensation hits the back of my sinuses. "I had no clue who he was, or that he was going to kill Dad."

She lets out a choked sob. "But you are with him?"

I bite my lip, saying nothing. A tear slips free, not for any reason but the betrayal in my mom's tone. I never want her to feel that way. That I betrayed her in any way.

"Is Reign Whitmore really the slasher?" she chokes out. "The police have been here multiple times looking for you and him. Tell me it isn't him. I let that boy into *my home*."

I roll over until the couch cushion wipes my eyes. "I can't talk about this, Mom. Please don't ask questions I can't give you."

"What am I supposed to tell them when they come back?" Her voice rises, becoming nearly hysterical. "Are you part of the murders, Lakyn? Did you kill any of those people?"

I give my hair a tug, needing the pain to focus somewhere besides every inch of my body. "Mom, I'm not talking about this. I won't be able to talk to you for a while, okay? Just… don't tell them anything. I never called you, okay?"

"They can get the phone records, Lakyn. Then they'll consider me an accomplice."

I roll my eyes. Fucking dramatics. "Then tell them you spoke to me, and I didn't tell you anything, which is the absolute truth."

"But, Lakyn—"

"Mom, I have to go." I glance out the window, wishing Reign would be here, but I see no shadow of a person outside. "I don't know when we'll talk again. But I want you to know… I love you."

She starts crying, and my heart clenches. "I love you so much, Lakyn. Please don't do this to me. I can't lose you, too."

I wipe my eyes. "You won't lose me. I just have to go for a little while, okay?"

She cries harder, and I can't take it.

"Bye, Mom," I whisper, hanging up the phone before she has a chance to keep me on any longer. I swallow down my sob, clutching my phone so tightly it starts cracking in my grip.

Blinking away the blurriness, I roll onto my side and scroll aimlessly through my phone, though each second only brings more anxiety, because all people are talking about is Creed's death, the lighthouse, the slasher, and the girl who I attacked—Celia Loken is her name. I've seen her at school before, but I've never spoken to her. We don't run in the same crowds, and she's never even been slightly close to Creed.

Which only angers me more.

The articles and posts don't say whether she's dead or alive. I don't know which one I'd rather be true.

A video pops up on my screen, and I pause when I see a girl in a Halloween costume, the black makeup around her eyes streaked down her cheeks.

I click on it, and the sound pops up.

"The look in her eyes sent chills through my spine. Blackness. Only darkness in her eyes. It's like she wasn't even human. I've never seen anything like it. It makes me wonder what is wrong with her. It also makes me wonder… did she actually kill Zane?"

My breath catches in my chest as I press Pause, letting out a huge breath. I stare at her face, the sparkling look in her eyes, the way she looks excited and full of rage. It makes my muscles lock up, and I can't help myself as I press the small triangle, starting the video again.

"I think she did, and it makes me so fucking angry that she's probably in on all these murders. She has something to do with this, I know she does. She's not going to get away with attacking my best friend, killing all these people in our town, and then just skating away?" she scoffs, her head shaking as a tear slips out. "No, not in the slightest." Her eyes narrow, anger filtering into them. "Lakyn Ashford, if you see this video, just know I'm going to figure out this entire story, and when I do…" She takes a deep breath, looking straight into the camera lens. "You're going down."

I click out, seeing the name of Braylin Carter on top of the video, but then immediately click on it again.

I can't stop watching the video as the front door opens, and Reign steps in with an armload of wood. The moment he sees the look on my face, his arms drop to his sides, the wood falling to the floor as he storms toward me.

"What the fuck happened?" he growls.

I can't say a word, only a slight shake of my head as I lift my phone toward him. He grabs onto it, replaying the video. I listen as she repeats the words that are already engrained into my mind. I can even see her face as she says them, as if she's in front of me this very moment.

The tear sliding down her cheek.

I shoot off the couch, walking toward the kitchen. I begin pacing, the linoleum tiles soft under my feet.

"I mean, what the fuck are we supposed to do with that information? This girl is going to find out everything, and I'm going to be… *holy shit I'm so fucked*," I wheeze, my palms slamming against the worn counter. My nails dig into the cracked surface, pressure building on the tips of my fingers as I squeeze with all my might.

"Fucking hell!" I scream, wanting to hit something.

Wanting to hit her. Kill her.

"Lakyn," Reign commands.

I can't listen, I can't focus. He's going to try and make me see reason—funny, the serial killer—but I know he will, because he grounds me when I begin floating away.

I want to. I want to lose my absolute shit because I've been keeping it contained for way too long. Being the governor's daughter comes with a price at being prim and proper at all times, but now that he's gone, the need to be as wild as I can be comes roaring to the surface.

I lift my gaze to him, staring him in the eyes. "I want to kill her."

He watches me with a clenched jaw, ticking over, and over again. "Lakyn…" he warns.

I lift my chin. "I want to. I want to do it, and I want you to show me how."

His eyes narrow. "Do what, now?"

Grinding my teeth together, I can feel the ache in my jaw as I face him. "I want to kill her."

His lip curls. "You're being a fucking idiot, Lakyn. Quit talking."

Shoving off the counter, I walk toward him, my heart pounding in my ears. I plant my hands against his chest, giving him a shove, but his fingers wrap around my wrists and he holds me tightly, keeping me secured against him.

"You want to commit a murder, baby Lake?" he asks with a cocked brow.

I think of this girl, with her fake sadness and her legitimate anger. She isn't someone who will just drop it out of boredom. She looks like someone who will dig until her nails bleed.

I can't let that happen.

"Yes. Yes, I do."

He brings his hands across my jaw, sliding down until his fingers wrap around my neck. He gives me a little squeeze, with his fingers that have taken so many lives. The blood which has been spilt from these hands is so many, it could fill a river.

"You think you could take a life, Lakyn? You really believe you could end a life, watch someone take their last breath of air at your hands? Could you watch the life drain from their face as they plead for help?"

I swallow beneath his fingers, feeling them tighten with each second.

"I don't know. I think I could. I want to." I narrow my eyes. "I want to hurt her," I whisper.

He smirks, and it looks evil. Menacing.

"You can't do it, and even if you could, I won't let you."

He releases me, taking a step back.

My eyes narrow, my mouth falling open. "What? Why?" I shriek.

He turns his back to me, heading toward the front door. "Because I'm not going to let you fucking kill someone. Think of what Zane's death did to you. How it fucking affected the rest of your life."

"This is different," I snap.

He sneers, a vicious look entering his eyes. "Why? Because you aren't fucking her?"

My hands clench into fists at my sides, my nails creating crescents against my skin. "Because she deserves to fucking die."

His hand goes to the door, and he unlocks it before he swings it open. "You aren't killing anyone, Lakyn. It's not in your blood, don't pretend otherwise."

"You know nothing, Reign!" I shout at him.

Anger filters into his gaze. "I know a shit ton more than you do, Lakyn, and you aren't doing it, so quit fucking asking."

Stepping outside, he gives me one more glance before he pulls the door closed behind him, leaving me alone.

I draw in a shaky, rage-filled breath as my feet pound toward the front door. I pull it open angrily, watching as he stalks into the woods.

"Reign!" I shout at him, rushing out the door.

He glances at me over his shoulder, and I can see his body tense from here. "Go back in the house, Lakyn."

I keep rushing toward him, fear and anger commingling into a hurricane of emotions. "Where are you even going?"

He shakes his head. "I've got shit to do, Lakyn. Go back inside." He keeps walking away from me, like we're not on the run from the police or sleeping in some creepy shack in the middle of the woods.

"You just got back! Where the hell do you have to go already?" I shout at him. I don't want to be left alone. Why does he keep leaving me alone in this creepy wooded cabin?

He groans, pointing to the pile of wood next to the front door. "I got wood, Lakyn, but I have things to do before it gets too late."

"Can't I come?" I cry out. My breaths come out as pants, and I feel winded as I reach him. He's left me before. With the blink of an eye, he disappeared, fear clutches me that it'll happen again if I look away long enough."

He tilts his head to the side. "No, Lakyn. You can't come. I need to get an update on how things are in town. Check in with a few people. Like I said earlier, if I have to focus on you, I won't be able to protect either of us if shit goes down."

I take a deep breath, wanting to fight him, but the anger emanating from him brings chills down my skin.

"I'm so mad at you," I whisper. For so many reasons. The list is endless.

He smirks, leaning down, his lips pressing against mine. "You love me more. Now get the fuck back in the house," he growls.

He releases me, and I take a step away from the tree, my tongue thick with words to lash at him, but I say none of them.

Instead, I head back toward the house, knowing this conversation isn't over.

Whoever Braylin Carter is, I'm going to find her, and I'm going to kill her.

CHAPTER SIX

REIGN

D amn, she pisses me off.

But I can't get enough of her.

The balls on her wanting to kill someone. She thinks she has it in her? She doesn't, not in the slightest.

She wants to pretend because she was able to do it once that she has the ability to do it a second time, or a third.

She thinks she's as demented as I am.

And the worst part is, I think she is.

The darkness which has seeped into her eyes is apparent. Her soul has darkened over the years, only further darkening once she met the masked man—*me*.

But I don't think I made her this way. I think it's how she's been all along. It's been hiding, lying dormant. And I've awoken it.

The real question is, do I allow her to fully open the gate into the darkness, or do I protect her from it?

She isn't wrong, this girl from the video needs to die.

She'll be pissed as fuck if I do it without her.

But I don't know if she can handle killing without losing herself completely.

There's this fine line of being able to take a life without becoming a monster. Still being a human and living among people normally without being a complete psychopath. I do it daily, no one would've ever assumed I was the masked man if Creed wouldn't have been there when the door opened.

But he was, and I was revealed.

The death of Zane is stained across Lakyn's face like red paint. It's obvious she's killed someone. It's in the haunted look in her eyes. The way her soul has stepped into the shadows. She doesn't have a scar, yet she appears to wear it like a badge of honor.

I fear if I give her the loaded gun, she'll take down the world.

She could do it. Easily, she could do it. But how will it affect her? How will it change her?

I don't know, but I know she's not going to stop until she gets what she wants. That's how Lakyn is, it's how she's always been.

I pull my phone from my pocket as I head through the woods. It isn't that far away from town, but Lakyn doesn't know this part of the woods like I do. Head straight north and you'll end up in Canada. Head south and you'll be in Hellcrest Heights.

We're stuck somewhere in the middle, hiding from the world in hopes we won't get caught.

Unlocking my screen, I see a missed phone call from my father.

With a sigh, I realize it's time to call him back. He's the one that sent me out here. And now the world knows I'm the serial killer, I have no idea how he's going to react.

Pressing his name, it starts ringing, and I head through the woods as I make my way to town. It only rings twice before he answers.

"Reign," he barks.

I run my fingers through my hair, irritation already rolling through my veins. "Yes."

"What in the fucking hell have you gotten yourself into?" he roars through the phone.

I pull the phone away, listening as his voice carries through the woods. "What exactly are you talking about?"

He laughs, though there's no humor. "I don't know, son. Why don't we start with why your name and face is plastered all over the local and national news?"

My head tilts toward the sky, and I stare at the naked branches basked in the dark night sky. "Because shit got fucked up at the Halloween party."

He lets out a sigh. "I don't know how anything could get fucked up when you were given simple instructions. Get in, take care of her, get out. Why on earth have you been ignoring my calls? It can't be that difficult to wipe a person out. She seemed to do it with no problems."

I swallow, though the groan still breaks free. "It's not as simple as just *taking care of it*. But you wouldn't know, since you pay everyone else to deal with your deeds."

"Watch your fucking mouth, Reign," he growls.

My finger goes to my jaw, and I rub at the tense muscles. "I'm not going to kill her." And that's the first time I've spoken the truth about it. Though my initial intention when I returned home was to take her out and go. But when the feelings came back, they were twice as strong as they've ever been.

I'm in love with her.

He pauses a beat, not saying a word.

"What do you mean, you aren't going to kill her?" he asks, his voice quiet.

My eyes narrow. "I mean, I'm not going to do what you want me to do."

"Was that ever your intention, Reign, or were you playing me all along?" His voice sounds betrayed, angered.

I grind my teeth together, feeling my molars crack. "It was the plan, but plans change. I'm not doing it anymore."

He lets out a growl. "Then I'll have to find someone else to take care of the fucking deed for me!" he barks.

A laugh escapes my chest. "I can assure you, if you or anyone else tries to hurt her, I'll gut your stomach until you're nothing but an empty cage."

A heavy, calculated breath comes through the speaker. "Are you telling me you'll choose some bitch over your own father?"

The phone cracks in my grip. "Call her a bitch again, Dad. I dare you."

"She killed your brother!" he barks.

"They all did," I grit through my teeth. "She wasn't the sole killer."

He laughs. "You okay to fuck someone your brother has fucked?"

All I can see is red. Pure rage that filters through my blood and bones. "Let me tell you something, Father," I start, and I can hear the chair creak from the other end of the line. He's leaning back, and I can already tell there's a smirk on his face that I'm itching to carve off.

"You, and anyone you know, isn't going to even touch Lakyn. If someone does, you'll regret it more than all of your enemies combined. Leave her the fuck alone. *She's mine*," I growl, baring my teeth.

He lets out a chuckle, and my head tilts to the side. "I'm done having this conversation. I won't be available for a while."

"Going to prison? Won't be able to protect your girl from there." His tone is mocking, like he's that much smarter than I am.

I know the possibility of going to prison, which is why I never intend to leave her. I'll do whatever needs to be done. I'll take down the entire fucking police force if I have to, to keep her safe. I'll burn down the world.

"We won't be going to prison."

He lets out a laugh. "You want to run for your entire lives? They'll find you eventually, you know."

Here's the thing about my father. He's always been loyal to his own blood, but when he's betrayed by one of his own, when he feels as if he's been backstabbed in any way, he will sweep the rug out from beneath your feet. He's been burnt by blood, by enemies, and by his closest allies. My father trusts no one. He's bitter, jaded, and cold as ice. The permanent frown lines and crease between his brows shows his displeasure with the world. He'll show it to you easily. He'll laugh as you get buried.

That's my father.

Spencer Whitmore.

I won't be there for him anymore, because he wants Lakyn dead for killing Zane. Part of his blood. But Lakyn means more to me than a half-brother who shares nothing with me but blood. I won't defend him any longer, not now that I have Lakyn back.

This pisses him off, because I'm my father's strongest weapon. He won't have anyone to use as his assassin. He'll no longer have the wall between him and the world. Who will protect him? It won't be me.

It isn't because I'm his son, it's because I'm his shield. His gun.

"We won't be on the run," I say simply. Because I'm not worried. I have no qualms that it isn't going to be a rough road, but we'll get there, because I'll protect her.

I'll protect the girl who means the most to me.

He lets out a chuckle, and it's bitter, angry. "And you're okay sticking your dick in the girl who was railed by your own brother?"

He has to dig that comment in. More than once, apparently.

My teeth crack as I grind my jaw, and I reach forward, gripping a branch so tightly it begins crumbling in my grip. "Say another word and I'll slice your neck like I did all the others."

I can hear his chair creak again in the background, and I can picture him standing and walking over to the small shelf near the wall in his office. The rattling of glass sounds, and I know he's pouring himself three fingers of his finest scotch. Can never drink too early in the day, I suppose.

"You going to threaten your own father, Reign?" he rumbles, his voice echoed as he tips his glass to his lips.

I let go of the broken branch, stepping farther into the woods. I can't leave Lakyn for much longer. I know she'll grow antsy, and even though I told her to stay inside, I can never trust Lakyn for too long. She's a loose cannon, honestly. A wick sitting too close to the fire.

I loosen my grip on my phone, tilting my head to the side, and listen as it lets out a loud crack. "No, Father. I'm done with your bullshit. I only wanted to call and tell you that whatever death wish you have on Lakyn, let it go. It's over. The feud is over. Unfortunately, Zane got twisted with her when he never should have in the first place."

"And what happens when she turns her back on you, too? You ready to be buried in the ground by her filthy hands?"

If she gives me death, I'll take it gladly, as long as it's her hands which give it to me.

Death by her would be a pleasure I couldn't resist.

"It's not going to happen."

He sighs, as if he thinks I'm foolish.

"I'll be unavailable for the foreseeable future. Don't make any wrong moves. I'll always be one step ahead of you," I clip.

I can hear him gearing up for a retort, but before he can say anything, I hang up the phone, tucking it back in my pocket.

Shaking my head clear, I head toward town, knowing I have to check out how deep law enforcement is.

But that's not all I have to do. And this one will be a surprise.

CHAPTER SEVEN

LAKYN

My eyes flutter open to the heat of a body falling over me. I jolt in place, glancing up and seeing my masked man hovering over me. The mask situates over Reign's face, his hard body molding to my soft one. I can feel the anger rolling through him.

"What's wrong?" I whisper, sleep thick in my throat.

He shakes his head, not saying anything as his fingers trail down my side. They tickle against me gently, and I can feel the hairs raise in their wake.

No, not his fingers.

My eyes glance down, and I see a knife in his grip. Not the one he's had before. This one is new, the blade smooth and free of scratches and blemishes. The handle is black and flawless. It glints against the setting sun, brightening the dim room. I let out a shaky breath as a shiver rolls through my body. I stare up at him, my fingers lifting into his hair. I tug on the damp strands, as if it's been drizzling, or maybe a slight snow is falling. I'd glance toward the window to look, but I can't take my gaze away from him.

I can feel the storm building beneath his mask.

"You're troubled," I whisper.

He shrugs away from me, the knife sliding down my side until he reaches the hem of my shirt. He grips it with his gloved fingers, completely dressed in his masked man attire. With his other hand, he drives the tip of the blade through my shirt, shredding it quickly all the way up to my neck. I hold my breath as the blade rushes toward me, fear choking me that the knife will go straight through my throat. He pauses, though, just as the tip of the blade pierces beneath my chin.

I can feel the warmth of blood as it drips down the smooth end of the blade.

"What's wrong?" I whisper again as he shoves the fabric of my shirt aside, revealing my plain black bra. He lowers the blade to my bra, and I see the silver blade painted with a trail of red. He slips it between the strap between my breasts, flicking the blade until the cups slide to each side of my rib cage.

A shiver rolls through me, my nipples peaking against the cool air. He lowers his face to my quivering stomach, and I can feel a grazing of the mask against my skin. Smooth yet rough, weathered yet strong.

His gloved fingers slip under the waistband of my pants, pulling them down quickly. They slip over my knees, and he rips them off my ankles, tossing them aside until I'm lying in only a pair of cream-colored cotton panties.

He lets out a hum under his breath as he lays the flat end of the blade against my ankle.

"I have a present for you," he says, and surprise shoots through me when I hear the voice box, distorting his voice.

Fear slowly trickles in. I haven't seen him this closed down since before the Halloween party. He doesn't seem like Reign. He feels like the masked man, and it puts my guard up and makes my heated blood cool to ice.

"Do you hear me, Lakyn?" he asks, and I let out a noticeable shiver as I glance at him.

"What present?" I croak.

He chuckles, "How badly do you want it?"

He drags the knife up, over to the inside of my ankle, and then starts lifting it, until I hear the light scrape as it slides against the fine hairs on my leg.

I huff out a small laugh. "You're the one who told me about it." Asshole. He toys with my mind and my body, making me crumble so easily in his grip.

The knife gets to the crux of my thighs, and he presses the tip of the knife against my cotton panties.

He grunts. "You're already soaking the fabric, baby Lake. How far would you like my knife to go?"

I squirm against the blade, holding myself against the lumpy cushions as he presses the blade in, pushing the fabric between my damp folds.

"I'll keep going unless you tell me to stop," he warns, and I can feel the edge of the blade sharp against my sensitive skin.

He pushes further, and I can feel the pinch of pain.

"Stop," I shout, and he withdraws the blade, easily flicking the blade as he cuts the panties from my hips. He pulls the fabric of my panties away, leaving me completely naked beneath him. I sit up slightly, and he brings the blade up to my breasts, nicking the skin. I can feel the blood dollop around my nipple before dropping to my stomach.

He brings his glove forward, swiping it and making it turn from a dark red to a light pink.

"Give me my present," I demand, and his shoulders shake with his chuckle.

He scrapes the blood with his knife, then slides the knife between my lower and upper lip. I clamp down, my teeth sliding against the smooth metal as I look at him with wide eyes.

"Who's got the knife, baby Lake? I think you should rethink your demand before you end up with more blood dripping down your body." He presses in further, and I can feel the sharp end of the knife cut into the corners of my lips.

"Do you hear me?" he growls.

I nod slowly, not wanting to cut my skin any more than it already is.

He slides the knife out from between my lips, dragging it along my jaw. "Close your eyes."

My brow furrows, and I say nothing as I feel the faint taste of blood hit my tongue.

His mask tilts to the side as he cocks his head.

Another nick. This time to my cheekbone. He brings his head forward, sliding the hard plastic against my skin, smearing the blood. I can feel the droplet smear, the warmth quickly cooling.

"Close your eyes, Lakyn, if you want to see your present."

As if on his command, because I can never fight against Reign, and never can I win, I slowly shut my eyes, feeling my lashes flutter against my cheekbones. My fingers grip the cushion on each side of me, and I can feel the air shift as he leans over my body, his body hovering over mine.

The distorted voice crackles through the small speaker, sounding monotone as it goes right in my ear. "Open."

Taking a deep breath, I let my eyes flutter open. They quickly widen when I see what's right in front of me.

A mask.

Nearly identical to his.

Though this one looks like it's made for a female. It looks like it was made just for *me*. The eyes are black, and the lips are as well, made into a smile, the center in the shape of a heart. It's scary as hell, but also gorgeous.

I love it.

"Is that… for me?" I whisper.

He gives one slow nod.

What does it mean? That he will show me?

"What does this mean?" I echo my thoughts.

He grabs the mask, unused and unblemished, sliding the strap around the back of my head as he slips it over my face. It fits perfectly, curling around the sides of my cheeks and molding to my face.

We stare at each other, our masks only inches from one another.

"It means you're going to stay there like a good girl and let me do whatever I want to do to you," he rasps through his voice changer.

Another shiver rolls through me, and I stare at him, intaking a shaky breath.

His gloved fingers linger down my sides, curling around my hips before they slide around to the backs of my thighs. He grabs me behind the knees, pulling me to the edge of the couch, until my legs hang over the edge. He slides between them, keeping a tight grip on my limbs as he dips his face between my legs.

I can feel his warm breath as it slides beneath his mask and onto my sensitive skin. He brings his hand to the bottom, shoving it up above his lips. Dipping forward, his tongue darts out, sliding between my wet folds, flattening his tongue against my clit.

I jolt in his arms, my hips bucking into his mouth. His free hand comes down, the knife landing right above my sex. He holds the blade against my skin as his face dives down farther, his lips and tongue and nose burrowing into my sex, his tongue sliding across every fold, licking up every drop of arousal that drips from my sex.

I can feel a hum begin in my lower belly, spreading across my limbs like wildfire. A moan cracks from my throat as my neck arches, my head tilting toward the ceiling. I can feel the tears leak from the corners of my eyes, sliding beneath the mask and into my hair.

I watch as he drops the mask back down over his mouth, his fingers expanding wide as he slides them up my body, gripping my hips as he lifts me in the air. I feel weightless against him as he slides onto the couch, depositing me onto his lap. I circle my legs around his hips.

He lifts me slightly with one arm while using the other to shove his pants over his hips. His erection springs free, and he grips it tightly, slapping it against my still pulsating sex. I swallow down a moan, my head tilting forward, my face burrowing in the crook of his neck. He nudges my head up, and I stare at him, able to see his dark eyes through the holes of his mask.

I'm sure we look wild, two people gripping each other, masks covering our faces. He grips his erection with his fingers, sliding it to my sex. I sink down, rolling my hips as I seat myself fully. He leans back, and I bring my hand to the hem of his shirt, shoving it up to his pecs, showing off his tattoos, his ripped abdomen. My fingernails scrape down his tense skin, and my mouth waters as it ripples with my fingers.

"Move," he growls, his hand going to my hip. He grips me tightly, and I can feel his fingers as they begin to bruise my skin. A moan slips past my lips, and I press my palms against his abdomen as I start working against his body. I shove myself up, feeling my soaking walls grip him tightly, holding him in a vise grip. I squeeze, and he twitches inside of me, growing impossibly harder.

I roll my hips again, lifting my hands and dropping them against his mask. He growls at me, and my fingers trace the blood, the scratches, the little surface injuries. The pads of my fingers slide across each shred in the surface, feeling the roughness scrape against my soft skin.

His other hand falls to the other side of my hip, and he lifts me, moving me as he wants, taking control. I shift my hips, slowing down slightly, attempting to take back some control. He leans forward, his hand going to my shoulder. He pushes down, keeping me in place as our masks knock together.

"You think you have all the power, baby Lake? Let me tell you something." He moves us together, until our masks completely collide, where our lips would be touching if our masks weren't between us. "You have no control. I have it all. Every piece. Every inch. Every breath you take, it's mine. It's all fucking mine," he growls.

Before I can even react, he grabs onto my hips, lifting me off of him and spinning me around. My knees slam against the wooden floor. The heat of his body curls around mine, his finger slamming against my clit. He rubs meticulously as he slides his cock back inside me.

I let out a moan, my spine rippling with tension as I feel him bury himself deep. He rolls his hips, curling his fingers around the back of my neck, the other on my hips, keeping my ass in the air.

He pulls out before shoving back in quickly, aggressively, until I can hear the slap of our skin connecting.

And again.

And again.

And again.

He picks up his pace, until my body creates a wave with each thrust, the gravity overwhelming from his aggressive thrusts.

A scream breaks from my lips, and I can't help the pleasure and pain-filled cries as he demolishes me, commands me, manipulates me exactly as he wants me.

I can feel the heat build in my lower belly again, warming my blood even as goosebumps break out along my body. This orgasm will be vicious, ripping through me so violently I almost wonder if I'll faint. My fingers curl against the floor, my nails scraping against the aged wood.

"This pussy is mine, Lakyn. You realize that? Not anyone else's. Never has been, never will be. It's mine."

I nod my head, my forehead knocking against the floor.

"Tell me, Lakyn," he commands.

"My pussy is yours, Reign. It's always been yours."

His grip tightens against my skin, bruising me as he lets out a growl. "Mine, baby Lake. Mine," he snarls. His panting quickens, until he's groaning above me.

"Now make that fucking pussy come all over my cock."

I do as he commands, the walls of my pussy fluttering as I come. He follows suit, his cock twitching violently as he empties himself inside of me.

His body curls over mine, holding me tightly for a moment before he stands, taking me with him. I'm limp in his arms as he walks to the couch. He sits down, keeping me in his arms as he holds me tightly. Curling my head up toward his, I watch as he shoves his mask over his face, and I stare at his dark eyes.

"You bought me a mask," I whisper, shoving my own over my face.

"I did," he rasps.

My lips purse. "What does that mean? Can we go after that girl?" I plead, my hand curling above his pec as excitement fills me.

He tilts his head to the side slightly. "You aren't doing anything alone, Lakyn. It'll be the both of us, so don't think I'm opening up the door and going to let you just go wild."

"Well, when can we go?" I'm eager, my blood thrumming through my veins with the need to get back at them, at every single one of them.

They put me in hiding. Their loud mouths and constant gossip.

This girl, Braylin, whoever the hell she is, shouldn't be sticking her nose where it doesn't belong.

Most of all my business.

He shoves me off him, depositing me next to him on the couch. His hands grip my wrists, my hands pinned above my head as he glares down at me. "Never if you keep acting like a fucking rabid dog. Quit thinking this will be a slap in the face, it's nothing of the sort."

I attempt to tear my arms from his grip. "I know it won't be a slap in the face. I understand how horrible it will be." I lift my head, staring him in the eyes. "And I don't care. I want the messy, Reign. Give it to me."

A smirk flutters against his lips briefly before they flatten. "This was a bad idea."

I shake my head, sitting up. "It's not! Just tell me what you need me to do, and I'll do it."

He shoves off the couch, pacing back and forth a minute. Then turning to the kitchen, he tears his mask from his head and sets it and the knife down.

"Well, first off, you need to not be so fucking eager, because that's going to come with mistakes."

I shrug, "Or it'll make me be more on my game." He glares at me, and I lift my hands in the air. "Sorry, less fucking eager. Okay." *Damn.*

"Two." He slides his hand behind his back, pulling out a knife similar to the one he just set on the counter. "Learn how to use a weapon."

I glance toward his stomach. "I do."

He shakes his head. "If you knew how to use a weapon, I wouldn't be here."

Well, shit.

"Okay, so what do I need to learn?" I ask, so fucking eager, but not wanting to show him in fear he won't let me do it. He'll kill her himself, and he'll do it without me knowing.

Fuck, I'd be so pissed.

"First off," he starts, when his phone starts ringing inside of his pocket.

He narrows his eyes, letting out a sigh as he pulls it out. A line creases between his brows, and it puts me on edge.

"Who is it?" I ask him.

He lifts his eyes to mine. "Archer."

My heart pounds in my chest, and I take a step toward him. "Are you going to answer it?"

He lifts it slightly when it stops ringing, only for it to start up again.

"Answer it," I tell him.

He lets out a sigh as he connects the call, putting it on speaker phone and setting it on the counter.

"Reign," Archer barks into the phone.

Reign says nothing.

"Where are you guys? We need to come talk to the both of you."

My mouth opens when Reign cuts me off.

"It's not happening," he says simply.

Archer sighs into the phone, and I can imagine him running his fingers through his hair, exasperation in his tone. "If I wanted you guys to get fucked by the cops, I would've led them up to Lakyn's bedroom."

"They could follow you," he says.

Kyler laughs in the background. "Who the fuck does he think we are? Being tailed by the police."

"What do you need? Just say it over the phone," Reign growls.

Archer and Kyler start mumbling through the phone, and I curl my toes against the floor, glancing down at my naked body. I'm suddenly unsure how I'll even do this. Reign tore my clothes, and now I have nothing to wear.

I certainly can't go out into the world without clothes, mostly when my face is posted literally everywhere.

"Reign," I mumble. He glances at me for a moment, his eyes flaring when he sees my naked body. I gesture down to my chest, and he tilts his head to the side, when Kyler and Archer start barking through the phone again, and his mind is once again on his conversation.

"Give me your coordinates," Archer snaps.

Reign shakes his head before Archer has even finished talking. "You aren't fucking coming here, Archer. Fuck that. You're just going to bring trouble."

Archer curses under his breath. "Fuck you, Reign. I'm done with your shit. Tell me where you are so we can quit with this back and forth shit."

Reign glances over at me, and my heart swoons at the way his hardened face tenses, the sharp cheekbones along his face enough to cut glass. "Fuck you, Archer." He hangs up the phone, and I step forward, a sudden chill filling the air. Goosebumps break out along my skin, and I swallow down my fear.

"What do you think they want?" I whisper.

His fingers fly across his phone. "I don't know."

I shuffle forward again. "What are we going to do?"

His eyes lift toward mine, though his face stays tilted toward the floor. "I'm going to let them come here and hope I don't have to kill any more of my fucking friends."

I swallow over the lump in my throat. "You're going to let them come here?"

A few more seconds and he drops his phone to his side before he shoves it into his pocket. "There's only one way to find out what he needs. I have to, Lakyn."

I nod, knowing he's right. Could Archer fuck us over? Completely. But honestly, he would've done that already if that was his plan. The fact that he wants to come over here randomly tells me he isn't looking to screw us over, but maybe help us.

At the end of the day, Archer is my best friend, and he won't fuck me over.

With a sigh, Reign rips his sweatshirt off. Walking over to me, he shoves the hoodie over my head. I shove my arms through, my hair slipping across my face. He steps forward, brushing the strands off my face. "I'll have to go and get you some clothes."

"And stop ruining mine." My eyebrow lifts.

His head cocks to the side. "I'll cut off every scrap of clothing if it means I can have what's underneath."

My chest thumps inside my chest, and the heat between my legs begins to throb. Reign knows me, and he can see the way my face heats, the way my body responds without him even touching his skin against mine.

"I'd fuck you again right here, right now, Lakyn, but I've gotten to the point where I'll kill anyone if they see you naked, and my ass won't be able to handle it if Archer or Kyler walk in here and see your fucking legs spread with my cock sliding between your creamy thighs."

I let out a whimper.

He steps up to me, his fingers sliding past my jaw, curling into the messy strands of my hair. He pulls my head to the side, my eyes cocking just below his. He stares down at me, his head hovering above mine.

"You're mine, Lakyn. This time I'm not letting you go," he growls.

"I don't want you to," I croak.

His free hand slides across my lips, and he dips them around my chin, sliding down my neck until his fingers span around my throat. He grips me tightly, and my eyes dart between both of his, seeing the possessiveness, the darkness lingering in the depths.

"Fall with me, Lakyn," he rasps.

I press on my tiptoes, gaining height until our lips are barely grazing. "I've already fallen," I whisper.

He lets out a growl, dropping his lips to mine, and I can feel the passion, the desperation and need in the way his lips connect with mine. His lips mold to mine, and I slide mine against his. I moan into his mouth, and he kisses me deeply, giving me all the emotions he isn't able to say. He nudges my lips open with his, sliding his tongue between them. They become tangled, tousling together, my tongue gliding against his quickly, aggressively, as our heat becomes a combustible fire that is unable to be tamed.

His hands slide around my waist, around my hips, and his fingers curl around my thighs. He lifts me into his arms. I circle my legs around his waist, holding him tightly as he stomps across the living room. We end up at the couch we slept on, and he spins around, sitting down, his back slamming against the back of the couch. I burrow my fingers in the back of his hair, tugging on the long strands as I grind myself down on him.

His hands fall to my ass, and he slides them beneath the fabric of his sweatshirt. My skin feels like it's on fire, and I can't help the whimper which cracks from my chest.

Knock, knock, knock.

I let out a groan at the same moment Reign's head slams against the back of the couch.

Knock, knock, knock.

"Let us the fuck in," Kyler groans. "It's cold as tits out here."

Reign's hands move back to my waist, and he lifts me off his lap, depositing me down beside him. He moves off the couch, glancing at me at the last second. "Behave, Lakyn."

My face pulls into a sneer, and I instantly want to backfire a retort, but decide to say nothing.

He adjusts the erection straining against the front of his pants as he walks to the front door. Flicking the lock, he swings it open, and my heart pounds in my chest when I see Archer, Kyler, and Posie all standing there. My eyes widen when I see a light snow falling around them.

Posie's hair is speckled white with flakes. She stares at me blankly, and I instantly slide off the couch, walking toward Reign.

"Posie," I whisper, wanting for my best friend to forgive me.

She steps around Archer and walks inside, glancing around at the small cabin which is no more than a small studio apartment.

"Where'd you find this place, Reign?" Kyler asks as he steps inside.

Reign's eyes narrow slightly. "You get a few things up your sleeve when you've been to prison."

Archer digs into his pocket, pulling out a packet of cigarettes he rarely smokes. He slips one between his lips, pulling out his lighter and sparking it up. "FBI showed up. There's a manhunt going on. Locals are getting together tonight to scour the woods."

I swallow.

"They won't find us. We aren't even technically in Hellcrest Heights," Reign says. Uncaring, unafraid. He's ballsy, and maybe being a little stupid.

"Reign," I murmur. "Maybe we need to go. Run somewhere? Anywhere?"

His gaze slowly turns to mine, lazily, maybe a little bored. "Where the fuck do you feel like going, Lakyn?"

My hands fling up in the air. "I don't care. Anywhere. Somewhere that isn't here, where we're bound to get caught."

He shrugs. "We aren't in Hellcrest Heights. The police don't have jurisdiction here."

"The FBI do," I snap.

He rolls his shoulders back, standing a little straighter as he steps up to me. "We don't have to worry about the FBI, Lakyn," he growls under his breath.

"I really think you do, Reign. It isn't just a few guys. You've got a whole department here ready to take you down," Archer warns.

I let out a groan, rolling my head to the side and letting out a crack. "We're so screwed."

I watch as Reign steps up to Archer. "Is this why you came here? To make Lakyn fucking panic? I can assure you, it's not needed, Archer."

Archer's hands go up to Reign's chest, and he gives him a shove. They come toe to toe, and I'm worried they are about to tear each other to pieces when Kyler steps between them, his hand going to each of their chests and pushing them away from each other. "Stop. Both of you, fucking stop."

"This isn't why we came, Archer. Chill the hell out for a second," Posie snaps before turning to me. "Are you doing okay?"

My heart gallops, and I can't help the tears that spring to my eyes. "I don't know," I whisper. "Did I kill that girl?"

She winces, taking a step back toward the door. "Does it matter whether you did or didn't? You fucked up, Lakyn."

My eyes narrow. "It definitely matters whether I committed murder or not."

"Did you see the video?" Reign cuts in, clearly not nearly as concerned about me murdering some girl in front of a ton of people.

Archer pauses a moment before he lets out a single nod. "That's why we're here."

"Where is Eloise and V?" I cut in, curious where my best friends are.

Posie scoffs. "You really think Vienna is going to come here when *he* is here?" Her gaze cuts sideways to Reign, and I squeeze my hands into fists at my sides so I don't scream.

"Shut up," Kyler says, waving his hands about. "Yeah, we saw the video, and from the sounds of it, she's going to try and dig up everything."

"It's already dead news." Reign spins on his feet, walking toward the kitchen without another word. "Plus, don't worry about her. We've got it handled."

Silence.

"*We?*" Archer says quietly.

Reign's eyes turn to mine, and he's giving me the warning, or the option to speak up if I want to.

It's my choice. I can tell them, or I can keep my mouth shut.

Fall with me.

I turn toward my friends.

"We've got it handled," I say simply.

Archer watches me silently, and I can see the way his eyes turn and calculate, contemplating what it is I just said. His pupils widen and darken as he comes to the realization of what I'm about to do.

For some reason, him realizing how dark I am is a fire in my gut, as I realize how far across the line I've really wandered.

My hand goes to the side of my head, and it's like the truth smacks me in the face, and I can't stop it.

I'm dark.

I'm just as dark as Reign is. Possibly even more so, honestly. There's always been a darkness inside of me, and it's something I've tried to keep locked down, hidden from the world, while only allowing glimpses to shine through when the cracks grow wide enough.

And then I cover, repair, and wait for the next time my life comes crashing down around me.

Though now, as Reign has shown me his own compass in the dark, I realize it's always been a façade, trying to be someone I'm not. I'm not the pretty princess. I'm not the queen between my best friends.

I'm not just a governor's daughter.

I'm Lakyn Ashford, and I'm just as dark as the guy who owns my heart. Whatever path he decides to head down, I want to be there beside him. I want to hold his hand in the dark and find our path.

I'm not a normal girl. I never have been and I never will be, and I think I'm okay with that.

I was honest when I said I wanted to kill that girl from the lighthouse. A need, a desire, a fucking desperation that roared through me at that moment, barreling against my weakened heart.

The feel of the girl who I destroyed, the way her skin shred against my knuckles, the feel of her thick, warm blood as it coated my palms and dripped from my fingers. It was a high, a hit that I didn't realize I was craving.

And now, all I want is more.

More, more, more.

I'm a fiend for the high. I don't want to tear apart people who don't deserve it.

But I do want to tear apart this girl who wants to ruin my life. I want to give her exactly what it is she deserves.

Death.

Posie's jaw clenches as she stares at me. "You're going to go after her, aren't you?"

Kyler starts laughing, turning so his back is to us. All I can do is watch the fabric of his shirt vibrate against his trembling back.

"What's so funny?" I ask, my face twisting.

He shakes his head, his laughter only growing louder.

The footsteps of Archer walk up to me, and my body stiffens as he stops in front of me. I can feel the tension in the room grow, Reign stepping closer to me, ready to pounce at any given second.

"Archer," he warns.

Archer's fingers grip my chin, and he moves my face to his, until our eyes clash, his angry ones against my hesitant ones. They burn into me, melting me in place, placing shackles around my ankles until I can't move. Can't breathe.

This is Archer, it always has been. The guys have me locked in their soul.

I'm theirs. Their best friend. Their girl.

Though only one owns my soul.

My eyes drift to Reign, and I can see his jaw cut like glass, ticking, ticking, ready to explode like a bomb.

"I always knew you were crazy," he murmurs.

I tilt my head to the side, my eyes narrowing slightly. "This isn't new, Archer."

He smirks slightly, though beneath the humor is a danger I don't want to test. "You're crazier than I ever thought you were. Untamed, Lakyn."

I swallow audibly.

His fingers drop. "We could place all the rope across your body, secure you with all the shackles in the world, and you'll still find your way out of them. You're wild, baby Lake. Wilder than I ever realized."

Kyler stops laughing, turning around and glancing at me. "There's only one person that can take care of you, baby Lake, and it isn't us."

I take a deep, shaky breath as I stare at Archer. He smiles, and it's not forced, though he isn't fully friendly, either. Taking a step toward me once more, he smiles as he brushes his fingers along my shoulder. "Reign is the only one who can take care of you, Lakyn. It's not for me anymore. Your wild and his wild match. Me and you," he shakes his head. "We're in the same puzzle, Lakyn, but we don't fit together."

I know we don't. We're best friends. Maybe even soul mates, in a sense. All of us are to each other, but that's as far as it goes. He's not my heart.

The man standing dangerously close beside me is. Completely. Wholeheartedly. Forever.

"What changed, Arch? You were about to kill me yesterday. Why the sudden change in demeanor?" Reign barks.

Archer steps away from me, glancing at Reign. "This isn't about you, Reign. This is about her. She's our world, and if you're the one who she needs to be with, then forgiveness will come with time." His eyes narrow. "Though, we'll never forget."

The silence stretches on, and the air grows taut with tension that ripples between the two men.

Posie breaks the silence, as if she knows it could quickly escalate to violence, if it goes on much longer. "So, you two are going after her, then?"

I nod my head slowly, my eyes disconnecting from Archer's as I look over at her, worry cooling my bones at the thought of her hating me for doing what I know is necessary. This isn't just to protect me, it's to protect everyone inside and outside of this cabin. We're all involved, and I'll do whatever needs to be done to protect my people.

"When?" Archer asks, pulling his phone out of his pocket.

"Why?" Reign clips.

Archer looks up at him. "Because we'll fucking distract them so you can go take care of it. We don't want this bitch digging any more than you do."

They want to help.

My heart gallops in my chest, and I clench my hands into fists at my sides as I turn to Reign. "When can we go?"

Reign shakes his head at me slowly before turning to Archer. "There's a lot to discuss before we do anything. Nothing is set in stone yet."

Kyler cuts his phone through the air. "Take a look at her latest video and I can guarantee you aren't going to keep wanting to do the sit-and-wait approach."

I step forward instantly, my blood pumping wildly through my veins as I pull his phone from his grip, sliding it from between his fingers. A video is paused, and I can already see her stupid dark hair pulled into a ponytail behind her head, her frozen face distorted, though there's an eagerness in her eyes that shows me I'm already not going to like what it is I'm about to see.

Reign lets out a breath as he tenses behind me. I glance at him over my shoulder, and he looks closed off, tense.

"You've seen this?" I ask, already knowing the answer.

He stares at me a moment before giving me a slow nod. "Yeah, right before I came back."

My finger hovers over the play button, and after a moment, I click Play, scrolling back to the beginning of the video. She's walking through the woods, and all I can hear is her heavy breathing, the sound of her boots cracking the branches under her shoes, and the light sound of wind whistling through the speaker.

"It's cold out, but I wanted to get out here because I learned about something today I thought was worth sharing." She takes a deep breath before pulling the camera closer to her face. "Zane is related to Reign Whitmore. Reign's father had a bastard child—aka Zane. Both of them have a history with Lakyn. The real question is, why was the slasher protecting Lakyn instead of killing her? Lakyn basically betrayed Reign by sleeping with his brother. Or maybe Zane betrayed Reign." Another shake of her head.

"Either way, the betrayal runs deeper than I realized. But it gets even more sticky. If anyone has ever spent any amount of time in Hellcrest Heights, you'll realize what type of relationship these guys have with Lakyn Ashford. They treat her like a queen. Royalty. My suspicions? Lakyn Ashford may have had a hand in killing Zane, but I think it was the guys. I think they were so jealous that Lakyn found someone out of their circle that they decided to kill him, without knowing the blood relation."

Her phone starts shaking, or wait, no, that's my phone that's shaking.

"But the best news of all, is that I'll be meeting with someone tomorrow, and I'll be getting evidence that will incriminate all of them. Every single one of them." Her eyes narrow. "You're going down, bitch. You and your entire fucking weird posse."

Kyler's phone is ripped from my grip, my fingers still curled as if the phone sits in my hand.

"Such fucking bullshit," Posie whispers under her breath. "I'm so fucking mad at you, Lakyn. You and Reign, both. A part of me doesn't think I'll ever forgive you. Not completely, at least. But this shit has to stop, and your little psycho boyfriend is the only one I know who goes and murders people left and right."

I stare at her, knowing I'll never fully be forgiven, but wanting to take this chance and prove to them I can be what they need me to be. I can help them, save them, be who they know I've always been, plus more.

Plus this new me.

The new me who is desperate to watch someone's life fade in front of my eyes.

"We need to go now," I whine, turning to Reign. "She's going to uncover a ton of shit. She's digging, Reign, and now she's going to talk to someone, and we're going to be actually screwed. Let's go finish this before it even starts."

"It's already started, Lakyn," Archer snaps.

I raise my hand toward him, staring at Reign with wide eyes. "See? It's already fucking started."

Reign glances at Archer. "I'll let you know when we decide to go. Tomorrow."

Archer's jaw clenches as he watches him, and after a second, he lets out a small nod. "Let's go."

Kyler turns toward me, a forgiveness in his hard eyes, though he doesn't say a word as he gives me a small nod before walking toward the front door.

The floor creaking in front of me has my eyes turning to Posie, and my arms automatically open when she walks toward me with her arms extended. Tears flood my eyes as her petite arms wrap around my waist.

"I don't understand, but I guess I don't really have to, huh?" she chuckles sadly.

I shake my head. "I don't think I even fully understand."

"But it feels right?" she whispers against my shoulder.

I nod, "He feels right."

She nods. "I know. It's always been him, Lakyn. It's not a secret. I just wish the cards weren't dealt for you two as they are."

That's the thing, though. I'm glad they are. I really am.

She gives me one more squeeze before her arms drop, and mine do after hers, letting her step away from me. A strong arm wraps around my waist as Reign holds me, the both of us watching the three of them head to the front door.

"Tomorrow, Reign. If she's really meeting with someone tomorrow, we don't have much time before we're all screwed."

Reign nods beside me, and I bring my hand to his, giving him a squeeze.

The guys have almost reached the door, and I'm shocked when Reign calls Archer's name.

Archer turns around with his brow lifted. "Yeah?"

Reign is silent as he steps toward them. My body tenses as fear rolls through me, fear that they're going to get into a fight, that Reign will go full slasher and gut Archer right in front of me, just for putting his hands on me.

Reign extends his hand.

Archer narrows his eyes, staring at Reign's extended hand. "What the fuck is that?"

Reign drops his hand, running his fingers through his hair. He looks uncomfortable as he stands there, as his chest rises slowly and falls. "I'm... ah, shit," he groans, tilting his head toward the ceiling. "I'm fucking sorry, man. For how everything happened. For fucking Creed, man." He shakes his head, and my chest hiccups with emotion.

Shit, Reign.

"I'm sorry for how shit went down. You have to know I never, ever wanted Creed to die. I tried to... I tried to save him." His throat grows thick with emotion, and he clears it. "I just wanted to let you know that I'm sorry. I'm sorry for it all, and more than anything, you guys are fucking family. Shit might have been fucked up, but death for my family isn't what I wanted."

Archer stares at him for long moments. I'm almost worried he's going to storm off. Kyler steps around Archer, grabbing Reign in a tight hug.

"Thanks, man," Kyler rasps.

Reign nods.

Posie smiles softly, tears in her eyes as she and Kyler turn around and walk out the door.

Archer still stands there, watching Reign.

Reign stands still as a statue until he finally steps back, ready to accept defeat.

"Wait," Archer says, stepping forward. He pauses a second, and then grabs Reign's arm, hauling him to him. They end up in a bro hug, which is so much more than a typical bro hug. They hold each other for many moments, not saying anything.

Until Archer steps back, keeping his head tilted toward the ground. "I'll talk to you," he grumbles before walking out.

I walk up to Reign, wrapping my arms around his waist from behind. He lays his hand on my arm, giving me a squeeze.

"That was brave," I whisper, nudging my nose against his spine as I inhale him.

He sighs, not saying a word.

We stand like that for many moments until he finally releases me.

"What if we went tonight to deal with Braylin? If we wait until tomorrow, we might be too late. They're going to search tonight? What if they find us?"

He shakes his head. "They aren't going to come this far. They'll only go to the border of Hellcrest Heights and in the woods there. We are too far off."

"But—" I start, ready to complain yet again, but he cuts me off with his fingers wrapping in my hair. He pulls my head back, until my eyes clash with his.

"Enough, Lakyn. We lay low tonight. Tomorrow morning I'll show you a few things and we'll go deal with her." He's not in the mood. Got it.

Deal with her. Kill her.

I nod, my fingers raising to his hair. Bending down, he secures his lips with mine, and he takes my breath away with the way he possessively steals my soul.

CHAPTER EIGHT
REIGN

"Not like that. Like this," I growl, shaking my knife in front of her as I try to show her how to grip the knife properly.

With the way she's holding it, she's either going to hurt herself, or she'll barely be able to get it through the tough meat of a human body.

"Like this?" She holds the knife incorrectly again, her thumb curling over her fingers, holding the handle too low to the bottom, her grip not nearly tight enough.

I shake my hand, and with my free hand, I grab the blade, sliding it from her grip way too easily.

"You aren't even holding it tightly," I groan, stepping up behind her.

We're standing behind the cabin, in the thick brush of the trees where even if we had an intruder or someone curious to travel this far in their search, they wouldn't see us all the way over here. The trees are thick, and we're dressed in dark, mixing in with the branches and the dark foliage.

I curl my front around Lakyn's back, bringing my hands around on either side of her. With her knife in my grip, I poise my hands in front of her, and she watches me intently as I show her exactly where my fingers go.

She nods as she watches me place them where they need to go. Then I hand her the knife, watching her closely as she holds the knife similar to how I was, but it's still just not where it should be.

I reach forward, adjusting the handle in her grip until she holds it tightly, properly.

"Good," I praise, pivoting the both of us until we're in front of a tree. Releasing her, I step to the side.

"Okay, pretend she's coming toward you head-on. How are you going to react?"

She shoves her knife out directly in front of her, and I'd laugh if she wasn't planning to go do something so drastic.

I shake my head. "No, like this."

Gripping my own knife, I walk up to the tree, swiping right so the sharp end of the blade nicks the tree. A large part of the wood chips away, flying through the air before falling to the ground in a light plop.

"Shit, Reign," she mumbles, staring at me in awe. She stares at me like I'm a saint, a god.

She's silly, because a man like me would never make it into Heaven.

I turn to her slightly as the corner of my lip quirks. "I want you to be the same, Lakyn. If you fuck up, she could gain the upper hand and we could be screwed. So pay attention to what I'm doing and do the exact same."

Her eyes narrow. "It's going to take time for me to be as good as you, Reign. You have practice. I have none."

I step to the side, giving her full access to the tree. "Which is exactly why we're here. Practice. You need to be perfect, Lakyn. There are no other options."

She takes a deep breath, moving forward a step. The light coating of snow on the ground crunches under her oversized shoes. They are about a size too big, but it was the only thing I could find. I left early this morning, before the sun was up, making my way to the edge of Hellcrest Heights.

There's a strip of older homes, most of them elderly people who have lived there their entire lives. As expected, the first home I went to was unlocked, and I was able to score Lakyn some clothes so she wasn't subjected to living the rest of her life naked underneath my sweatshirt.

I wouldn't have complained, but she also wouldn't never been able to leave the house.

"She's not moving. Attack her," I snap, and she lunges forward without a second thought, plunging the old rusty knife we found in the kitchen straight into the cold bark.

"Less Jason Voorhees and more psycho killer," I say.

She growls under her breath, pulling the knife out, needing to wiggle it back and forth until the tip flies free from the thick bark. She steps back, and then lunges forward, slicing into the branch slightly as she shoves the knife in. It goes in farther than before, but still gets stuck when the tip goes in.

"Good. That's better. Now. Try on me," I say, stepping in front of the branch.

Her eyes widen, and she takes a step back, leaving the knife inside the branch. "No, I'm not trying anything on you."

I cock my head to the side, my brow lifting. The sudden fear in her voice has me questioning if she can do this at all.

"Why not?" I lift my own knife toward my chest. "I'd try it on you, Lakyn. Shall we?" I tilt the knife toward her and watch as her entire body tenses.

"No, Reign. Let's just do it on her."

I give a slow shake of my head. "Not until I know you're ready."

She shivers. "Reign, no."

I point my knife at her. "Get ready, Lakyn. I suggest you get your own knife out of the tree unless you want to have more marks on your skin than the healing ones you already have."

Her eyes cut toward the branch with her knife sticking out of it. Her cheeks are rosy, her nose pink from the crisp air. In a split second, she grabs for her knife, pulling it out with all her strength before leaping to the side, ready, a little sloppy, but ready.

"She could be armed, you know. If she's smart at all, she would know we're coming for her. She could have a gun, but we'll pretend she only has time to grab a kitchen knife. She's coming after you, Lakyn. You'll have to defend yourself. What are you going to do?" I question her, wondering how much she's learned from me being the slasher.

Her face twists a second, and I watch her contemplate, wondering how she'll be able to get out of this on top.

"Weak spots," she whispers.

I nod after a second. "Which are?"

Her knife tilts toward her neck. "Neck. Heart."

I nod as I step toward her slowly, and she tenses as I drop my knife to her upper thigh. "Don't forget the vein near the inside of your thigh. Cut it correctly and she'll bleed out quick. If you're somehow at a disadvantage, you can always cut the thigh and she'll drop quickly. But honestly, get her anywhere and you may be able to gain the upper hand."

She nods, taking in every bit of information I'm giving her.

Time to test it.

Fuck, I hope she gets me.

I freeze, tensing my body as I stare at her. She wobbles to the side before freezing herself, watching me closely.

I lunge.

Leaping forward, I rush toward her, snow kicking up behind me as I make my way to her. She swings her knife out, and it cuts against the fabric of my sweatshirt, tearing a tiny hole in the arm. I swing my knife to the side, ready to cut her hip, when she moves to the side, out of my reach.

She swings the knife around, pretending to slice into my right lung. She slices again, and this time I can feel the blade as it cuts into my skin. I let out a hiss between my teeth as I feel the metal blade sink beneath the fabric of my sweatshirt.

Baby Lake wants to play.

Letting out a growl, I quit playing around and step toward her again, this time grabbing the knife and swinging it in front of her. She leans back, but my free arm swings out, and I whisp it around her neck. She lets out a whimper as the blade connects with her throat. Not enough to sink into the skin, but enough to cause her to freeze, panic in fear.

Her back sinks against my front, and I curl my spine as I press the knife in deeper. Taking a deep breath, I inhale the heady scent of blood as it fills the air. Glancing over her shoulder, I can see the way a dribble of blood drips from her neck and down the silver blade.

Perfection.

"You're going to kill me," she whispers.

I shake my head against hers. "No, baby, I'm not going to kill you. But take this as a fail. Don't let her gain the upper hand. Only I'm the one allowed to have a taste of your blood." Bringing the knife toward me, my tongue slides out and swipes against the blade. I can taste the thick crimson as it coats my tongue, and it's so fucking delicious, a burst of flavor exploding on my tongue.

She shivers against me, and I smile as I lick the blade clean. "Ready to go kill someone, baby Lake?"

She nods. Only once. "Yes."

The large two-story home in front of us is lit with lights inside. Halloween decorations are finally down. Soon the Christmas lights will be up, and I can already imagine a house like this will be extravagant. As are most of the homes in Hellcrest Heights. Unless you live on the shitty end of town, then you have no decorations at all.

"Do we just walk in?" she whispers beside me.

I shake my head, bringing my gloved finger up to my lips. I nod my head toward the side of the house, walking around the perimeter. It's cold, and in the middle of the night. After talking to Archer, he informed me was going to be calling the police station and talking to the detective, letting them know he thinks he saw us down by the lighthouse. If all goes well, they will all be down there, which is on the opposite end of town.

Hopefully he pulls through for us.

We had to walk all this way, and it took us over an hour of walking through a flurry of snow, the crispness in the air kissing our cheeks.

The light on the second level is lit up, and as we walk around the side of the house, I see a flash of brown, and I smirk, knowing Braylin is up there. She usually is at night, from the location on her phone the last two days. She goes out during the day, when she knows she'll be safe. At night, she worries about us, it's apparent. So, she goes home, and if I were to bet, her alarm system is on. The moment we walk through the front door, it'll go off.

Which means we have to disconnect it before we go inside.

"Garage," I whisper.

We walk around the side of the house, and I eye the side door on the garage. Digging into my pocket, I pull out my lock pick and shove it into the doorknob. It only takes a second before I hear the click, and I smile, shoving it open and stepping into the heated garage.

Braylin's Porsche sits nestled in the middle, the other two spaces empty.

Her parents are gone. Which, from what I've gathered, they always are.

I turn the flashlight on my phone, shining it around the wall of the garage.

"What are you looking for?" she whispers.

I shake my head, my eyes connecting with the local security company's system installed in the back corner. I nod my head toward it, pressing my finger to my lips again.

Slipping my knife from my pocket, I bring it to the security box, using the blade to pop the top open. Various colored wires come into view, and I grind my jaw, having no idea where to begin. Taking a deep breath, I read the instructions on the inside of the cover before I pull a few, enough to turn the sound off and disable the entire alarm.

"Wow," Lakyn whispers behind me, and I can hear the breathlessness in her voice.

I nod my head toward the door heading into the house. "Come on. It's disabled and won't alert the security company, but we only have so much time before they realize it's disabled."

Lakyn nods, and we head toward the door leading into the house. I glance at her as I walk up the few steps, making sure she looks ready.

She nods.

My gloved finger grips the silver knob, and I turn it slowly, opening the door to music filtering down from the second story. Lakyn's gloved fingers wrap around my hip, and we step inside. I pull the door closed softly behind me before glancing around the mudroom. It's simple, though updated.

Lana Del Rey plays through the surround sound speakers, and I turn to Lakyn, her mask firmly on her face, the hood of her black sweatshirt covering her hair, and her black leggings molding to her thighs.

She looks fucking sexy as a slasher.

I turn the knife to her, spinning on my feet as I press it against her neck, shoving her against the wall. I can feel the way her breathing picks up, her heart thundering against her chest. I bring the clean blade against the small sliver of skin between her sweatshirt and her mask.

She tilts her face up to mine, and I can see the way her eyes darken through the small holes of her mask. She stares at me, her eyes probing mine, and I swallow down the groan at the way her eyes secure to my soul.

Mine. All mine.

I knock my mask against hers, wishing I could kiss her, but I refuse to reveal her face or mine. So instead, I take what I can, which is every bit of her I can touch.

My hands slide from her shoulders down around her ribs and to her waist. I grip her tightly, and she trembles in my hold, unable to move barely an inch besides beginning to crumble in my grip.

"Your scent fills the air, baby Lake. It seems the anticipation of killing has you turned on."

She lets out a small growl, and I press the knife into her more firmly, turned on by her eagerness.

"Come on, Lakyn. No more time to waste." I pull the knife away from her neck, dropping it to my side, and step into the kitchen. The place is dim, with the lights on above the sink and a few tealights lit around the counter. It's clean, the granite countertops shining, the tall barstools, the matte stainless-steel appliances. It's all in pristine condition, like not one person actually has done any work in here.

The music turns off suddenly, making me stiffen briefly before it switches to a new song. The floor creaks upstairs, and Lakyn tilts her head up. My eyes fall to her gloved fingers, and I look at the knife in her grip, her fingers tensed tightly around the handle.

"I want her," she whispers.

I smile. She's fucking perfect. "You can have her."

Lakyn's arm goes around my neck, the one holding the knife. I bend with her pull, securing my lips against hers for a brief second. Our kiss is hot, demanding, possessive, and gone before I can even breathe. Or maybe it's just Lakyn, stealing my breaths as she always has.

Lakyn slides her hand from my neck, walking around me and toward the front of the house. She sees the grand staircase, the shining oak bannister glinting against the moonlight. Her gloved fingers slide against the surface, her fingers poised and delicately curved as she wraps them around the railing, sliding them up as only Lakyn can. Dangerous, beautiful.

Deadly.

She's transformed, I realize. She isn't the Lakyn I came home to, though she was already on her way. The entire process of being stalked by a masked killer, coming to find out she may have feared him, but fear wasn't the main emotion. It was a need—a desire that she fought against as if she could run from herself. She could never run from who she was becoming, it was going to overtake her like a giant storm. No matter which direction she ran, it was still going to demolish her where she stood.

It wasn't until she realized who the masked man was, that it was me, and she nearly murdered someone in front of the entire town, that the real her become unglued. The real Lakyn came out, as if her metaphorical mask finally came off.

And now she's here, someone different entirely, and if I were to be honest, the girl who walks in front of me up the stairs is the girl I've been in love with since I first met her. I knew she was this beneath her clothing. This girl, this dark and dangerous woman, was the real Lakyn.

And I've been waiting for her all this time, I just didn't realize it.

But now that she's here, I'm helplessly in love with her, and I'll spend my entire life being dark and depraved for her as I pull out her dark and depraved side.

"Lakyn," I whisper over the music, Lana crooning something that sounds too fucking romantic for my ears. She continues walking, and then it's as if she hears the tone of my echoed voice around the notes of the music. She glances at me over her shoulder, and I smirk at her, though she can't see the way my cheeks turn to stone, or the dangerous lift of my lips.

"I love you, Lakyn," I growl under my breath, and she shivers, as if she can feel the vibrations from here.

Her masked face tilts to the side, and I can imagine the soft gaze in her eyes. "I love you, Reign."

Her eyes glow before she turns around, and she tightens her hold on her knife, grabbing the handle as she gouges it into the railing. Shavings of wood curl around the blade before sliding down to the ground. She makes it to the top of the stairs, and the music is so loud it drowns out the sound of the knife against the wood. She makes it to the top of the stairs and glances right, then left, where the shower is running from the bathroom.

She glances over her shoulder at me briefly before she steps toward the bathroom. This is about to be bloody, and I should warn her that when the blood mixes with water, it always looks like there is more than there is, but I won't warn her.

It's time for her to figure everything out on her own.

Turning toward the bathroom, she nudges the corner of the door open with her boot, and music blares out of Braylin's phone which is connected to a speaker system. Braylin sings through the shower door, the spray pounding down around her body as she washes the soap from her hair.

I can see as Lakyn begins practically vibrating beside me as she steps into the bathroom, the room surrounded with light while she's cloaked in black. She steps into the shower farther, extending her knife out and tapping it onto the marbled counter.

Ting.

She tilts her head to the side, her gloved finger reaching out and tapping onto the phone. She turns the music off, and the sound throughout the house cuts off abruptly, Braylin's voice singing off-tune before it breaks at the end as she settles into the silence.

"What the hell?" she mumbles.

I stare at the shower, watching through the clouded door as she turns to face us. Her body tenses, and she steps back, until her naked form hits the back wall of the shower.

"What are you doing in my house?" she screeches from behind the shower door.

Lakyn giggles, and I almost wish she had a voice alternator like I have, but there wasn't enough time to get one. Plus, Braylin knows who we are anyway. The masks are a means of a disguise, because we don't need to be noticed more than we already are.

"Step out of the shower and I'll tell you," Lakyn says, her voice holding a slight bit of husk in it.

Braylin freezes, and I can see her eyes widen from through the shower door. "Oh, my God. Reign? Lakyn?" she shrieks, a cry bursting from her lips. "What the hell are you doing here?"

I laugh. I can't help it. "If you have to ask, you're one stupid bitch."

She lets out a scream, her palm slapping against the wet tiled wall. It makes a loud slap, water flinging across the shower. "Get out! Get out, get out, get out of here!" she screams. "You guys are murderers!"

Lakyn takes a step closer to the shower and Braylin starts screaming wildly. "You'll never get away with this! They'll know exactly who it is! Everyone knows I'm this close to taking you all down." She pinches her fingers together until there's only a hair's breadth between her fingers. Then her hand flings toward the door, and she slaps her palm against the glass. The walls shake, rattling metal against glass.

Lakyn takes another step, her knife going out, the blade tapping against the glass wall. "I know who you are, Braylin, and I know what you've done. I realize that everyone will know it's me, and see, at this point, I don't care. I don't care if the world knows I killed you, because the alternative…" She takes a deep breath. "The alternative is letting you live, and that would involve my friends all going down for this shit, and I just can't let that happen."

She starts hyperventilating, through the steamy shower and the pelting water, she starts to shiver, though I know from the heat of the room it's still hot water pounding against her skin. "I won't say anything! I'll stop my podcast. I won't make another video!"

Lakyn drags the knife down the glass wall until she reaches the door. Pulling it open with her gloved hand, steam pours from the shower and there stands Braylin, naked, trembling, absolute fear and terror in her eyes.

"I'll delete everything. I'll make a video and take it back. I'll retract every word." She wheezes, fear cloaking her throat. "Please," she croaks.

Lakyn laughs. "No," she says simply, shoving her knife forward. Braylin leaps back, her body slamming against the wall. Lakyn growls, lunging through the doorway of the shower. She shoves the knife straight into Braylin stomach, and my eyes widen, my mouth watering when I see the fear in Braylin eyes. Her mouth opens on a gasp, her hand slapping against the knife as she searches for the wound.

Lakyn pulls up with the knife, and I swear I can hear it tear through her skin. She slides the knife out of her skin, and blood soaks the knife, dripping from the tip of the blade and falling to the bottom of the shower. The blood dilutes to a light pink, surrounding both of their feet and growing until the entire ground is filled with blood. It looks horrific, but I don't sense a nervousness or fear in Lakyn's form. She is in control, angry, violent, and vibrating with a high.

I know that high. It's euphoric, one you only get from the scent of blood and the feeling of holding someone else's life in your hands. Braylin cries, weeping hysterically while her hand presses against her stomach as she attempts to keep her insides from spilling outside.

Lakyn lifts the bloody knife above her head, her chest heaving as the water pelts the front of her black sweatshirt. It looks heavy, inky as it molds to her form, water sprinkling across both of them and spraying out of the shower. The floor gets drenched, clear with a tinge of pink water soaking into the cream-colored mats.

Braylin stares at the opening of the shower with tears in her eyes, and with a groan, she lunges forward, attempting to get away from Lakyn's impending knife.

"Get away from me!" Braylin screeches.

Lakyn laughs, grabbing onto Braylin's hair and tugging it toward her. Braylin flies back, her feet slipping on the ground, and she begins to fall. Lakyn's laughter turns to a growl and she swings the knife down, plunging it directly into Braylin's neck. Braylin chokes, and Lakyn immediately pulls it free before shoving it back into her neck. In and out she shoves the knife until the ground is no longer pink, but a dark red, the entire ground filled with Braylin's blood. It smells tangy in the bathroom, humid and nearly stifling as Braylin goes limp and Lakyn pulls the knife from her body for the last time. The sound of skin against metal makes a sound that makes the hairs on my arms stand on end.

Lakyn turns toward me, shoving the mask over her face, revealing pink cheeks and a damp hairline.

"Holy shit," she whispers, her chest heaving with each breath. She glances at the knife, her eyes glowing brightly as she stares at the thick blood. The knife slips from her fingers, falling on top of Braylin before clamoring to the ground. She turns her gaze to mine, and I shove my mask up, staring at her darkly.

"Baby Lake…"

There aren't words to explain how beautiful and epic she was as she took a life. My girl, my baby Lake, she's as much of a monster as I am. She took so easily, with not an ounce of remorse, and doesn't look like she has a lick of fear in her eyes.

Only elation.

"Did I do good?" she whispers, her voice raspy.

I nod, stepping into the puddle of bloody water. My hand snakes out, and I wrap it around her waist. Her clothes are soaked, the warmth turning cold quickly as I haul her body against mine. She molds to me perfectly, sinking her curves against my hard form. My hand goes to the small of her back, and I press her into me, smirking down at her.

"So good, baby. I'm so fucking proud of you," I murmur, leaning down and pressing my lips against hers. The soft plushness of her lips against my commanding ones. I take from her and show her exactly how proud of her I am with my kiss, breathing her in and giving her life with my lips.

She whimpers into my mouth, moaning against me, her bloody hands falling to my shoulders. She squeezes the muscles, her nails digging through the fabric and into my skin. I can feel as she creates small crescents against my arms, and I groan, relishing the pain. I press into her harder, nudging my erection against her lower stomach.

She steps over Braylin's body, her boots squeaking against the tiled floor as she climbs into my arms. I wrap my hands underneath her thighs, holding her tightly against me as I spin around and make my way to the counter. My gloved hand comes out, swiping away the makeup and clothing piled on the counter. Settling Lakyn down on the cool surface, I nudge her thighs open as I settle in between them. She curls her fingers around my shoulders, hauling herself forward until the crux of her thighs press into my erection.

Gliding her hands up, she cups her fingers around my neck, painting them red with her bloody hands. I can feel the blood stain my skin, and I tilt my head to the side, pressing my lips against her neck. My lip curls as I bare my teeth, sinking them into the sensitive skin of her neck. She trembles in my arms, dropping her hands to the belt of my jeans. I can hear the clank as she undoes the belt. Her hands tear at my pants, loosening them enough and shoving them over my hips.

I growl as I reach forward, grabbing onto her leggings and tearing them down her thighs. I can hear the sound of the threads popping from my aggressive pulling. They pause around her ankles, stuck above her boots, and I release them, pressing my hands against her bare knees and shoving them apart. Her wet folds come into view, glistening and dripping with arousal.

My gloved fingers reach forward, and I press them against her wet folds. The warmth seeps through the fabric and melts into my fingers. I press my fingers forward, sinking deep inside of her and feel her walls clench around my digits. I curl them forward, and she bucks against me, letting out a throaty moan as her eyes roll in the back of her head. I sink my teeth into her again, feeling her skin break, the warmth of her blood coating my tongue.

She grips my erection in her fingers, squeezing tightly as she shimmies her hips toward me. Needy. Wanton.

"What do you need, baby Lake?" I rasp against her neck.

"You. I need you," she moans, pressing my erection against her wet folds. My hands snap behind her, and I grab onto the curling iron, my fingers gripping the cord. I pull her hands behind her with my free hand, wrapping the cord around her wrists, tying them back. I wrap the end around the sink faucet, keeping her arms pinned there. Her shoulders are pulled back, her chest jutting out toward me.

I smirk at her as I crouch down in front of her, pulling my knife from the back of my jeans. Her eyes widen, flaring as she sees my clean blade.

"What are you going to do?" She shimmies again. "I need you."

I exhale against her writhing pussy, the warmth of my breath kissing her sensitive skin. She shivers as I pull the knife forward, pressing the tip against her naked mound.

"Marking you," I murmur darkly, pressing down on the blade.

She tenses as I drag the knife down her skin. Not too deep, but enough that it'll leave a scar. She whimpers as I carve into her skin, my hand steady while my insides vibrate wildly, animalistically, as I mark her.

I take my time, making each swipe perfect until I pull the knife back, bloody on the tip, and stare at Lakyn's skin. Rivers of blood coat her pussy, seeping between her folds. She rubs her thighs together, and it smears the blood across her skin. I bring my fingers to my teeth, tearing the glove off before planting my palm against her skin. I swipe away the blood and watch as Lakyn tilts her head to look between her legs.

Right on the top of her pussy are the letters RW. My initials carved into her skin. Her eyes widen, her mouth dropping open in shock.

"Yours," she whispers, glancing up at me through her damp eyelashes.

"Mine," I growl, pressing my fingers against her skin, feeling the raised skin of my initials against my palm.

Standing up, I grip her behind her knees, pulling her toward me until I'm lined up. I stare down at her bloody pussy, my cock harder than it's ever been, pulsing with a need to claim her.

"Mine," I repeat, thrusting forward slowly, sinking into her fully. My cock pulses as the walls of her cunt tighten around me. I grab her by the hips, and her ankles lock behind my back. My fingers burrow into her skin as I pull out and sink back into her, her wetness clinging to my skin. I let out a groan as I thrust into her. Her head tilts back, her arms still pinned behind her back as I speed up, until her body rattles against the sink.

"Oh fuck, Reign," she moans. Glancing up, her eyes flit over my shoulder, and I can see in the glossiness of them, lays Braylin. "I killed someone," she gasps, tears flooding her eyes. They aren't sad tears, or remorseful. They are a new beginning, a new life, one where we can be wild and free. Where we can thrive in the madness and create absolute mayhem.

"You killed someone," I grunt, shoving into her roughly.

She groans deep in her throat, tilting her head back. Her tears trail down her temples, falling into her damp hair. "I killed someone, and it felt so good," she gasps.

I drag my hand from her hip, around to her stomach. I slide it up, between her breasts, until my fingers wrap around slender throat. I squeeze tightly, smirking at her devilishly. "You've never looked so beautiful, Lakyn. Taking the life of someone else, the confidence in every step you made. You've always been stunning, Lakyn, but tonight there wasn't anything that could've been more beautiful than watching you take another life as you did. So fucking perfect."

She whimpers, glancing up to look at me. Our eyes lock, and I become in a trance as I watch her, memorize her, mark her, consume every inch of her. Lakyn is mine, and she will be mine long after she takes her last breath.

"I'm going to come," she moans.

I squeeze her neck. "You'll come when I say and not a second sooner."

She writhes on the counter, and I grip her tightly as I speed up, bruising the insides of her thighs with my hips, growing to stone inside of her.

"Come, baby Lake. Wake the dead with your screams."

Her shoulders jut back, her nipples peaking through her wet sweatshirt as her breasts bounce lightly against her chest. The walls of her pussy clench around me as her orgasm takes hold. I can feel my balls clench, drawing up as I empty myself inside of her. I bruise her skin with my fingers, staring down at her skin painted red. I shove into the hilt, clenching my cock as I empty every last drop inside of her.

She lets out a gasp as I pull out of her, staring down at the initials on the top of her pussy. I bring my fingers down to her skin, brushing my initials lightly.

"Braylin?" Comes a voice from the hallway.

My eyes simultaneously widen with Lakyn's, and I snap my hand back, untying her hands as quickly as possible. Two voices come closer, mumbling to each other quietly.

Knock, knock.

"Braylin? Are you in there? The alarm wasn't on."

Shit.

We didn't reset the alarm. Fuck.

Lakyn leaps off the counter, pulling her pants back up as I tuck myself back into my jeans. I'm doing up my belt when I hear one more knock on the door.

"Coming in, Braylin," a masculine voice says, moments before the door opens, and there stands Braylin's parents, dressed to the nines in a dress and suit, and absolute horror on their faces.

"Braylin?" her mom screams, glancing over our shoulder and at her daughter, dead and bloody on the shower floor.

"Oh, my God!" Braylin's dad shouts, his gaze swinging to the both of us. "No!" he roars, stepping forward a second before pausing. He looks a cross between angry and terrified. He wants to go to his daughter, he wants to run, and he wants to hurt us, all at the same time.

Lakyn turns to me, but I don't take my eyes off the parents. Squatting down slowly, I grab my knife from the ground, clutching the handle in my grip. I swipe my glove up too, shoving it quickly into my pocket.

I know what I have to do, yet I don't know if Lakyn is capable of taking a life she's not prepared for.

"The police have already been called. They will be here any minute. I suggest not doing anything stupid," her dad says, leveling me a look.

Well, that's just not okay.

I step forward, the knife in my grip as I lunge toward him. He's an imbecile, though, because instead of running, he rushes me, attempting to take the knife from my hand.

"You fucking murderer!" the father roars, and I swipe the knife, cutting through his suit coat and up his arm.

The mom screams, and I can hear Lakyn rush behind me. The sound of metal scraping gives away her grabbing her own knife. I shove the dad on the ground, hating that Lakyn has to do this, but knowing we don't have a choice. It's them or us, and I will always, always, choose us.

"Get off of him!" the mom screams, coming up behind me and hitting me in the back of the head with her purse.

I attempt to shake her off, pressing my knee against his chest. He wheezes as I press my knee between his pecs, cutting off his breathing.

"Bitch, don't touch him," Lakyn growls, and my body tenses at the sound of a knife sinking into skin. The mom falls off me, and I use the moment to my advantage, pulling the knife up before shoving it down above my knee, straight into his heart. He lets out a gasp, his eyes widening as he starts choking. His hands shove at my arms, but I grind my teeth, putting more weight into his wound. Blood fills his mouth, and he coughs. Bloody spittle flies from his mouth, coating my face.

Glancing over my shoulder, I watch as Lakyn stabs the mother in the back, again and again. The mother is dead, her eyes open as a trail of blood seeps out of the corner of her mouth. She lays face down on the bathroom floor, her knee-length dress wrinkled with blood splatter across the creamy material.

"Lakyn, she's dead," I grunt, pulling the knife out of the father's chest. He chokes, and his wide eyes begin to narrow, growing cloudy with each passing second.

"She's not dead enough," Lakyn breathes, stabbing her yet again.

I bring the knife to the father's neck, swiping it across his jugular and watching as the rest of his blood quickly flows from his throat.

I wipe the knife on his expensive suit jacket and turn to Lakyn. "We don't have time for this. If the police are on their way, then they'll be here any—"

The sound of sirens ring out down the street, and I tense into stone.

"Lakyn, stop. We have to go," I growl, leaping off the dad and glancing around the bathroom, making sure I've left nothing else behind.

She pulls the knife from the mom, her face covered in blood splatter. "What are we going to do?" she whimpers, glancing through the doorway, as if they are going to come pounding up the stairs at any moment.

"We can sneak out the side of the house, but we have to go now." I grab onto her wrist, hauling her out of the bathroom.

This shit is really testing my patience.

We race across the hall and down the stairs as the sound of sirens grows closer. Our heavy pants with our pounding footsteps are the only things heard as we race back through the mudroom and through the garage. We rush out the side door, and the lights light up the trees in the yard.

They're close. Too close.

"Lakyn, you have to run as quick as you can," I snap as I glance at her. We race through the yard and across the street, just as three squad cars pull up on the street, followed by dark SUVs behind them, which I assume is the FBI. Their headlights shine on us, and we both freeze.

"Oh shit," Lakyn whispers.

"Run!" I roar, picking up my pace and running into the yard across the street.

"Stop where you are!" a megaphone shouts through the night.

"Don't stop. Don't stop," I breathe, my feet keeping their pace. I glance toward Lakyn, seeing her running with me, her arms pumping wildly from side to side. Tears flow down her face, pure terror painted in her eyes.

"I'm going to get you out of here, Lakyn. Just fucking run," I grunt.

"We will shoot. Drop to your knees right now!" an officer shouts in the distance.

"Reign! They have guns!" Lakyn screams.

"Just keep going. Don't look back."

If any of them shoot Lakyn, I will light this entire fucking town on fire.

Bang, bang. Bang, bang, bang.

Shots fire through the air, and Lakyn jolts beside me.

"If you stop, you're dead. Don't fucking stop," I snap.

"They're going to shoot us. We're going to die. Oh my God," she cries out, and I reach out, squeezing her hand as I glance at the woods in the distance.

"We need to get to the forest. Once we get there, we'll lose them. Don't stop, Lakyn. We're so fucking close."

She shakes her head, letting out a cry as she picks up her pace.

Bang, bang, bang.

A searing fire roars through my shoulder as I'm jolted to the side, but I don't fall off my feet. I keep running. I refuse to give up. I can't, not with Lakyn by me.

"Were you shot?" Lakyn screams, glancing at me. "Oh, fuck! You're bleeding!" she cries out, her pace slowing slightly.

I shake my head, leaping off the last curb and crossing the street. The sirens are behind us, the speeding cars, the constant megaphone telling us to stop. And the gunshots, growing closer, and closer.

I cut left into the edge of the woods, away from the small cabin in the woods.

"Where are we going?" Lakyn asks.

"Follow me," I growl. The sky lights up behind us.

They're close. Too close.

I rush into the woods, instantly encased in darkness, though the sound of car doors slamming alerts me they are going to follow us into the woods.

I grind my teeth together, my body turning numb while aching wildly at the same time.

"Where are we going? The cabin is the other way," she whines, her breaths coming out in small pants. "I'm getting tired, Reign. I'm not going to make it."

I turn my gaze toward hers, keeping our pace quick as we race through the woods. "You will not give up on me, Lakyn. Not now. You hear me?"

She nods her head, unable to say a single word.

"Put your hands in the air! We've got you surrounded!" an officer shouts, and I turn to Lakyn with a pain in my shoulder and pain in my heart.

"Lakyn," I murmur.

She turns to me, and it's almost in slow motion as she looks purely frightened. "Reign," she breathes.

"I love you," I say moments before my hand shoots out, and I shove her as hard as I can. She stumbles to the side, letting out a yelp as she falls down the small hill.

And right off the cliff. Into the water below.

CHAPTER NINE

LAKYN

"I love you."

Those are the last words I hear before he shoves me so roughly I am whiplashed to the side. My body jolts as I stumble down the small hill.

And right off the cliff.

My scream gets lodged in my throat, and I can't say or speak a word as I tumble through the night air and toward the water below.

The moment my body hits the surface, it's like glass shards spread across my body. The cold water is like knives against my skin, and I gasp in a painful breath as quick as I can before I'm submerged beneath the surface.

I suck in a breath moments before I'm plummeted toward the floor of the water, attempting to swim against gravity. My arms windmill around me as my butt hits the ground. My shoes shove against the ground as I push myself back to the surface. The cold water nearly paralyzes me, the cold so vicious it feels like lead seeps into my skin.

I shove off as hard as I can, kicking my way to the surface. The moment my head breaks free, I arch my back, allowing in as much air as I possibly can. I glance up toward the top of the cliff, hearing voices in the distance. A flashlight shines down at the water, and I quickly go back under the surface, swimming toward the edge of the cliff.

My back presses against it as I break through the water, intaking sharp, shallow breaths as I wait for the sounds of shouting to pass.

He pushed me over the edge.

He's trying to save me.

My heart sinks into my feet, and fear clutches me tightly as I fear the worst.

Did he allow himself to get caught?

I glance up at the cliff, wishing I could see him looking down at me, but I can't, and he's not there.

I silent sob rips through my chest, and I float onto my side, kicking softly around the side of the cliff. I'm as silent as I can, and eventually, the noises drift away.

They're gone. Did they get him? Is he in the back of the police car?

I shake my head, silent tears tracking down my cheeks and mixing with the ocean water. I paddle heavily against the waves until I find a clearing, almost like steppingstones up to the forest above.

I drag my weak, cold body to the top of the cliff, my fingers raw as I grip onto the sharp and dull stones. Once I reach the top, I collapse, falling onto my stomach on the forest floor. Shivers rack my entire body.

"It's so cold," I whisper, wishing Reign was here to protect me. But he's not, and fear grabs hold when I realize I don't know where he is.

Please don't leave me.

I dig my fingers into the dirt ground, my nails becoming embedded with pebbles and twigs. I can feel them pierce my skin, and it's so painful as I pull myself up, my body so cold, so tired.

I grip onto each tree branch as I wander through the woods, knowing the general direction of where the cabin is, but worried I won't be able to find my way.

"Help me," I whisper, my cheeks drenched with tears, my teeth chattering as I glance left and right.

Where the hell do I go?

I pull myself through, the only light is the crescent moon shining down on me. It lights up the forest, only slightly through the branches, and I stumble north, swallowing down my cries as my body starts to ache.

I can feel it shutting down.

I can feel my entire being shutting down.

My knees eventually give out, and I fall to the ground, my palms slamming against the rough forest floor.

"Lakyn," the voice sounds so far away, but I gasp, knowing his voice anywhere.

"Reign?" I choke out, sniffling my runny nose and attempting to blink through my blurry tears. "Reign? Where are you?" I whimper.

"Look," he mumbles.

I blink, blink, blink, and eventually, through the thick trees, is the cabin in the small clearing. Sitting on the front steps is Reign. He's hunched over, gripping his shoulder as he stares at me in pain and awe.

The sob finally breaks through my chest, and I crawl forward, all the way across the woods, the clearing, and up to the front steps.

He stares at me, his face filled with worry and hesitation, fear, relief, anger. It's all there, and all I can do is reach forward and grip onto his ankle.

"I thought you were gone," I whisper, my face falling to his shoe.

He leans forward with a grunt, grabbing me beneath my arms and hauling me up. A groan breaks from his throat as he lifts me into his arms, shoving himself to a stand. "Never, Lakyn."

"Where'd you go?" I whisper as he opens the front door and steps inside.

He says nothing as he pulls me across the living room and kitchen, into the small bathroom.

He drops me, but keeps his arm around my waist as he holds me up. His jaw clenches as he watches me. His hands drop to the hem of my sweatshirt, and he pulls it over my head and drops it to the ground in a wet plop.

"Where'd you go?" I repeat, staring at him. "How did you get away?"

He shakes his head. "I just… bolted."

My brow furrows. "Why'd you push me over the edge? I could've died."

He shakes his head. "I would've never been able to get away with you with me, Lakyn. I had to run, and you were growing tired. I couldn't risk it, Lakyn. I did what I thought I had to do. So, I pushed you."

I let out a shiver as phantom pains of the cold water lashing across my body come back to me. "You couldn't warn me?" I growl.

He leans over the tub, turning on the water. The pipes groan, the faucet sputtering before a weak spray of water shoots out. "I know you better than that, baby Lake. You would've never gone along with it if I told you what I was going to do."

This is true.

"I could've died," I whisper.

He steps over to me, grabbing onto the waistband of my pants. He rips them over my hips, crouching down to take my boots off and tear my pants over my feet. "We both would've died if we got caught. We just did a triple murder, Lakyn."

I take a shallow breath, knowing it's possibly the truth. It doesn't hurt any less, though, physically or mentally.

The bathroom grows warm, and my erratic trembles turn to small shivers. He shoves my clothes to the side and stands up, taking his own clothes off. His shoulder has stopped bleeding where the bullet grazed him, and I brush my fingers against it, but he flinches. "I'm fine," he growls.

He tosses his clothes on top of mine before stepping up to me. Wrapping his arms once again around my waist, he hauls my body to his. "I told you I wouldn't let anything happen to you."

I tilt my head back, my cool hair trickling across my shoulder blades. He lifts his hand, removing my mask from the top of my head and tossing it onto the ground. "We'll have to get out of here soon, you know."

He grabs me by the waist, lifting me into his arms as he steps toward the tub. The spray is warm as it pelts my body. Reign reaches out, grabbing onto the edge of the shower curtain and pulling it closed, encasing us in the dim light.

"I thought you said we were safe here," I murmur, dropping my head to his shoulder as the spray warms my back.

"We are, and we will be, at least for a little while. But sooner or later they will scope out this entire forest, and we need to be long gone by then."

I tighten my legs and arms around him, leaning my head back to look him in the eyes. His eyes are dark, possessive, protective.

"Where will we go?" I whisper.

His hand reaches out, and he brings his thumb to my jawline. He grabs a droplet of water that's trickling down my skin, blocking it with his thumb. My breathing picks up as he watches me, his eyes flaring with a darkness that'll lead to more blood spilt, only this time it'll be mine.

"We could go anywhere we want. South America, Alaska. Wherever you want," he rumbles from deep in his chest. He bends down, his scratchy jaw itching my cheek.

He brings his fingers to my hair, clenching them tightly in his grip and pulling my head back, letting the water filter through my messy strands.

"I want to go wherever you will be," I moan, enjoying the warmth seep into my bones. They begin to thaw, and the pain dissipates with Reign's body against mine.

"We can go anywhere, or everywhere." He takes a step forward, until I'm no longer in the spray, but he is. My spine presses against the tiled wall, and he pins me against the cool tiles with his hips. I can feel his throbbing erection between my legs, needy and hungry for me.

My hand lifts to his hair, and I run my fingers through the warm, wet strands, pulling them away from his face as I look him in the eyes. "Everywhere," I whisper.

He leans down, his lips pressing against mine. My mouth opens with a gasp, and he slides his tongue between my lips. I moan into his mouth, and his teeth sink down in my lower lip as he drops a hand between us. I can feel as he lines himself up with me, and his hips shift forward, he cock entering me in one smooth thrust.

My head tilts back, knocking against the wall as a moan escapes my throat. His lips nudge against my throat, his teeth baring as he bites down gently, followed by a swipe of his warm tongue. His hips begin to move, grinding against me until my body shifts against the wall. Bringing his hands to mine, he grabs my wrists, hauling them above my head. He opens my fingers, wrapping them around the faucet of the shower. His fingers come down around mine, pinning them tightly against the warm metal. "Hold on tight, baby Lake."

I do as I'm told, gripping the shower head tightly as he begins to move quickly. My body slams backward, and each moan that escapes my chest echoes through the shower. The steam fills up in our little hidden cove, making breathing difficult, my body shivering, not with cold this time but an overwhelming sense of pleasure.

He drops his hands from my wrists, and I keep hold of the faucet as he brings his hands to my hips, burrowing his fingers into my skin and bruising me, marking me.

His hand shifts forward, until his fingers brush against the wound above my mound. His initials, ones that will be marked there for the rest of eternity. "Mine, baby Lake. You've always been mine."

I nod my head, too overwhelmed to speak with the way he fills me so completely, until I can feel him in my stomach, stretching my walls, hitting every single sensitive spot in my being

"I could never get enough of you," he growls, his thumb pressing into the scar. I let out a cry, the pain somehow bordering on pleasure.

"Fuck, Reign. It feels so good," I moan.

He slams into me harder, until the shower curtain vibrates with our thrusts. He turns manic, wild as he fucks me ruthlessly underneath the warm spray of the shower.

He grows impossibly harder inside of me, until a tinge of pain hits me. "Come for me, Lakyn. Come now," he groans.

His command grips me. A flush of warmth spreads across my body and floods my limbs. A scream breaks from my throat, and it barrels through the room as Reign grips me, slams my hips against his, his own moan roaring from between his lips.

His thrusts slow, until we're slowly rocking against each other, our breaths panting from our chests. The grip of his fingers loosen, and I drop my hands to his shoulders as he slowly lowers me to the ground.

My knees shake, and I balance against him as I gain my footing.

Reign brushes the hair from my face, combing the strands with his fingers. "We don't have much time here, Lakyn. I need you to be ready. When it's time to go, we'll have to go, and we can't wait."

I nod, a lick of fear rolling through me.

"So be ready, Lakyn, because when the time comes, Hellcrest Heights will be nothing but a memory."

CHAPTER TEN

REIGN

My eyes pop open to the sound of gasping, wheezing. I shoot up, looking over to see a dark figure standing over Lakyn. A pillow is in his hands, and he's pressing it directly over Lakyn's face. She thrashes from side to side, attempting to get him off of her, but it's useless with the hold he has over her face.

Fuck no.

I leap up from the couch, lunging onto the ground where she must have fallen. The man sees me a second too late, his body freezing as I crash my body against his. The pillow flies off Lakyn's face, and she inhales, gasping as she sits up, tears streaming down her cheeks.

"You okay?" I growl, turning back to the man. He shakes his head from side to side, gaining his bearings as he turns toward me. He has a ski mask on his face, and I bring my fist back, crashing it straight into his cheek. He falls onto his back, and I climb on top of him, grabbing the top of his mask and tearing it from his head.

My eyes narrow when I see one of my dad's longtime workers watching me in a mixture of fear and anger. A large red mark paints his cheek, and

I bring my fist back, powering it forward as I smash my knuckles into his other one. He lets out a groan, bringing his knees up as he attempts to kick me, shove me, fight me off in any way possible.

"Motherfucker. I'll fucking kill you," I growl.

"Reign," Lakyn cries.

I look over my shoulder, seeing her sitting there, fear in her eyes as she clutches her chest in terror.

Anger roars through my body, and I turn back to the man, my bones vibrating with rage. "You're fucking dead," I snap, and my entire body explodes. I pummel him with my fists, hitting his face over and over again. The only sounds which can be heard are the sounds of my knuckles hitting his bones. My fingers drip with red, and I grab onto each side of his head, swinging up and slamming the back of his skull against the wood floor.

Again and again I pound his head into the ground until he's nothing but mush. Until he's no longer fighting, but limp beneath me, and a pool of blood surrounds us.

"Reign, he's dead," Lakyn chokes from behind me.

I take a breath, my tense fingers releasing his head. Whatever is left of it drops with a plop, a mushy slap against the ground. Blood is in every direction I look, and I lean back, my hands planting into the puddle of blood on the floor as I move off him.

"Holy shit," Lakyn whispers, crawling over to me. I turn to her, seeing her wide eyes, her flushed cheeks. The way she breathes heavily as her eyes flit from the man and back to me.

I turn to the door, seeing it wide open, the night air gusting into the small cabin. The fire I created before bed is nearly extinguished, only a few embers still glowing beneath the logs.

"Who is he?" Lakyn mumbles.

I stand up, stepping over the dead body and walking toward the door. I shut it, and lock it, noticing how the lock has been manipulated.

How the fuck did I sleep through that?

I grab a couple logs near the front door and set them in the fire. Bloody handprints are left across the surface of the wood.

"He worked for my father," I clip, anger rolling through me.

I told my father to not mess with her. I warned him, and he sent someone after her anyway. He went against my word, but I suppose I knew my father never listens to anyone but himself.

Either way, he came after her when I told him not to. I need to keep Lakyn safe, even if it means taking out my own blood.

"Wait… what?" she breathes.

I turn toward her. "My father sent him here, Lakyn. To kill you."

Her breathing picks up, her brow furrowing as she stares at me. "Why would he do that?"

I grind my teeth together. "Because he's pissed at me. He wants you dead, Lakyn, and nothing is going to stop him until he gets what he wants."

I watch as the color drains from her face slowly, as if it's dripping out the end of her body. "He's going to kill me."

I shake my head. "No, Lakyn. He's not going to kill you."

She clutches her neck, as if she pleads with herself to get air. "How do we stop him from coming after me? Some weird goon just came in and tried suffocating me in the middle of the woods in the middle of the night!"

She's growing hysterical.

I step toward her. "I'm going to kill him. I'm going to take him out."

Her eyes flare. "You're going to kill your father?"

I have no other choice. It's him or her, and I'll always choose her.

"Yes, I am." I walk around her, heading toward the kitchen, and turn on the faucet. My bloody hands go beneath the tap, and I watch as the bottom of the sink turns a light red from the blood. I splash water on my face and wash off every drop I can, but I still feel full of the dead man that's laying on the living room floor. "I'm going to kill him now."

"Now?" she shrieks.

I turn to her with a fierce glare, anger lighting my skin on fire. "Yes, now. I'm not waiting for him to send someone else." I walk toward the front door. "Stay here."

She leaps in front of me, her bare foot slapping into the puddle of blood. "No, wait! Let me go with you."

A laugh bursts from my chest. "No, Lakyn. You're staying here this time."

Her mouth twists in anger. "Fuck no, Reign. You don't get to walk out this door and leave me here alone, again. Not this time. We just committed a triple homicide together, so why can't I come help you?" There's an edge and rage in her voice that causes her body to tremble. She's mad at the situation, she's mad at me. She's fucking mad at my father.

I'm much worse than she is.

"Because I can't fucking watch out for you!" I roar in her face.

Her hand raises, and she jabs her finger in my chest. "I don't need anyone to look out for me, Reign! I can look out for myself!"

I grab her finger, pulling it down slightly. "You think you can take care of yourself?"

Is she capable of looking out for herself? She just murdered two people. She ran from the police. She plummeted beneath the water and found her way back to the cabin. She survived it all, and she doesn't have a look of fear in her eyes at the prospect of having to do it again.

She wants to, and she wants to stand on her own two feet when she does it.

"Of course I can take care of myself," she snaps, yanking her finger from my grip. "I want you, Reign, but I'm also my own person. You aren't the only person who has a darkness inside of them. I do, too, and I can handle myself."

I know she can, and that's what fucking scares me.

I take a step back, narrowing my eyes at her. "You think you can come with me? You want to show me you can take care of yourself?"

She gives me one single, short nod.

"Then I'll bring you with me, and you fucking prove it to me. I'm not going to hold your hand, and I'm not going to baby you. You think you can do it?" I lean forward, getting directly in her face. "Then prove it to me."

"I will prove it to you," she says, standing a little taller, her chin tilted back.

I smirk at her. "Then show me what you've got, baby Lake."

"What are you doing?" Lakyn asks as I park along the side of an empty road.

I pull the wires underneath the steering wheel, turning off the car. We found this car on the road to town. Unfortunately, we couldn't walk the entire way to my father's house, which meant we had to hot-wire a car.

It was easy, though I know the authorities will be called for a stolen vehicle, and I'm sure they'll connect the dots. We only have a limited amount of time before the police are looking for us and the car.

So I parked far enough away from my father's house, instead of being a fucking idiot and parking in the driveway.

"Can't park too close. We'll have to go from here on foot." Opening up the driver's side door, I step out into the dark. It's got to be nearing four in the morning, only another hour or two and the sun will start to come up. Our time is limited, which means we have to move. Fast.

"How far away is it?" she whispers as she steps out of the car.

I nod my head down the long, wealthy neighborhood street. "His house is at the end of the road."

She nods, and we hop onto the sidewalk, making our way down the street.

"Does he have any guards? A security system? Anything?" Lakyn asks after a few silent minutes.

I shake my head, pulling my mask out from the back of my pants. Lakyn does the same with hers. "My father is too cocky to have any guards. He thinks he's too powerful and people are too worried about him. He's an idiot. As for a security system, yes, he does, but it's been the same code since I was a kid."

She nods, slipping her mask over her face, our feet silent as we make our way to the end of the road. After a few minutes, we turn the corner of a large birch tree, and there sits my father's estate.

Large, grand, surrounded by an acre of sprawling green grass. Hedges cut to perfection, the grass green without a flaw on the landscape. The large, wide steps lead up to a dark oak wooden door, but we bypass that as we head toward the backyard. The lack of neighbors for my father—with the wealthiest and largest home in the neighborhood—is something he wanted when he moved here two years. He likes to stand out. He wants to have the house that everyone ooh'd and ahh'd at.

Well, he got it. Unfortunately for him, his dream house will be short-lived. Or, well, I guess, he will be.

We walk around the exterior of the house until we make it to the backyard. The large pool expands behind a black iron gate, with unused pool chairs, couches, and tables. There's even an outdoor kitchen, with a grill and bar area.

We bypass the area until we get to the back door. I pull on the handle, and as expected, it's locked. I dig into my pocket, pulling out the small pins at the bottom and shove them into the lock. I jimmy them around until I can feel the latch release. Shoving the pin back into my pocket, I slide the door open, hearing the alarm beep.

I press in my date of birth and smirk when I see the device turn green.

"That easy, huh?" Lakyn mumbles beside me.

I grab my knife from the back of my pants, not saying a word as I walk through the kitchen and toward the staircase.

I can feel Lakyn's tension build behind me, and I pause, turning toward her with narrowed eyes. Slipping the mask over my face, I tilt my head at her masked face and smile behind my mask. My hand goes out, and I brush my gloved fingers down the side of her face.

"You're beautiful, Lakyn. And now it's time to show me how much of the madness really consumes you."

She reaches out, her hand going behind my neck as she pulls my head toward hers. The foreheads of our masks knock together until it's just us, staring at each other through the eyes of our masks.

Mine.

I drop my hand to her heart, feeling her wild heartbeat underneath her sweatshirt. I memorize the beat against my palm as I step back and nod my head toward the stairs.

She nods, and we walk in that direction. Our boots paint dirty prints on the cream-colored carpet, leaving what's bound to be more clues and evidence to bury us into the ground.

Only if we get caught.

Lakyn pulls out her knife beside me, and we walk the rest of the way up the stairs. Once we get to the landing, I nod my head to the left, and we quietly stride down the hallway and toward my father's master bedroom.

The door is open a crack, and I press my boot against the corner of the door. It quietly rolls open, and I see his large king-size bed sitting in the middle of the room, a lump on the side underneath the covers.

And a lump on the other side as well.

Shit. He brought a whore home.

I glance over my shoulder and can see Lakyn's eyes narrow underneath the mask. I nod toward the girl, and tap my knife against my chest as I gesture toward my dad.

Lakyn nods, stepping around me and making her way into the bedroom and to the side of the bed. I step around the other side, watching as Lakyn tiptoes her way toward the woman in the bed.

The woman's hair lays in blonde tresses along the crisp white pillow, the rest of her covered by the Egyptian sheets. I step up to my father and see the back of his head buried into his pillow.

Fucking dick. Sleeping soundly knowing he sent someone to kill Lakyn.

My hand shifts over the bed, and I get ready to rip the sheets off both of them when my dad jolts, a knife slipping out of the bed, and swiping across my thigh.

Burning pain rips through me as I let out a hiss, staring at his bloodshot eyes as he glares at me with rage.

"I knew you were coming. Took a little longer than I expected, though, to be honest."

I growl, stepping back as I feel rivers of blood slide down my legs. The girl awakens from the other side of the bed, letting out a gasp as she glances over at us.

"What the hell?" she shrieks, ripping the sheets off her naked body.

Lakyn laughs as she reaches forward, grabbing her by the hair and dragging her to the ground. The woman lets out a cry as she fights against Lakyn, kicking and attempting to pull her hair out of Lakyn's grip.

"I thought I told you to stay away from Lakyn," I growl at him. "You fucked up."

My father laughs, pulling the sheets off the bed. He goes to a stand with his boxers on. He looks just like me, only older. With his tall, trim form and dark features, his medium-length hair a mess on top of his head. He has the shadows of a beard coating his jaw. He's a man that is handsome to many, but a cruel monster to most. The devil in sheep's clothing.

Unfortunately for him, I'm cut from the same cloth.

"You think I'll fold because my own child demands it of me? Who the fuck do you think I am?" he chuckles.

I step toward him, my jaw clenching like mad. He quickly darts to the foot of the bed. A quick glance on the other side reveals Lakyn pinning the woman against the ground, her hand slapped against the woman's mouth. Lakyn brings her knife out, pressing the edge of the blade along the woman's neck.

I glare at my father. "Take another step and I'll have her cut your whore's throat."

My father laughs, his knife bobbing as he points it in my direction. "You're funny, son. You think I care about that woman? My only ask is you take it downstairs and not on my nice carpet."

I sneer at him.

He tilts his head to the side, a pitiful smirk on his face. "You're a fool, son. If I've taught you anything, it's to never trust a woman or her intentions. Never get attached. Never fall in love. They are simple rules to follow." He lifts the blade closer to me. "One you epically failed at, by the way."

"Kill him, Reign. Don't listen to his bullshit," Lakyn barks at me.

I grind my teeth to dust as I stare at my father, his words echoing in my ears.

He has given me those life lessons throughout the years. I've known his inability to love, or his lack of desire to call a woman his. He's a soulless man, with no need to have a companion. It's how he's always been, and it's how he'll always be. I don't know why he is the way he is. Possibly it's because the woman who he did love—my mother—walked out and never looked back. Maybe it's because he doesn't have a heart in his body. He's grown up with his companion of work and illegal dealings. He's a corrupt man, one who would kill his own son just to save his own ass.

"You feel that way, Father, for one reason, and one reason only," I say simply.

A crease forms between his brows. "Humor me. Why would that be?"

I step forward, and he takes a step back, standing directly between Lakyn and I.

"Because you never found your Lakyn. If you did, you would realize what it means to protect her. To stand by her. You'd rather see blood spilt than open yourself up to anything more than hate."

His head tilts to the side slightly. "Ah, so this is for love. Well, let me tell you something, son."

My body tenses in anticipation of his ridiculous answer.

I say nothing.

"Love is a fool's game. You'll end up dead or alone, just like every other fool in this world. She'll stand over you one day, with a knife in her hand, and your blood dripping from the tip. Are you ready for that?"

I glance at Lakyn, and she stares at me blankly. It's a possibility, but it's also a possibility that she would be laying underneath me, with a bloody knife in my grip.

I think both of us realize our love might end in death, but I don't think either of us care too much. Every second of life with her is worth the inevitable death at her hands.

"Whichever way death ends, I am certain you won't be there to see it," I growl.

Lunging forward, he anticipates my move. He rushes to Lakyn's side of the bed, wielding the knife in her direction. She shouts, grabbing the woman and pulling her up, using her as a shield. My father plunges his knife down, right between the breasts of the naked woman.

She chokes, coughs, lets out a cry as pain rolls through her body. Lakyn tosses her to the side, and I can see the rage in her eyes through her mask.

"Bought her a psycho killer mask, just like you, huh, son?" my father growls, stepping toward her.

Lakyn stands quickly, lifting her knife. "Get the fuck out of my face," she snaps.

My father laughs, and then he bolts, rushing behind Lakyn and grabbing her arms, hauling them behind her back. He brings his knife up to her neck, pressing the bloody blade against her throat.

My entire body freezes, turning to stone as I stare at my father hold a knife to Lakyn's throat.

I take a step forward, and he takes one back, pressing the knife harder to Lakyn's throat. "Ah, ah, ah, son, careful where you step. This knife might slip and nick a main artery."

I grip the handle of my knife harder, feeling the blood cut off from my fingers. "Don't you fucking dare."

He smiles behind Lakyn's back. "Why don't you walk out of here, Reign. I'm sure you don't want to see this."

My eyes flit to Lakyn's, and I can see the fear through her mask. My father reaches forward, pulling her mask below her chin. Her face is pale, not an ounce of blood left beneath her skin.

"Please help me," she whispers.

And the thought goes through my mind on how I can possibly allow anyone to put any ounce of fear inside of her.

"Put the knife down, Dad," I command.

His eyes narrow slightly, the humor wiped from his face. "You couldn't possibly think I'd allow her to walk out of my house, right? You're an idiot to think otherwise. This was all a setup, Reign. From the man I sent to your house, to changing my security code to your birthday, to bringing a whore here. Life isn't that easy, Reign, I just made it seem to be that way."

He's an idiot. Of course this is a setup. My father might be an idiot, but he's one of the smartest men I've ever met in my entire life. Never in a million years would anyone be able to walk into his house and stab him in his bed. He's a clever man, and I'm almost disappointed he would think otherwise.

I stare at Lakyn, telling her with my eyes exactly what I need her to do. We're the same, and she instantly knows, swallowing and narrowing her eyes slightly.

Prove it to me, baby Lake. Prove to me you can do this.

"Let her go, and I might spare you," I lie effortlessly, turning my gaze back to his.

His shoulders drop slightly, "You're disappointing me, Reign. I figured you would put up more of a fight for he—" Lakyn grabs the second blade from the back of her pants, swinging it back into my father's thigh. The knife drops from Lakyn's neck, and he stumbles back a step, his hand flying to his thigh. "Fucking bitch," he growls, lifting his gaze to Lakyn.

I step forward, grabbing onto Lakyn's arm and pulling her behind me. "No. That was the first and only time you'll ever put your hands on her." I tear my mask from my face, since there's no reason to hide from him. He shouldn't die at the hands of the masked man, the slasher. No, he should die at the hands of his son, his heir, his fucking weapon.

His own weapon that's turned on him.

Fear trickles into his gaze, and he stumbles back, blood trailing down his thigh. "Get the fuck out of here, Reign. You're going to regret it."

I shake my head, taking another step toward him. "I can assure you, this will be the last thing in the world I regret. I'll very much enjoy taking your life."

He lifts his knife, pointing it at me. "I'll kill you. Don't think I won't do it." He stumbles back another step, tripping over air.

I lunge toward him, my free hand grabbing his neck. He darts the knife forward, and it swipes against my arm. I ignore the stinging pain as I squeeze his neck as hard as I can. He chokes, the knife falling from my arm as they grow limp at his sides.

I throw him onto his back, his spine meeting the creamy carpeted floor. Looming over him, I growl, "Say goodbye to Lakyn. She'll be walking out of here tonight. You won't."

"You're a coward. Choosing a spineless bitch over your own father," he spits at me, his eyes going bloodshot in stress. "You'll regret it."

I lean over him, my feet on each side of his waist. "The only thing I regret is letting you speak at all." My hand shoots forward in the blink of an eye, swiping across his neck. I can't even see the knife, but can only hear the swipe of the blade against his skin. Moments later, blood pools from the slice, trailing down his neck and onto his naked chest.

He chokes, his brow furrowing, almost as if he's in shock this is happening. His hand raises to his neck, and his fingers dive through the blood, swiping it across his skin. He stares at his blood-covered fingers before his hand falls to the ground.

His eyes watch me, but I can see the life drain from his eyes by the second. Until there's nothing there, besides his dark eyes staring lifelessly at me.

"Reign," she whispers. I say nothing, staring at the man who raised me to the monster I am today. Who made me his own weapon. Who led me to a life of crime, solitude—a weapon. He doesn't deserve life. He doesn't deserve happiness or wealth.

He deserves the blood he is drowning in. He deserves to swim in it until he's nothing but a corpse, a shell of a man he once was.

"Reign," Lakyn repeats.

I snap my gaze to hers, watching her watch me with a worried expression.

"Are you okay?" she whispers.

I plant my hand on his chest, feeling the warmth of his blood against my glove. I shove to a stand, slightly in shock, a little numb, and a fucking lot relieved.

"I don't know, but we have to go," I mumble, grabbing my mask and walking through the master bedroom. The girl is dead, my father is dead, and I did what I came to do.

Why does his death not feel like enough?

It's a hunger that can't be satisfied. I want to tear apart the world, everyone who has ever wronged me, wronged Lakyn. I want to tear apart the world and watch it crash to the ground.

I can hear Lakyn as she follows me through the house. I leave the alarm off, stepping out through the back door. The sun has started to rise, cresting over the treetops and lighting up the sky.

I slip my mask into the back of my pants, picking up my pace as I jog down the sidewalk.

"We took too long. We have to hurry," I mumble.

"Is it too late? Are we too late?" she whimpers behind me.

I shake my head, seeing the stolen truck up ahead. "Let's just go," I snap under my breath.

We rush to the car and hop in. I grab the wires under the dash, tying them together once the truck rumbles to life. Lakyn breathes heavily beside me, both from running and fear.

"We'll be okay, Lakyn," I say, glancing down at my gloves that are covered in my father's blood.

The death toll slowly rises, and I wonder if it'll ever be enough.

Shifting into drive, I pull off the curb, peeling down the street and out of the neighborhood. It's going to be much more difficult to drive across town with a stolen car during daylight, but we have to do it. We can fucking do it.

I take as little main roads as possible, cutting down side streets and back roads where I can.

"Shit, cop!" Lakyn shouts, pointing across the street.

My eyes widen, and I pull off the road, turning down a back alley.

"Fuck," I grumble, pulling behind a tree and parking in a way that I can see the cop through the thick tree. He sits on the side of the road between two buildings, where he is slightly hidden and can see every oncoming car. He has dark aviators on, but from the looks of it, he didn't see us. "Can't go that way." I turn around, waiting until he's looking down the road and pull out, rushing down the opposite street.

"Did he see us?" I ask.

Lakyn turns around, looking briefly before shifting in her seat. "No, he's still there."

I nod. "Good."

I drive past the docks and the lighthouse, seeing the remnants of the Halloween party gone as a light snow covers the ground.

We're close. We're so close.

"Cop," Lakyn mumbles, pointing up ahead.

I take the first left, turning down a small neighborhood street and pull up to the curb. "This will have to do. We can walk from here," I say.

Lakyn stares at the snowy ground. "It's cold, Reign, and it's far."

"The streets are too hot, and there are too many cops looking for us. We just have to go, and we have to go now."

I hop out of the car, and the door groans, the old pickup more rusty than not. Lakyn slides off her fabric seat, shutting the door softly behind her. "It's not safe to be out here," she says, glancing in every direction.

"It's not safe to be anywhere," I glance down the street, and then in the other direction. "Let's go."

I bolt across the street, Lakyn right beside me as we dive into the woods. The tree branches are covered in a light dusting of snow. Every step brings a crunch against our boots as we weave in and out through the trees.

"Speed it up, Lakyn," I growl.

She huffs behind me. "Do you think they're in here?" She glances around. "They might not even be in the woods."

"Oh, we're in the woods. Put your hands up." My eyes widen, and I grab my knife in a flash, spinning around and jolting my arm forward at the same moment I duck, a gunshot ringing around and powering over my shoulder.

Lakyn screams, dropping to the ground and crawling behind a tree. The FBI dressed in black stares at me, his eyes wide as he falls to his knees. I pull my knife from his gut, watching as drops of red seep into the white snow.

He lifts his arm, pointing his gun at me. "Put your knife down," he chokes.

My arm swings out, and I bat the gun out of his hand. It flies across the air, burrowing into the thick white snow.

"You son of a bitch. You'll never get away with this," he groans, staring at me with tears in his eyes. His hand goes to his stomach, and he pulls it away, wheezing. There's a lot of blood. Too much blood. I got him good.

"I've already gotten away with it," I chuckle, stepping forward. The tip of the knife drips blood on his neck, and he flinches away from every drop. Leaning down, I shove the knife into his chest, directly above his heart.

He chokes, his head falling to the side as blood starts seeping from his mouth. "Fuck," he chokes. "Stop."

I shake my head. "No." I twist the knife, watching as his tense body slowly relaxes, the snow around him turning pink with his blood.

In front of my eyes, I watch as his life fades away. He eyes settle closed, and I quickly pull the knife from his chest, wiping it across his clothes before I turn around.

"Lakyn," I snap, looking around for her.

She bolts out from behind a tree, her eyes wide as she stares down at the dead man. "Is he dead?" she whispers.

I nod.

She can't take her eyes away from him, shock in her eyes. "Who is he?"

I shrug, kicking him to the side slightly when I see his FBI badge attached to his pants. "FBI," I mutter.

"Fuck, Reign," she whispers. "This is bad. Really bad."

I know. I really know.

"How will we ever be able to live a life? We'll always be on the run," she whispers, tears flooding her eyes.

I step up to her, my hands going to each side of her face. I grab her tightly, pushing her against a tree. Her cheeks become painted red, and I wipe it, only smearing it across her face. "I told you, baby Lake. I'm going to take care of you. I'm going to make sure you're safe. I'm not going to let anything happen to you. You and I are going to get the fuck out of here, and they'll never be able to find us."

She shakes her head between my palms, fear in her eyes. "How will we ever be able to cross a border? We'll never get out of here alive," she whispers.

I give her a single nod. "We'll find a way. Because there's no other choice."

She stares at me, her eyes probing mine. She looks so fearful, each of her eyes darting between the two of mine. After a moment, her chest deflates, her shoulders dropping as she gives me a nod. "Okay."

"Okay." Leaning down, I give her a quick kiss before pulling back.

"Now, let's get back to the cabin."

With one last glance at the dead man behind me, we rush through the trees and make our way back to the cabin. We're silent, only our short breaths and puffs of air in front of us.

"Cop," I whisper, leaning forward and gripping Lakyn's arm. She jolts in my arms, and I haul her back against a large tree. I pin her there, with her back against the bark and my front against hers. I glance over her shoulder, keeping the both of us flush against the trunk as I stare at the cop in the distance. He glances around, clearly another FBI from the badge attached to his side. He has a gun in his grip, walking through the snow quietly as he glances around the trees.

Lakyn lets out a shaky breath, and the cop stops, narrowing his eyes as he glances around.

I lift my arm, pressing it against Lakyn's mouth while the man stands where he is, his eyes narrowed as he waits for another sound.

Not one comes.

It takes him a few minutes, with Lakyn trembling in front of me, until the cop decides to move on. He brings his walkie-talkie to his mouth, and I hear a beep. "Walker, copy."

He waits a second, but when a response doesn't come, he walks away, heading farther away from the cabin.

Fuck. This isn't good.

Once the FBI is out of sight, I grab onto Lakyn's arm, pulling her with me through the woods. I lift my finger to my mouth, pressing my pointer to my lips before I keep racing through the woods.

After a few minutes, I can see the cabin in the distance. I pick up my pace, running as quick as we can, when I see two police officers circling the house.

Shit.

"Hey! You! Get on your knees!" an officer shouts, lifting his gun in my direction.

"Fuck!" Lakyn cries.

I shove Lakyn to the side. "Go hide!" I bolt the other way, getting the officers to come in my direction. I rush between the trees, hiding out of sight and luring the cops in my direction. I can hear their loud steps in the snow, their heavy breathing.

"Come out, Reign Whitmore. We know you're here," one of the officers says.

I grab my knife, still stained lightly in blood from the dead FBI officer. I stand with my back against a tree. When one of the officers comes close enough, I snap away from the tree, my knife swinging out and swiping across his neck. He lets out a shout, his gun falling from his grip as he reaches for his neck. He falls to his knees, and the other officer comes up to me, his gun pointed in my direction.

Fuck.

"Put your weapon down," he orders, his eyes flitting to the dying officer beside him and back to me. "I've got you. Don't make any stupid moves or I'll pull the trigger."

I lift my hands in the air, knowing I'm at a loss when he's at a distance. If he were closer, I'd have a chance, but as it stands right now, with his gun pointed at my forehead, I'm fucking screwed.

He stares at me in rage, in absolute fury. His hand is steady, unwavering as he directs the barrel at my forehead.

"Put your knife on the ground and get on your knees," he commands again.

With a deep breath, I lower my knife slowly, dropping it to my side. I stare at him, unblinking as I begin to kneel.

Footsteps ring out of nowhere, moments before the officer's eyes widen. He stares in the distance in shock, and then I see the shadow of Lakyn as she pulls her knife from the man's back. She shoves it in again, this time above his shoulder, directly into his neck.

I step forward, batting the gun out of his hand and onto the ground. The man falls to his knees, then falls forward onto his stomach, his face down in the snow.

"Shit, Reign," Lakyn breathes beside me. "What are we going to do?"

I shake my head. "I think this place is done. It's been found." I glance at the cabin, wondering how many officers know about this. "Let's go inside. I don't want to be seen out here by anyone else."

Lakyn nods, staring down at her bloody knife. I grab her wrist, pulling her gaze to mine. "Lakyn, look at me."

She does as I ask, her head tilting back and her gaze turning toward mine.

"You had to do what you had to do. Don't feel guilt or remorse or it'll eat you alive. Live with it, swallow it down, and let the worry die in the bottom of your gut. If you didn't kill him, he would've killed me. It's as easy as that."

She nods, just as we hear the sound of tires peeling through the snow. We both freeze, our bodies turning to stone as we turn toward the noise. I reach for my knife again, ready to fight until I'm nothing but bones and blood on the snow, when I see Archer's car whip between the trees. He pulls up to the house, slamming on the brakes so quickly his car slides across the snow.

Lakyn's body relaxes in mine when she realizes who it is, and I release her. Both of us head toward Archer's car as the doors open up. Archer, Kyler, Posie, and Eloise all slip out of the car, staring at us in shock.

Eloise points to the dead bodies on the ground. "Who the hell is that?"

Lakyn shakes her head, a slight lick of shame entering her features. "They were going to kill Reign."

"I'm guessing you haven't seen the news," Archer cuts in, narrowing his eyes at me. He's giving me a warning, that whatever I'm about to see is something I'm not going to like.

I shake my head at him.

"Come on. You've got to take a look," Archer nods toward the house, and we all head inside.

"What are we going to do about the bodies?" Lakyn asks as we step inside.

"Well, burning them will attract people. The ground is too hard to bury them." I narrow my eyes as I walk to the kitchen, dropping my knife in the sink. "We're going to have to take them out of here, but we don't have a car."

"Fuck you," Archer laughs, and I turn to him, knowing he's our only chance unless we are supposed to drag two full grown men through the forest in the snow, when we're being hunted. "Where the hell are we supposed to take them?"

"We could drop them outside of town. We could put them in the woods up north a little. Deep in the forest," Posie suggests quietly, and I watch as everyone's eyes whip toward hers.

"Really?" Lakyn asks breathlessly, her eyes glowing. "You'd do that?"

Everyone is silent as we contemplate what to do. I know there's no way out of this. There's no going back, so the real question is, how do we move forward?

"We'll take care of it. But that's not why we're here. Take a look at the news." Archer steps forward, bending at the waist as he turns on the TV. It's pure static, but once again, the news anchor, Bridget Bofield from Fox 7 News is on the TV, this time in front of Braylin's house.

I can barely make her face out, and she splits in half and bobs back and forth with the static, though her voice is clear. "This is Bridget with Fox 7 News reporting from Hellcrest Heights here in Maine. The masked killer, who we now know as Reign Whitmore of Hellcrest Heights, has struck again. A triple murder of the Carter family has risen the death toll and we suspect there will be more. It appears Mr. Whitmore has added an accomplice who we now have identified as Lakyn Ashford. The brutal and heinous slayings of the Carter family have the town in fear of who may be next. The police are asking the public if they have any—" She frowns, pressing her finger to her ear. "Oh, one moment please." She nods her head a few times until her eyes widen and she looks directly at the camera.

"It seems there are two more deaths which have just been discovered. It appears the father of Reign Whitmore, Spencer Whitmore, has been murdered by his own son. There is an unidentified female on the property who has also been reported as deceased. More information to come soon. George, back to you." She nods, and even through the static I can see the unease in her eyes. The desperation to be done reporting on this case.

She should be nervous. Those who get involved end up dead.

Archer switches the TV off and turns toward me. "Your time is limited, Reign. It's time you guys get out of here. If you waste any more time, you'll be surrounded, and you might be able to take down two, but you won't be able to take down an entire police force once you're both surrounded."

I know. It's time to go.

"Lay low. We'll take care of the bodies, and we'll be back tomorrow. We can get you outside of town and you guys can go wherever you need to." His eyes flit to Lakyn's. "Just get her out of here. Get her safe."

I nod, my jaw clenching. "I plan to."

"Creed's funeral is tomorrow. Obviously you guys can't go, but I thought you might like to know," Eloise says.

Lakyn sighs, and I turn to her, seeing her eyes darken with sadness. "Oh," she whispers.

Posie steps up to Lakyn, and I watch as Lakyn's body curls over slightly in pain. "Lakyn, we'll get you out of here. Just stay strong, okay? Don't get caught."

Lakyn nods, her eyes growing watery. "I'm so sorry. For everything."

Posie shrugs, giving her arm a squeeze before she steps back. "Don't be sorry, Lakyn. Just stay safe."

Archer steps up to Lakyn, and my body grows tense as I watch them. The connection they have which I know doesn't slip into anything more than friendship, yet there's still a discomfort in watching their connection.

"You're so beautiful covered in blood, baby Lake," he mumbles, his fingers grazing her chin.

She tilts her chin up, narrowing her eyes. "It's just me, Archer."

He steps back, his hand dropping to his side. "I know it is." He turns his gaze to mine. "Both of you. You belong together."

"Let's go, Archer. I need to make sure Vienna is okay before Creed's funeral tomorrow," Eloise interrupts, and Archer takes a step back.

"We'll grab the bodies. Stay inside until we get back tomorrow," Archer says, and I nod at him, thinking that's the smartest thing we could do.

If only things could ever go as planned.

CHAPTER ELEVEN
LAKYN

"I'm going," I growl.

Reign clenches his jaw, standing in front of the front door. "You aren't leaving this house."

A laugh bubbles in my chest, and I can't help but chuckle. "I'm going!"

He steps toward me, while still blocking the front door. "You aren't going to his funeral, Lakyn. Head into the back room, say a fucking prayer, and put him to rest. You don't need to be standing over his grave to say goodbye."

Tears flood my eyes, because I feel like I do have to be standing over his grave to say goodbye. I don't feel like he'll ever forgive me for what I've done, and I need to see him. I have to.

"I want to go, Reign. I have to go to him one more time. I won't ever have this chance again." It's true. If we run away, will I ever come back to Hellcrest Heights? Most likely not, and I'll never have this chance again.

"You can't, Lakyn. You go, you get caught. It's as simple as that," he snaps at me.

My brow furrows. "I won't even go by them. I'll stay far away from the funeral party. I just want to go there. I want to… I need to be there."

He shakes his head at me. "No. That's my final answer."

I glance down at my leggings and black zip-up sweatshirt. My oversized black boots. How my hair is pulled into a messy bun because I don't have a brush. I have no makeup on. I'm a wreck. A mess, but I don't have any other option here. I'm not dressed for a funeral, but I want to go. I need to go.

I step toward Reign and his eyes narrow at me. He knows I'm not going to back down, and we can either fight until he lets me, or he can step aside, come with me, and I can do what I need to do.

"Come with me, Reign. Come with me and say goodbye to Creed. I know you need to as well. Please, Reign," I plead. "Please."

His bod slowly loosens, until he's standing in front of me, staring at me blankly. He steps forward, his hand going to my chin. He tilts my head up, until he's watching me. His fingers are warm, strong as they pinch my chin. I inhale, smelling the heady scent of Reign as he envelops me.

"There's something about you, Lakyn, but I can never say no to you. We can go, but we'll stay away, and you will not walk up to the funeral at all. If we see anything off, we fucking bolt. You hear me?"

I nod. I hear him.

"Thank you," I whisper, emotion bubbling in my chest.

"For you, baby Lake, I'll give you the world. Even if it means I wouldn't survive," he rasps, and my heart fills, if even for this one moment.

I slide down, my spine sliding against the bark of the tree as I stare at the oversized crowd across the cemetery. A cloud of black, from students to family members, all dressed in the color of death, surround the grave plot with the large, dark oak coffin propped above the dug-up hole in the ground.

A light snow falls from the heavy gray clouds which hang low in the sky. Each flake is perfectly formed as it falls on my arms, instantly dissipating into the dark fabric. I'm cold. It's cold outside, but I'm also cold inside.

Filled with so much death I've caused and had a hand in. Remorse doesn't ring through me, but a heaviness does, as if the fear and sorrow of all the dead cling to me, weighting me down into the earth. I can't do a thing but allow myself to grow numb to the death and absorb it as if it's my own bones.

"Creed was one of the good ones," Reign mumbles beside me.

I nod my head, pressing my bare hands against the snow. The cold seeps into my veins as tears flood my eyes. I watch my friends at the front of the crowd—Vienna most of all, standing near his parents as a constant sob racks her spine. She leans forward, her hand planting against the surface of the coffin. She looks so sad.

The pain of losing the one who owns your heart is one you'll never recover from. Of knowing no more breaths you take will be surrounded by him. No more kisses, or touches. You'll never feel their skin against yours.

I reach out, clutching onto Reign's hand. I lost him before, and I will never be able to lose him again.

"What do you think they're saying over there?" I whisper, snow mashed between our palms.

Reign sighs beside me. "I think they're saying how loved he was. That he had so many friends and family that loved him. That he was smart, someone who was going to go far in life. That he met the love of his life at such a young age and was one of the luckiest guys in the world. That he was handsome, forgiving, funny, and loyal to those around him. How generous he was to even those he didn't know." He clutches my hand tightly, and I allow the tears to track down my face in fast rivers. "How he had the greatest friends anyone could ever have, and how he'll miss all of us, just as much as we'll miss him," he mumbles, emotion heavy in his voice.

A sob breaks from my chest, and I curl over, my forehead pressing against my knees as I cry, hoping that Creed is still watching over us and wishing he would know how sorry I was for everything I'd done. That I would take back every second of this if I could.

"He doesn't hate you, Lakyn. Not even a little bit," Reign says, and it only makes me cry harder.

"I feel like the worst friend in the world. Why did he have to die? Why did Creed have to die? He didn't deserve this," I sob.

I can feel him shake his head beside me. "We can't take it back, no matter how badly we want to. All we can do is move forward from here. He lived a good fucking life. We make sure Vienna lives a good life. That's what he would want."

My chest aches painfully in my chest, a grief that feels never-ending. I want the pain to go away, I'd do anything for it to disappear, but it won't. There isn't anything I can do to make the pain go away.

"It'll all be okay, Lakyn. In time, it'll all be okay," he rasps in my ear, and his warm lips press against my neck. I lift my head, looking at the crowd, watching as funeral workers lower the casket into the plot. My brow furrows as I watch the wave of black shake, as if every single person is simultaneously sobbing in pain.

"Police are in the parking lot. We need to go," Reign whispers in my ear. I turn my head to the parking lot, seeing the two FBI SUVs pull into the back parking spots. They are mostly hidden, yet at the same time stick out like a sore thumb.

"If we get up now, we'll be seen," I mumble.

He sighs. "If we stay here, we'll also be seen. We need to go. When I say go, we need to dart behind this tree."

"Archer brought us here, though. We can't go get him," I stare at the crowd, watching Archer who has his arm around Posie. She cries in his arms, both of them looking distraught.

"We're on our own," I whisper to myself. Reign understands what I mean, though.

"Yeah. Let's go. Now," he snaps under his breath, and we move, shoving off the sand and making our way behind the tree. Reign's arm shoves against my chest, and he keeps me still against the trunk as he glances around it, toward the parking lot.

"Clear. Let's move." He grabs onto my wrist, hauling me across the cemetery. Our feet crunch against the snow as we bolt away from the FBI. Glancing over my shoulder, I don't see anyone following us, no FBI, no one from the funeral party noticing us.

It's just us.

At the end of the day, that's all I need.

"Lakyn." My name is whispered above me, and my eyes crack open. All I can see above me is Reign, standing there with the yellow glow from the fire illuminating his eyes. He stares at me with a coldness in his eyes, one that leaves my body shivering even when my body prickles with heat from the nearby flames.

After we safely made it back to the cabin, both of us quickly fell asleep by the warm fire in the living room.

"What's wrong?" I whisper, my fingers lifting to his cheek. I brush the shadow of his beard, the rough hairs scratching my fingers.

"We need to go. It's time to get out of here." His fingers drop to my neck, and trail down my chest, landing on the curve of my hip. He squeezes tightly, holding me against him.

"Where are we going?" I whisper, my hand dropping to his shoulder.

"Wherever we want to go," he murmurs as his face drops to my chest. He kisses a path along my collarbone. His hand shoves up his shirt that I'm wearing, until my panties are showing, and then my breasts are revealed. His mouth darts to my nipple, his tongue swiping along the hardened peak.

"Don't we have to go?" I moan.

His teeth scrape along my flesh, and I jolt in his arms. "I changed my mind. I want to have a taste of you first." His free hand goes to my other breast, squeezing roughly as he bites at my nipple. "I want to taste all of you."

I arch my breasts into his mouth, and he wraps his arms behind my back, holding me in his arms as he ravishes my body. I pull at his clothes, and he leans back, grabbing the fabric behind his head and tugging it over his head. His naked, tattooed chest comes into view, and he leans down, connecting skin against skin. He's warm against me, and the other side of my body prickles with heat from the flames of the fire.

"If this is our last night together, I want it to be the best night of our lives," he rasps in my ear.

He slides down my body, his hands gripping my thighs. He lifts them over his shoulders, and I relax my legs open, my eyes settling closed as the warmth from his breath floods between my legs.

"Your smell is intoxicating, baby Lake, and I'll never get enough of you."

I arch into his mouth, and my mouth opens on a gasp when his tongue flattens against my silky folds. He covers me with his tongue, humming out a moan when he tastes my arousal. "You taste like the most delicious, sweetest fruit I've ever tasted."

He flicks his tongue against my clit, and I let out a moan, my hips bucking against him. He moans deeper, gripping my thighs with his fingers as he pulls me close. His face burrows between my legs, and a cry escapes my lips.

"That's it, baby. Scream my name to the world." His fingers brush against his scarred initials above my pussy. "Who it is you belong to you?"

"You, Reign. It's always been you," I cry out.

He hums deeply, his tongue flicking madly against my clit. Again and again until every flick creates a jolt against my body. I can feel the warmth settle in my lower belly, an electricity which has my body racked in tremors.

"Come on my tongue, Lakyn," he commands, and my body shoots off, like a match that's lit it's fuse, and I explode into his mouth, crying out his name as my body feels as if it's levitating.

He sucks my clit into his mouth, and I let out a shout as I grab at his hair, pulling on the strands and wishing he would come closer yet move away at the same time.

Removing his mouth from my wet folds, he climbs up my body. Grabbing onto my hair, he wraps the strands around his fist as he pulls me upright. He pulls my shirt over my head, and I can feel the heat from the fire warm my back.

Reign stands, his erection straining against his pants. My hands reach out, and I trail my fingers along the seam of his jeans. It tenses against my fingers, and he grabs the back of my head, his fingers squeezing my hair in his grip. "Taste me, Lakyn. Taste all of me."

I grab the button of his jeans, undoing it and tugging down his zipper. His erection springs free against his briefs, and I pull them down. He's hard, the thick vein on the underside pulsing with need. I grip him in my fist, squeezing him tight at the base.

Leaning forward, my tongue slips out, and I smack his erection against my tongue. He groans, squeezing my hair to the point of pain. "Don't tease me, Lakyn. Show me how good of a girl you are for me."

I wrap my tongue around him, sucking him into my mouth and going down as far as I can. He hits the back of my throat, and I allow the saliva to pool in my mouth, spreading along his silky skin.

"Fuck yes," he groans, thrusting his hips forward into my mouth. I choke as I glance up into his eyes.

He grabs me tightly, holding me in place as he stares down at me. His fingers graze along my jaw, sliding across my hollow cheeks before he wraps his fingers around my neck.

And then he fucks me ruthlessly, staring down at me with so much love in his eyes it makes my own water. His fingers wipe the tears as they fall, catching them on his fingers and then slipping them into his mouth. He sucks my tears clean as he fucks me, his cock growing endlessly large in my mouth, until my jaw aches, and I can do nothing but drag my tongue along the underside of him as he takes what he wants.

Which is everything.

And I give it, willingly.

He pulls out suddenly, leaning down and grabbing me beneath the arms. He hauls me up, pinning me back until the back of my neck hits the mantle above the fireplace. The flames are warm against my backside. Reign steps up to me, grabbing me around my thighs and lifting me into his arms.

My arms go over my shoulders, and I grip onto the mantle as he lines himself up and slides inside. I let out a moan, gripping the wooden mantle tightly as Reign positions himself just right.

He moves, and I hook my ankles together behind his back as he begins thrusting inside of me. Our bodies grow warm, damp with perspiration as we move together. Our eyes connect, hold and lock together as we move as one. His eyes swirl with emotion, and I let go of the mantle, leaning forward and gripping onto his shoulders. Both hands go to each side of his face, and I grip him tightly as I lean down, pressing my lips against his. My mouth opens at the same time his does, his tongue slipping between my lips. I grind my tongue against his, moaning into his mouth as his hands go to my upper back, keeping me pinned against him.

We grind against each other, our bodies becoming slick with sweat, and a moan breaks from my mouth.

His hands go to my hips, and he slides me down his body. Grabbing me by the waist, he turns me around, his front molding to my back. I reach forward, gripping the mantle as he slides into me from behind. My front prickles with heat from the fire, and we move together, sliding against each other. Every thrust from him hits the spot inside of me that has me seeing stars.

The slap of our skin connecting has me moaning, and he drops his hands back to my hips, embedding his fingers into my flesh as he thrusts into me again and again. He lets out a low growl, his nails creating crescents.

I tilt my head back, dropping my head to his shoulder. He bends down, pressing his lips against my forehead in a quick kiss. "Your cunt is fucking euphoric against my cock, Lakyn. I never want this to end."

"Then don't let it end," I moan, staring at the chipped ceiling paint.

"Everything has to end someday," he rasps, pulling me back before slamming back into me. "Though I'll never let you go."

Heat barrels between my legs, and I let out a cry as my second orgasm comes to a head, ripping through my limbs. I nearly lose my balance, but he holds me against him as his cock stretches my walls, emptying himself inside of me. I sigh, feeling his heartbeat pump wildly against my back.

"I never want you to let me go," I whisper against him, my front feeling on fire from the flames. I glance down, seeing my warm skin tinged pink from the heat.

He holds himself against me for a moment before he slips out, his hands sliding down my back. "I'll never let you go, but we can't stay here any longer, Lakyn. Grab your things, we're leaving."

My brow furrows, and I turn toward him. "Where are we going, though? For real."

He pulls his pants up and shoves his shirt back over his head. "North. We're heading north. It's our best bet."

I think of trekking north, through the cold snow. On foot. It sounds horrible, but it also sounds like our only bet.

"Okay. Let's go."

He nods. "Grab your things."

We work silently, getting our things together, packing the two small backpacks Reign found in one of the back closets. Once the cabin is as empty as we arrived, we stand in the doorway, staring at each other.

"Ready?" he asks.

I shake my head. "Not at all. Why are we leaving tonight?" I ask him.

He glances out the window. "Because if officers were here yesterday and were reported missing last night, we can guarantee there will be a horde of officers here when the sun comes up in a few hours."

I nod, knowing he's right. "Have you talked to Archer at all?"

He nods. "Yeah, a few hours ago. He thought leaving was a good idea."

I sigh, staring out the window. When will I see my friends again? Never? "I hope I can see them again. Someday."

Reign reaches out, grabbing onto my hand and giving it a squeeze. "I don't know, Lakyn. Maybe. I'll be with you, you know. Every step of the way."

I peek up at him, a sudden fear filling every bone and vein in my body. A small shiver rolls through me, and I look at him. "Please don't leave me alone. I won't know how to deal with this by myself."

His hand goes to my jaw, and he gives me a light squeeze. "Never, Lakyn. Not ever."

He presses his lips against mine, and then parts from me. "Come on, baby Lake."

He pulls the door open, and we slip out into the morning air. The sun has yet to rise, and as we step outside and glance up, I can see a light, fresh snow falling on the ground. The wind is nonexistent, but it's still bitterly cold out, each breath we take puffing a gust of air in front of us.

We walk silently, my hands gripping the straps of my backpack as I keep my eyes ahead—north. The woods will lead from here all the way to Canada.

"Do you know where we're going once we get there?" I whisper after a while.

He glances at me, his cheeks a light pink from the cold air. "We'll get to New Brunswick tonight. We'll cross the border at dark and probably find a hotel or something. Tomorrow we'll find a place to stay until we can find a place to settle down at. Figure out where we want to stay for good."

I nod, shaking out my legs and the numbness that's setting in. I have no idea if he plans to stop along the way or just keep walking, but I hope the temperature doesn't drop at all, because I don't know how much more cold my body can take. At least walking reduces the stiffness.

We slip back into silence, the only sounds are our feet crunching in the freshly fallen snow. The sun has started to rise, peeking through the thick trees.

Reign turns to me after a while, his hand rising to my nose. "Your nose is cold."

I bring my palm to my nose, cupping my fingers around it. "I can't even feel it anymore."

His brow furrows, and he stops for a second.

"Put your hands in the air! You're surrounded!" a voice shouts in the distance.

My eyes go wide, my mouth falling open as I look in the distance.

Reign freezes to stone beside me, his hand falling from my face. "Shit," he whispers.

"Get on your knees!" the officer shouts.

Reign looks directly at me. "Lakyn, I'm going to distract them, and I'm going to need you to run."

I reach out, gripping his hand. "Reign, no. Fuck no. I'm not leaving you again. We are not getting separated again. If you're going down, I'm going down with you."

He pulls his hands from my grip. "This isn't your choice, Lakyn. Run south. Go anywhere. Fucking hide."

I narrow my eyes at him. "No, Reign. I won't do it."

He narrows his eyes back at me. "You don't have a choice."

He shoves me away from him, shouting as he starts running toward the police.

"Get on your knees! Get on your knees!"

I watch him, frozen in place.

"Lakyn, go!" Reign roars, falling to his knees, putting his hands behind his head.

I let out a sob, choking on air as I start sprinting away from him.

"Run, Lakyn! Fucking run!" he roars, and I let out another cry as I run for my life. I book it through the woods, hearing officers follow me, but I weave in and out of the trees, quickly getting away from them. I don't stop, though, don't even slow down as I make my way through the forest.

"Lakyn Ashford, turn yourself in. You are under arrest." The voice is spoken through some megaphone, echoing through the trees.

My breath wheezes out of me as I continue running, until my legs have grown numb and I no longer have feeling in my face. My tears on my cheeks have frozen against my skin, and my lips are cracked, bleeding.

Where the hell am I going to go?

There's only one place I know where I can go.

I rush through the woods and make my way back into town. I weave in and out of neighborhoods and stay out of sight. The police are frequent, rolling down the streets and parking at the edges of the streets. But I steer clear of all of them, making sure I'm never noticed.

I'm so close.

I move from suburban neighborhoods to the other end of town, my entire body numb to the point I can't even tell I'm running anymore. It just feels like I'm floating above the ground. The houses thin out and the trees grow thick as I make my way to the one person I know will always help, even if he hates me.

Archer.

I bend at the waist, my frozen hands on my knees as I tilt my head up, glancing at the house in front of me. The cars are in the driveway covered in a light blanket of snow. A crow caws behind me, and I jolt in place, nearly stumbling over my own feet. Glancing over my shoulder, I watch the oversized bird perched on the branch, staring at me, it's mouth wide open.

"What?" I groan, not having the patience of being mocked by a bird. "I'm a fucking mess, I get it."

Its wings lift, flapping wildly as it starts cawing again. It flies away, shoving snow off the branch and letting it flutter across my shoulder.

I brush the snow from my sweatshirt, my fingers a very alarming dark red, almost purple color. Turning around, I walk up the driveway. The front door opens as I'm walking up the steps, Archer's arm snaking out of the door. He grabs onto my arm, an alarmed look on his face as he hauls me inside. Slamming the door shut, he locks it, slamming me against the heavy wood.

"What the fuck are you doing here? Where is Reign?" he snaps.

Whatever fluid is left in my body bubbles to the surface and I let out a sob, my cheeks instantly flooded with tears. "The police got him. They caught us," I cry, and I can hear footsteps pounding down the stairs as Kyler and Posie come rushing toward us.

"What's going on?" Kyler barks.

"They got Reign," Archer growls.

"Holy shit, Lakyn." Posie comes up to me, knocking Archer out of the way. She grabs my hands, lifting them to her face. "Lakyn, your fingers look like they're about to fall off."

"I can't feel them," I whimper, trying to curl them, but they won't move. "I can't feel anything," I cry, another slew of tears rolling down my cheeks.

"Shit, we need to get you warmed up." She pulls me away from Kyler and Archer, who are both trying to block her path.

"No, we need to figure out what's going on," Kyler snaps at Posie.

"Then you're going to have to come with, because Lakyn is in serious need of warmth, and you yelling at her isn't going to get any of us anywhere!" she shouts, pulling me up the stairs. I stumble behind her, staring at Archer and Kyler with disoriented eyes.

"Fine," Archer growls, stomping up the stairs behind me.

Posie pulls me into the main bathroom upstairs, releasing me near the sink as she walks to the bathtub. Archer instantly invades my space, his fingers curling around my biceps. "Tell me what happened."

"We left this morning, and we made it like an hour when all of a sudden, police surrounded us from all sides. Reign, h-he shoved me away from them and fell to his knees. He gave himself up so I could get away."

"Why the hell would he do that?" Posie shouts from the bathtub. She shuts the water off, wiping her hands on a towel before stepping up to me.

171

"Come on, Lakyn. Let's get you in the warmth."

"Obviously they wouldn't both get away. He saved her," Archer grumbles, and I keep my eyes locked on his as I'm being pulled away from him. "Just as any of us would do."

Posie grabs my sweatshirt and shirt, hauling them over my head. I cover myself, averting my eyes as I feel the gaze of both Kyler and Archer on me. Posie helps me out of my pants and boots, then shoves me into the bathtub, closing the curtain around me.

I settle into the tub, swallowing down a cry when pain hits my skin. The cold against hot leaves my skin feeling as if it's burning, as if my flesh is boiling from my bones. Hissing through my teeth, I grab onto the walls, settling down as comfortably as I can.

"So, the question is, what're we going to do now?" Kyler shouts from the other side of the curtain.

"We're going to get him out," Archer says simply.

My eyes widen, and I grab the corner of the curtain, pulling it around my head. "What do you mean?" My heart pounds against my chest, and I stare at Archer and Kyler, both who watch me with blank eyes. "How can we do that?"

Archer crosses his ankles, leaning against the sink. "We'll have to figure it out. Come up with a plan. I'm sure he's going to Hellcrest Heights Jail. Usually we could pretty much walk in there and grab him and get out, but with the FBI there, I don't know if he'll get transferred somewhere, or if the FBI have an extra watch on it."

I release the curtain, letting it fall closed. It grows dark around me as the curtain blocks the light in the bathroom. I sink deeper into the tub, until the water curls around my neck, closing my eyes.

"We'll get him out, Lakyn. Don't worry about it," Kyler says from the other side of the shower curtain.

Tears flood my eyes when I think of Reign looking at me in rage, telling me to run as he puts his hands in the air, falling to his knees in the middle of a ton of police officers. How he risked his life to save mine.

Fuck, please don't let anything happen to you.

Knock, knock, knock.

My eyes widen, and I grab the shower curtain, ripping it back. "Who is that?" I whisper.

Posie's face goes pale. Kyler bolts from the bathroom, going to the nearby window.

Archer rushes up to me, grabbing the towel over the curtain. "Get out, Lakyn. Get out now."

I stumble, my limbs a mixture of numb and in pain as I leap from the tub and straight into the towel. Archer wraps the towel around me, pulling me out of the bathroom. "Posie, get into the tub, now."

Posie nods, ripping her clothes off her body and jumping into the bathtub. Archer pulls me from bathroom, dragging me down the hallway. He ushers me into his room, opening his closet. It's a walk-in, and in the corner is a large chest. He opens it up, lifting me into his arms. "Sit in here. Don't move. Don't make a sound. If you're caught, this is all over. Do you hear me?"

Knock, knock, knock.

Ding, dong.

"This is the police! Open up!" an officer shouts from outside.

A broken cry breaks from my chest as I settle inside the hard, wooden chest. I'm cold once again, the water dripping from my body quickly cooling. A shiver rolls through me as I curl into a ball, staring up at Archer.

"Not a sound, Lakyn," he whispers, closing the chest door. I can feel something sit on the top, and my breathing instantly picks up, claustrophobia clutching my throat and holding me in its grip.

"Don't panic. Don't panic," I chant to myself, my fingers clutching the towel to my chest.

I can hear voices, though they're muffled and I can't make out the words. It feels like it goes on forever, each second making me feel like the air is growing thinner, my oxygen slipping away with every breath I take.

The voices grow louder, and I squeeze my eyes shut, my hands slipping from my towel and grabbing at the sides of the chest. I hold my breath, my lungs screaming at me.

I don't know how long it goes on for, but my vision fades in and out, and I feel like I'm near passing out when I hear movement above me.

My heart pounds in my ears as my eyes spring open, and I stare above me, ready for the moment the officer hauls me out of here and brings me to jail.

I'm a murderer. I'll never be free.

The chest swings open, and there stands Archer, staring down at me with a worried look on his face. "You okay?"

I gasp in a breath of oxygen, panicked and terrified. "Are they gone?" I whisper.

He nods, reaching down and grabbing me. He lifts me into his arms, carrying me out of his closet and into his room. He sets me on his bed and walks to his dresser, pulling clothes out, tossing them at me. "Get dressed and meet us downstairs. We need to talk."

I swallow, grabbing the clothes in my lap and pressing them against my chest. "Is everything okay?"

He levels me a look. "No."

"What's going on?" I ask, walking into the living room.

Kyler and Posie sit on opposite ends of the couch, while Kyler sits in a nearby chair, a class of liquor in his grip.

"Sit down, Lakyn," Archer mumbles, tipping his glass back. The ice tumbles around, and he lets one slip in his mouth, crunching it aggressively between his teeth.

My knees start to shake, and I walk to the couch, sitting in between Kyler and Posie. I tuck my legs up underneath me, Archer's sweatpants swimming around my waist. "Tell me what's going on. Is Reign okay?"

His jaw clenches, and he gives me a single nod. "He is, for the moment."

Kyler leans back, and I turn to him, watching as he stares at Archer. "We're lucky there isn't a death penalty in Maine, or else Reign would be headed straight to the electric chair."

My fingers go to my neck, and I squeeze at my throat as it clenches uncomfortably. "What?" I whisper.

"Reign was taken to Hellcrest Heights Jail this morning. He's being transferred to the Cedar Woods County Prison and will be there until his trial. He's looking at life without parole, Lakyn," Archer says simply.

I take a deep, shaky breath. Cedar Woods County Prison is about forty-five minutes from here. If he gets there, it'll be ten times more difficult for him to get out.

"What's our plan?" I say after a second, glancing at Kyler.

Kyler reclines in his seat, crossing his arms over his chest. He leans his head back on the couch cushion, turning his eyes to mine. "We have to get to him before they transport him. They said he will be at the prison tomorrow, so I think we really only have tonight, and that's it."

"We'll need all of us on board. Posie, you need to call Eloise and see if she's in. There will be a place for each of us. Lakyn, when we give you the go-ahead, you'll need to be at the back door, waiting for Reign. Once he's out, you bring him to our car, where Kyler will be waiting. We'll bring you as close to the border as we can, but then you guys need to go and not look back."

I nod, fear making my limbs tremble.

"When do we leave?" I croak.

Posie shoves off the couch. "I'll go call Eloise and see if she can come over here."

My eyes flit to Archer's. "Were they here looking for me?"

Archer nods, swallowing down the rest of his drink before he sets it on the table. "They were."

I bite my lip. "They didn't find me."

He nods. "But they know you were here. The unfortunate thing about it being winter is that your footsteps led you directly here."

My eyes widen, and I lean forward in anxiousness. "And? How did they not find me?"

He tilts his head to the side. "I told them you came here and I sent you away."

My brow furrows. "They believed you?"

He shrugs. "It doesn't fucking matter. You weren't found."

My body slowly begins deflating. "I want to save him," I whisper.

He nods, shoving off the couch. "We all do, Lakyn. And that's what we're going to do."

CHAPTER TWELVE

REIGN

"You can kiss your sorry life goodbye, Reign Whitmore." The words are lashed in my direction as my face is shoved into the snow. My skin burns from the icy cold, and I scowl as I'm lifted up, police and FBI surrounding me from every direction.

"You'll be going down for this, you sick fuck. Murdering all those innocent people."

None of them were innocent. Not a single one.

"I hope you become the little bitch to all the men in the prison. See what fear really feels like," one of the officers barks in my ear, his breath smelling like onions.

This early in the morning? Really?

I'm hauled into the air, my arms yanked aggressively behind me. The feel of cold metal wraps around my wrists as they shackle me in cuffs. They tighten them uncomfortably, until my circulation is nearly cut off from my hands.

They drag me through the snow, barking degrading comments in my direction as they haul to me a police car.

"You're a piece of shit. You deserve to rot in your cell."

"I hope they string you up by your balls."

"I'm going to make sure you get the worst penalty possible."

They go on and on, and I drown them out as my eyes scan the horizon, hoping for a glance of Lakyn, and also hoping she's long gone. She ran. I watched her run for a long time, but I have no idea if she hid to watch me, if she's waiting for me to get away, or if she left.

I hope she went to them. To him. He'll protect her like no one other than me can. She needs them. They'll keep her safe when I can't.

Fuck, don't let anything happen to you, baby Lake.

They open the back door to the police car, roughly shoving me in the back seat. The seats are plastic, hard against my body and extremely uncomfortable. I slide around, a constant chill running through my body.

One of the officers leans down, his head shoving inside the police car. "Piece of shit," he growls at me before slamming the door in my face.

I slide into a sitting position and watch the officers and FBI huddle into a circle, mumbling about me. I can't make out what their saying, but every once in a while one of them turns to glance at me, glaring at me with pure hatred.

Slouching down in my chair, I wait for them to be done talking to me when one of the main officers, a man in his late forties, with salt-and-pepper hair, a large puffy police coat, and his hand permanently attached to his gun holster as if he needs to warn me at all that he's armed, walks toward the driver's side of the car.

Sliding in, he turns it on, warm air instantly blasting from the vents.

"Want to tell me where your little friend went off to?" he asks as he turns the car around and begins making his way out of the woods.

I say nothing, my wrists aching fiercely behind my back, and I focus on the pain, instead of this man's line of questioning. Not going there. I refuse.

"If you help us get her, we might be able to reduce your sentencing," he says after a minute.

I let out a laugh, shaking my head. Saying nothing.

"Is something funny back there?" he barks.

I shake my head again. "Everything is funny."

"Like your little friend you let run away. Is she funny?" he pokes.

I cut my glare to him. "Don't fucking talk about her."

He grips his steering wheel, a smile taking over his face. "She hits the button inside of you, doesn't she?"

I tilt my head to the side. "You might be able to say that."

"Do you know where she is right now?" he asks after another minute.

My eyes narrow at him. "I thought I told you to not fucking talk about her."

He sighs heavily, glancing at me in the rearview mirror. "You'd rather have a longer sentence than give up the girl?"

I bare my teeth at him. "You act like I'm getting anything less than a life sentence. No amount of bargaining is going to lower that term."

He has nothing to say to that, just as I figured.

We fall into an awkward silence, and I shift my back against the seat, staring out the window.

Get somewhere safe, baby Lake. For me.

"We're headed to the jail for some questioning, and I'm guessing they'll be transferring you to the prison tomorrow morning. Get ready for a long day."

I grind my jaw together, keeping my eyes averted.

"You don't have to give up your friend, but we'll find her. Just like we found you, Reign Whitmore. Her time is limited."

I take a deep breath, my eyes shuttering closed.

Fuck.

My body is slammed into a small metal chair, my spine already in pain from the police car seat. I adjust myself, glaring at the officers who decided to treat me like a fucking bag of garbage. One of them squats down in front of me, wrapping shackles around my ankles. He tightens them up, and the chains between my feet slap against the cement floors. He locks the shackles to a bolt in the floor, as if I'd ever be able to get out of here anyway.

Fucking idiot.

My jaw clenches, and I stare at the wall in front of me, ignoring the way their eyes scream hate and rage.

They would kill me. If they had the guts, they would, but they don't. They're all pussies.

"So, Mr. Whitmore, you've created quite a stir in Hellcrest Heights," a detective says as he enters the room. One of the officers leaves, while the other one—the one who shackled my ankles—stays near the door.

I say nothing, watching as he adjusts his suit jacket and sits down. He pulls out a small notepad and pen, putting it on the table in front of him. He opens the top fold, going to a clean page. He clicks the end of his pen and presses it to the top of the paper before glancing up at me.

"Where should we begin?" he asks.

I stare at him.

"How about we start with the basics. Okay?"

Not a word.

"Name?"

I roll my tongue along my teeth.

He sighs, dropping his pen to the table. "We can sit here all night. My wife is at her sister's for the evening, so I've got nothing at home. Only when I get my answers will you leave here. And let me tell you, if you decide to not cooperate, your punishment, and the punishment of Lakyn Ashford, will be much worse. Is that what you want?"

"Don't touch her," I growl.

He smirks at me. "Name?"

My nostrils flare, my teeth grinding to dust as I clench my jaw. "Reign

Whitmore."

He nods, jotting down my name. "Age?"

"Twenty-six."

"Parents' names?"

"Spencer and Lydia Whitmore."

"Are you the slasher of Hellcrest Heights?" he asks, his pen poised to write *yes*.

I tilt my chin up. "Yes."

He nods, though it's already been a fact.

"How many murders have you committed?"

I lift a brow. "In my life, or in Hellcrest Heights?"

That has him pausing, and he chews on the inside of his cheek before his eyes narrow. "Are they two different numbers, Mr. Whitmore?"

I shrug. "Could be."

His eyes narrow further. "How about we start with the number in Hellcrest Heights."

"Ten."

He blows out a breath as he writes down the number seven and circles it.

"Who is Lakyn Ashford to you?" he asks after a beat.

This has my mouth clamping up.

He flips to a new sheet of paper, tapping his pen in the center. "Like I said, Mr. Whitmore, I have all night."

I lean forward, the shackles clanking together. "I'm not answering any questions about her. Next."

His head tilts to the side. "And why not?"

"Because she's off-limits," I growl through gritted teeth.

He sighs. "If you don't give me anything to go off of, you won't be cooperating much."

I shrug. "I don't care. She's off-limits."

He stares at me just as heavily as I stare at him. Finally, after too many minutes, he nods.

"Tell me a little bit about the murders," he says.

I stare at him, wondering how much I should divulge. It doesn't seem I'll be getting out of here. Not with all the deaths they have on me. Do I spill everything, or do I keep my mouth closed?

I guess only time will tell.

Clank.

The jail cell closes, and I'm once again locked in a cage. It's been years since I've been in jail, and yet it doesn't feel like I've been away from it for more than a day. Once you've been in one jail cell, it seems like you've been in them all.

"Hey." The voice comes from across the hall, and I lift my head, staring into the cell across from me.

A guy who looks to be in his late twenties stares at me, tattoos traveling from his neck up the side of his face. "You're him, aren't you?"

I sit down on the small cot, turning my head toward the wall. "Who am I?" I mutter.

"The slasher. You're the guy from Hellcrest Heights who was murdering all those people."

I narrow my eyes, turning my head toward his. I don't say a word, but I don't have to.

How does he know?

"Everyone knows about the manhunt that was going on looking for you, and then word was they caught you. I can tell a murderer from a mile away, and boy, your hands look covered in blood."

I nod my head, not saying a word.

"How'd they get you?" he asks, an excited lilt in his tone.

I swallow down my sigh. After being in the interrogation room for hours with the detective, the last thing I want is to have another story time, but maybe this guy is just bored out of his mind, or maybe he is interested in my story. Either way, I'll give him a bite.

Only a bite.

"I didn't get caught. I caught them."

It's the truth. I knew we'd only make it so far. I realized after speaking with Archer how close they were to us. The worst thing I could've done was wait it out, let them come to the cabin. Then not only would I have been caught, but Lakyn, too. At least while we're in the middle of nowhere, she has a chance to run. She had the chance to get away. I had to give her that chance.

"What do you mean?" he asks with a chuckle.

I turn my gaze to his. "I mean, I knew they'd be there. I walked right into their trap willingly."

"Why the fuck would you do that?" he barks.

I drop my head to the ground. "To save my girl."

Silence.

"Man, you're a fucking G. I'd never go to prison for life for any girl, man. I don't even know if I could do it for my own momma."

Because Lakyn isn't just any girl. She's *the* girl.

The only girl.

"Yeah, well, you don't know Lakyn Ashford."

CHAPTER THIRTEEN

LAKYN

"Are we good to go?" Archer says from the passenger seat. We're about a block away from the prison. It's late at night, and we only have about thirty minutes until shift change. Once the earlier shift goes home, we have to move. We have a small window to get in there, turn everything upside down, and get out.

Kyler is going to go in the visiting area and act panicked and say his wife is in labor. Posie is going to get behind the wheel of the truck and drive away, so when the officers come out to take a look, the car is going to be gone. Kyler will panic even more, and the officers will be sidetracked enough to look away from the jail for a minute.

In the meantime, Archer will go to the control panel of the jail and cut the power and steel doors. Eloise will get inside the jail and find Reign, telling him to go out the back door. I will be standing by the back door, and by the time Reign gets out, I'll be waiting for him, everyone will be back in the truck down the road, and they will take us as close to the border as possible.

Eloise hasn't forgiven me, and she certainly hasn't forgiven Reign, though we're a team. We don't do this alone. We've always done things together. Blood, sweat, and tears, and we aren't going to stop now.

The people at the jail will be so bombarded with everything that has been going on, they shouldn't notice Reign missing for at least enough time to give us a head start.

Who knows if it will work. If even one thing goes wrong, we'll be screwed. We could all be behind bars in only a matter of hours, or we could be on our way to the border.

"I'm ready," I breathe, clutching onto the coat Archer grabbed for Reign. However difficult this mission is going to be, he'll need a coat to get through this winter.

"Good to go," Kyler says from the back seat.

"Let's do this," Posie breathes from the driver's seat.

"I'm nervous at shit, but I guess I have no other choice," Eloise grumbles.

We all hop out of the car across the street and around the corner of the prison. Posie, with a fake belly underneath her hoodie, sits in the driver's seat. Kyler hops in the passenger seat, dramatically placing his hand over her belly.

"We've got this, Momma."

Posie's face wrinkles. "Shut the fuck up, Kyler."

I let out an unsteady breath, shaking out my arms and fingers as I hop onto the sidewalk.

"Just stay by the back door. There's a dumpster back there, so if you hear any noise, hide under it. Not behind it, but under it. Got me?" Archer levels me a look.

I nod, watching him closely. "Got it."

We pause on the corner beside an oak tree, and Posie pulls off the side of the road and makes her way across the street, to the visitors' entrance of the prison.

"Fuck, this could go so wrong," I groan, watching Posie park off to the side of the entrance.

Archer reaches out and grabs my hand, giving it a squeeze. I glance up at him, and he's watching me with an assuredness I didn't realize I needed. "We're going to get him out of there, Lakyn. We'll get him back for you."

I squeeze his hand, emotion bubbling in my chest, but I refuse to let it free. "Thank you, Arch. For everything."

He nods, pinching his lips together. "Anything for you, baby Lake."

The truck is shifted into park, and Kyler steps out, running his fingers through his hair about a million times. He gives a thumbs-up to Posie, and I can't help but crack a smile as a whole new persona overtakes him. He looks like a distraught father-to-be as he slouches a little bit, moving his hands erratically as he races to the entrance.

"Holy shit, he got ugly quick," Archer grumbles.

I chuckle, curling my toes in my boots as I wait for the go-ahead. Posie waits a few minutes, and then I watch as the taillights light up as she shifts into drive. She pulls around the parking lot and gives us a thumbs-up through the window as she drives around the side of the building.

"I'm going to go. I'll see you guys on the flip side," Archer gives us a nod before darting across the street.

I turn to Eloise. "I better go too. Wait by the back door. Will you be okay?"

Eloise stares at me a moment before giving me a single nod. "I'm going to head across the street, wait for Kyler to bring them out here and distract them and I'll slip inside. I'll see you in a bit?" Eloise is cold, which I feel is completely valid, but it still hurts to see her not the friendly, bubbly girl she used to be.

"Yeah. I'll see you in a bit," I mumble, and then I pull my hood over my head and dart across the street. I go in the opposite direction of Archer, making my way toward the backside of the jail.

Once I make it to the door, I crouch down beside it, my entire body coiled tight as I wait to see Reign.

I only saw him this morning, but it feels like I haven't seen him in ages.

I miss him, and I want him to be okay. I want him to know that I'm okay.

We'll be okay.

Please be okay.

CHAPTER FOURTEEN

REIGN

The low hum that groans throughout the building suddenly stops, and my eyes shoot open, staring at the pitch-black ceiling.

"What was that?" the guy from across the hall asks, standing up and walking to the bars.

A few other people start shouting too, and my stomach burns with realization.

She's here.

I stand off the bed, going up to the bars and staring at the dude on the other side.

"What do you think is going on?" he asks loudly over the shouting.

I shrug, keeping my eyes down the hall. The power went out, as well as whatever that hum is. The small, barred windows barely let in any moonlight, but my eyes have adjusted quickly.

"This has never happened before," he says, clearly wanting me to start up a conversation with him.

I stare down the hall, my body coiling tight with tension as I wait for something, anything, to happen.

Guards begin shouting, their voices close, but they quickly grow farther and farther away, until it's only silence. It's just me and the other inmates, all with our faces pressed to the bars, our hands wrapped around the cold metal as we hope it's one of us that are going to be saved.

"Something is happening," the man utters across the way.

Suddenly, light footsteps pound down the hallway, and I hold my breath when a flash of red enters my vision.

Eloise.

She stops in front of me, glaring heavily with so much hatred that if the bars weren't between us I'm certain she'd reopen my stab wound.

"Reign," she sighs, stepping to the empty guards' station. She narrows her eyes as she glances down, and I hold my breath, wondering what she's about to do, when she pushes a button, and all our cells simultaneously click.

My eyes widen, and I push against the metal bars. I listen to the creaky groan as other inmates do the same, and suddenly, it's Eloise and I, with a ton of felons.

I grab her wrist, much to her dismay, holding her close.

"How'd you get in here?" I mumble.

She tilts her chin, staring up at me in irritation. "If you have to ask, you're not as smart as I thought you were."

"Bro," my neighbor inmate steps up to me, and I realize how fucking tall he is. A few inches taller than me, at least, and I'm at six three. He turns his gaze to Eloise, and I stiffen next to her. "Thanks, babe. I owe you."

And then he's off, jetting down the hallway with a flood of other inmates.

Eloise tugs on my hand. "Come on, Reign. We need to go."

"Where is Lakyn?" I ask, following quickly behind her.

She glances over her shoulder at me, her hair flowing into her eyes. "Waiting for you, obviously."

She turns back around, dressed in all black as she darts down the hall. I follow after her, keeping close but away from the commotion of all the other inmates. Guards are shouting in the distance, and I listen as they try to gather them all up and get them back to their cells.

What's the most depressing is those who still sit in their cells, their doors unlocked but they just lay in their beds and watch everyone escape.

Yet they choose not to.

Inmates pause every so often, their eyes widening when they see there is a female in their midst. I growl at them, baring my teeth and daring them to get within touching distance of her.

We make it through the jail area, and Eloise drags me away from all the inmates flooding out the visitors' area and around to the back. I narrow my eyes at her, but don't say a word.

Eloise brings me through door after door until we reach one with the large neon exit sign above it. She glances at me, a slight smirk breaking over her face. "Ready?"

I nod, my body buzzing as Eloise pushes the door open.

And there, standing before me, is my baby Lake.

CHAPTER FIFTEEN
LAKYN

"Lakyn," he rasps. He's dressed in a gray sweatshirt and sweats, his hair a mess, his face pale. He looks like he hasn't slept in years, even though it was only this morning when I last saw him.

Tears immediately flood my eyes at his raspy voice. I step toward him on autopilot, and he meets me halfway, his arms lifting and curling around my trembling body. I mold perfectly to him, each curve and crevice a puzzle piece meant to be. He holds me tightly, his arms locked around my body as if he'll never let me go again. My eyes shutter closed as he presses his lips to the crown of my head.

"I was so scared," I croak.

"Hey, sorry, but we have to go. Like now," Kyler snaps from beside us.

I can feel Reign nod his head above me, and his arms drop to my hips as he pushes me toward Archer's vehicle. We all pile in the back seat, squeezing into too little seats with too many people, and Archer peels off, making his way out of the parking lot.

Sirens alarm outside the jail, and we all turn around and watch the inmates flood out the front door moments before we turn around the corner and go out of sight.

"Shit, hurry. Let's get the fuck out of here," Kyler cackles, slapping the dashboard. I watch it with wide eyes, waiting for the air bags to engage.

Archer takes the side streets before pulling out onto the main drag, making his way toward the highway.

"Where the hell are we even going?" Posie shouts from the back seat, her breath shooting from her chest in quick breaths. Her eyes are a little crazed, but I suppose everyone's are from the adrenaline.

"Getting out of Hellcrest Heights is our first fucking goal. Once we get out, head north," Archer clips, jerking the car as he whips down different streets.

I hold on to the headrest in front of me as I feel arms wrap around me. Glancing to my side, I see Reign staring at me with a heavy gaze. I relax back into his arms, giving him a small smile.

"Hey," I breathe.

His brow quirks, and his tongue swipes gently along his bottom lip. "You are a fool, Lakyn, but I'm glad you came."

I shake my head. "You think I would've left you in there?"

His arms tighten around my waist and he squeezes me against his warmth. "It would've been the smartest option. If shit went south and you would've gotten caught, we both would've been behind bars forever."

My head tilts to the side. "You're worth the risk, Reign."

His fingers release my waist and he brings his hand to my chin, pulling me close until our lips touch. Everyone talks, shouting wildly around us while my lips mold to his. I exhale at the same moment he inhales, and we breathe each other in as we become trapped in our own bubble.

"I love that you came for me," he mumbles against my lips.

"Shit!" Archer shouts. The brakes slam, and I'm ripped out of Reign's arms and thrown against the front seat. Scrambling up, I glance over the front seat and see police officers blocking the street in front of us. The main road out of Hellcrest Heights. "Fucking shit," he growls, reversing onto another side street.

"What are we going to do now?" I ask, fear clutching my throat.

"Take the woods. Your truck can take it," Reign says from behind me. "It'll be bumpy, but it'll make it through. There's a ton of ATV trails. You can head east around the coast and through the woods once you make it past town."

Archer slows to a stop, and I watch in the rearview mirror as his eyes narrow, contemplating this plan.

"We have to try, Archer," I whisper to him. "Please."

He glances over his shoulder, his eyes spearing mine. His hand reaches out, and his finger grazes across a fallen tear I hadn't known had shed. "Lakyn, have I ever given up when it comes to you?"

I shake my head, his fingers still attached to my cheek.

His eyes narrow, and he pulls his hand back. "Exactly. Sit the hell back, because this ride is not going to be an easy one."

He turns around, heading toward the coast, and enters the woods near the abandoned ship.

The truck rocks back and forth as Archer turns left and right through the trees. We pass our treehouse, which is covered in a light coating of snow. Everyone falls silent as the headlights illuminate the small flakes of snow as they flutter to the ground. We're all tense, constantly on the lookout in case there are police watching us, waiting for us.

There is no one.

"They all must be near the highway, waiting for us to make our move," Kyler chuckles. "Fucking idiots."

"It is the only way out of Hellcrest Heights. This isn't really an exit for a vehicle." Posie's voice jumps with every bounce of the truck.

"They're probably on the south end where the trees and less dense," Archer grits between his teeth.

We nod, falling back into a silence as the trees get thicker. As the sides of the truck brushes against them, the snow blanketing the branches shakes off, falling across the truck. We're in some winter wonderland of snow, and this moment suddenly feels life-changing.

The moment in our lives we'll never come back from.

Life-altering.

We reach the thickest part of the woods, where the edge of the water meets the end of town. Archer slows down, turning around the bend and heading north.

"We're close," Archer says, leaning forward as he stares out the window. We all lean forward simultaneously, and soon enough, finally making our way out of Hellcrest Heights.

"Holy shit," I whisper, letting out a small chuckle. I didn't actually think we'd make it. Like, I was almost certain we'd get caught, but I knew we had to take the risk.

And it worked.

Archer drives through the forest, and slowly, we all begin to relax. Settling back in our seats, we wait to get through the rest of the trees and turn onto the highway. Leaning over, Archer turns on the stereo, when an alarm blares over the speakers.

"What the fuck?" Kyler leans forward, turning the sound down.

"Hello, this is the United States Federal Bureau of Investigations reporting to you with a city-wide emergency. We are looking for a Ford F-150, black, with a license plate one-four-eight, J-B-Q. That's one-four-eight, J-B-Q. Vehicle was last seen near the jail and headed east. Local fugitives Reign Whitmore and Lakyn Ashford are among the passengers in the vehicle, most likely armed and dangerous. If seen, please do not approach, but instead call nine-one-one immediately to be transferred to the appropriate office. Hellcrest Heights Jail has also been breached, and a number of local inmates have escaped. We advise all residents to stay indoors until we alert you otherwise. Thank you and stay safe." The voice is automated as another alarm goes off and the message repeats.

I turn to look at Reign, and he's staring out the window with a clenched jaw. "Fucking hell."

"We're already out," Kyler says. "We'll be fine."

"We have to ditch the truck," Archer says. "Ditch the license plates, too, maybe."

"Where? And then what? We travel on foot? We'll stick out like a sore fucking thumb," Eloise snaps.

"We'll get a different car. Just make sure we ditch this one out of sight. Maybe in the woods across the river. There's a small town on the other side. We can probably find something there," Reign grumbles from beside me, his eyes outside the window.

Archer nods, hopping onto the highway and making his way across the river. It's close to five a.m. now, and soon the sun will be up and the roads will be flooded with cars, all of them with eager eyes as they look for us.

We don't have much time, which means we need to move now.

"There, get off there," I point to the next exit, and Archer immediately turns into the right lane, cutting quickly off the divided highway and onto a lone highway. There isn't a building in sight, but the woods quickly pick up again, and Archer turns toward them.

Kyler slaps the volume on the radio, turning off the incessant blaring of the alarm as the entire world begins looking for us.

"Are you guys going to be able to go back? I mean, they know it's your car, Archer. How will you get away with this?" I ask, suddenly nervous for the rest of my friends, not wanting them to take the fall with me.

He looks in the rearview mirror. "I didn't kill anyone, Lakyn." His eyes narrow. "Not today at least. I won't be going down. None of us will. My father will take care of it."

I nod, knowing it's most likely the truth. For Reign and me, I don't feel like we have that choice. I feel as if we have crossed the line too far, and we no longer have the ability to escape our fate. What we must do now is find a new life, a new way of living. And we can both do that.

Together.

Archer makes his way into the woods, following the river. Piles of white snow fall across the river, while the edges are lined with ice and the middle ripples with cold, rushing waters.

I follow the river with my eyes as Archer heads toward the small bridge up ahead, crossing it as he makes his way into the small town of Renville.

"Shit looks like it's been abandoned for years. How the hell do you know about this place?" Archer asks.

Reign sighs beside me. "I've been to a lot of places over the years. This was just another passing town I learned of."

I glance at him briefly, wondering how much he's been through over the years, with going to prison and getting out, staying away. Battling his father's demons while also tackling his own. Reign has lived a dark life, and in turn it has made him a dark man.

And he's found his dark companion.

I reach down, threading my fingers through his. I give him a squeeze, and in turn, he squeezes my hand back.

My heart melts, and I watch as Archer pulls off to the side in the woods, turning off his car.

"Well, it was a good run," Archer grumbles as he taps his steering wheel.

"It's so cold outside. How long until we find another car?" Posie asks, wrapping her arms around herself.

"There's a small strip about five minutes up the road. I'm sure we'll find some houses nearby and can take a car from there," Reign says, disconnecting from me as he scooches toward the door.

"What if there's police here?" I ask, suddenly nervous we'll get out and be surrounded by officers.

"No chance. This place is too far off the map. Too small. They'll be here tomorrow, maybe, but right now I'm sure they're focused in Hellcrest Heights," Kyler chuckles as he opens the door.

Instantly, a gust of wind and icy snowflakes fly inside, bursting across our faces. My teeth chatter, and a shiver rolls through my spine as Reign opens his door. I slide across the seat, and with Eloise and Posie next to me, we make our way out of the truck. Shutting the doors quietly, Archer moves to the front of the car. Using his key, he wedges the license plate off, and then goes to the back of the truck to repeat the process. With both of them in hand, he tucks them under his arm and turns to Reign. "Lead the way."

Reign nods, and we all trek through the snow. It's up to our shins, and each step feels like a step in place instead of a step forward.

It takes longer than ten minutes, and when I glance over my shoulder, I see a clear path of six pairs of footsteps making their way out of the woods. "Well, that'll be obvious," I grumble.

Reign glances up. "Snow is falling hard. By the time the sun is up, most of the prints will be covered."

I fucking hope so.

We end up in a small downtown area, which is less of a strip and more of five old-school buildings planted on one side of the road and a broken-down gas station on the other. The shops include a clothing store, an old bookstore, an art gallery, a coffee shop, and a jewelry store. All of which look as if they haven't been updated since the early two thousands.

"Look. There are some houses down there. I'm sure there will be a car that will be good enough to make it to the border," Reign says, pointing down the road.

"Are you sure? From the look of this place, the cars here won't be very reliable," Kyler chuckles.

Reign shrugs, and I know we don't have any other choice. We need to find something here and we need to get out of this town. Out of this country.

We see some old farmhouses up ahead, each one with their large yards.

"There," Eloise points to the house on the corner, an old-fashioned pickup truck in the driveway. It looks like it was a blue at one time which has now faded to an off-grayish color. Rust lines the bottom of the truck, and the top is packed with about seven inches of snow.

"There are literally only three seats on there," I grumble. "There's no way we will all fit in there," I clip.

"Guys," Kyler says. We all stop, fearful of his quiet voice. Turning around, our eyes land on an old-school station wagon. It would be a tight fit, but we could make it work.

"Better. In a sense," Archer says, turning around and making his way to the dingy car.

"I mean, I guess we'll all be able to fit inside, at least," I say.

Making our way across the street, we step into the yard of an old barn-style house. Archer and Kyler step around the car, using their sleeves to wipe off the piles of snow. Reign steps up to the driver's side door, and when he pulls on the handle, he meets resistance.

"Shit," he glances down at his jail uniform.

My eyes widen when I realize he has nothing to rig the car open with. "Here," I whisper, my cold fingers lifting to my hair that has fresh flakes on it. I take out one of my bobby pins, pulling it open and handing it off to him. "Try with this."

He nods, giving me a small smirk as he turns toward the door. Bending down, he bends the pin a certain way before inserting it into the lock. His eyes narrow as he moves it around, and slowly, a blanket of snow covers his back.

Click.

My eyes widen, and he pulls the pin out and opens the door. The smell of seventy-year-old smoke floats out, and the scent is somehow slightly comforting.

He slides into the driver's seat as Archer and Kyler finish wiping off the car. Bending down, he reaches under the steering wheel, pulling down the bundle of wires there. His teeth sink into his lower lip as pulls the wires apart.

I watch him in awe as he works as if he's done this a million times. For all I know, he has. But what would take me hours takes him seconds as he brushes the tips of the wires together, and the loud roar of the old station wagon rumbles to life.

"Good work, Reign," Archer says, hitting the unlock button before opening the door. Eloise, Posie, and Kyler follow suit as they all pile into the back seat together.

Kyler nods toward the passenger seat, and I walk around the front of the car as Reign closes his door. Opening up the door, I slip in as Reign leans over and blasts the heat. My entire body has become numb at this point, no more feeling left in my toes or legs. My nose constantly drips and I'm pretty sure my eyelashes have icicles on them.

Reign glances over his shoulder, glancing over at us. "Ready?"

"Get us the fuck out of here," Eloise chatters.

Reign pulls out of the snow-covered yard, leaving the headlights off as he drives slowly down the road. The car is loud, and my biggest fear is waking anyone up. This town is small enough they would probably know if something was amiss or didn't seem right.

We hold our breaths as we make our way through town, until he pulls around the other side of town and hops back onto the highway.

And off we go.

"We need to stop somewhere until tonight. We shouldn't be on the road now that the sun is up," Reign says a few hours later.

"I don't think you'll get so lucky as to find another cabin in the woods," Kyler grumbles.

Reign lifts his eyes to the rearview mirror. "Archer," he barks.

Archer watches him closely before he lets out a nod. "Got it." Pulling out his phone, he unlocks it and immediately starts working on it.

"What's going on?" I ask with narrowed eyes.

"Archer will get us a place," Reign says calmly.

I spin around, my thawed fingers gripping the fabric seat. "How can you do that without them figuring out where we are? Aren't they like watching our credit cards or something? Tracking your phone?"

Archer keeps his head tilted toward his phone as his eyes lift toward mine. "You really think I'm that stupid, baby Lake?"

I slouch in my seat, knowing better.

"No, I guess not." Turning back around, I fold my arms across my chest as glance out the window.

"My phone is untraceable, Lakyn, even to the FBI. I suppose they could crack it, but if they do, I'll get an alert and ditch it. So far, I haven't received anything. I'll use my father's card which isn't even listed in his name to reserve a VRBO. If they find out—which they won't—we'll be long gone before they do anyway."

A calmness settles over me as I smile. "Thanks, Archer."

He grumbles under his breath, but I couldn't hear a word he said.

"Really felt like going extravagant, didn't you?" Eloise chuckles from the back seat.

I look at the house in front of me, wondering how the hell Archer reserved something this nice in a matter of hours. Though, if I were to ask, I'd get another *are you stupid?* look.

Reign pulls up in front of the cabin—no, mansion—in the woods. The lights are already on, both inside and outside the home. A faint blue light shines, illuminating the morning sky. The house is three levels, with mostly glass windows and a sleek, dark exterior.

Reign reaches underneath the steering wheel, pulling on the wires until the car sputters off.

I'm surprised it's made it this far, honestly.

"Let's go check this place out," Kyler groans, stretching his arms above his head. "I'm tired of sitting in this ashtray of a car."

We all hop out of the car, gliding into the morning light as we slip into the snow. Our feet crunch loudly as we walk up the wide driveway that has been freshly plowed. Archer checks his phone as he walks up to the door. On the frame is a keypad, and he narrows his eyes on the screen of his phone as he types in the code.

The keypad slides open, revealing a small, gold key inside. Archer lifts it out, turning to the front door and shoving it into the lock. It turns seamlessly, and he opens the door, revealing expensive tiled floors. A massive, plush rug sits in front of the door, and we all step inside, slipping off our shoes and walking into the house.

The warmth of the tiled floors seeps into my damp socks, and I turn around and glance at Posie. "Heated floors."

Relief floods her face as she steps onto the tiles. "Shit, that feels so good," she groans as she walks down the hallway.

"Look at this place," Kyler smiles, running his fingers through his snowy hair.

We walk down the hallway, which opens to a large, extravagant kitchen. The counters are a crisp white marble which flow into dark gray cabinets. Stainless-steel appliances against a dark backsplash. The entire kitchen is a chef's dream.

Large, wooden beams extend across the vaulted ceilings. A large sectional couch sits in front a fireplace that's built into the stone wall which extends all the way up to the second story. Glass windows extend around the entire wall of the cabin, showing off the snow-covered trees.

Eloise and Kyler walk into the living room and plop down on the couch while Archer walks up to the fireplace and starts building a fire.

"How long are we staying here?" I ask, walking toward the kitchen. I haven't drank anything since before we broke into the jail. I open cupboard after cupboard until I find some tall, slanted glass cups. Going to the sink, I fill it up to the brim with water then swallow it down in three gulps. And repeat.

"This is what we need, not water," Posie grunts, and I glance over to the sound of clanking glass. She pulls out a bottle of wine, tilting it toward the ceiling. She smiles as she wipes her hand down the front label. "Perfect."

"Pour me a glass, Pose," Archer says, his voice echoing inside the firepit.

Posie nods, walking to the cupboard with the glasses. She presses on her tiptoes, reaching as far as she can to grab the rest of the glasses.

"Back to my question, how long are we staying here?" I ask again, grabbing one of the empty glasses and shoving it in front of Posie.

"We have this place booked until tomorrow. But I think we should leave in the middle of the night. We have to move when it's dark out," Archer says, staring out the back windows.

"How much longer until we get to the border?" Eloise groans as she puts her feet up on the coffee table in front of her. Kyler snaps them up, sliding them onto his lap. He alternates between rubbing and tickling her feet. She snarls at him, kicking him in the leg.

"Fucking stop," she groans and laughs.

"If we leave tonight, we can probably get there before the sun gets up." Reign turns toward me. "As long as we don't get caught."

I swallow, clutching my glass.

Posie points the bottle toward the hot tub. "Hot tub!" She turns to me, her face beaming. "For just a little while, can we not worry about our worlds ending? Let's fucking enjoy our night in this huge mansion and start panicking again when the sun goes down."

"I'm down," Archer says, standing up and wiping his palms against his jeans. He leans back, his hands going above his head. I can hear the joints in his back crack all the way from here.

"What do you say?" Posie says, turning toward me. "Feel like taking a dip in the hot tub?"

I shrug, glancing down. "No suit."

"Who cares?" Kyler chuckles, shoving Eloise's feet off his lap. He stands up, pulling his shirt over his head and tossing it onto Eloise. "Just go in your underwear and shit."

"And shit," Archer grumbles, pulling his own shirt over his head.

Posie smiles at me, sliding her coat down her arms and dropping it to the ground around her. She grabs the hem of her sweatshirt, pulling it over her head. A black sports bra molds to her chest, and she turns around, shrugging her pants off as she walks toward the back sliding glass door.

Unlocking it and sliding it open, a gust of cold air bursts through the door. Everyone gets up, making their way toward it.

"Can't forget the drinks," Archer grunts, swiping the bottle of wine off the counter and making his way toward the door as well.

Taking a deep breath, I set my glass down on the counter and slip my coat off. A warm arm wraps around my waist, and I jolt, glancing over my shoulder to see Reign standing there. He has a stone look on his face, and I turn in his arms, wrapping my fingers around his waist.

"Hi," I murmur, tilting my chin back to look up at him. He bends down, until his damp hair falls across his forehead and brushes against mine. It tickles against my skin, and I lean up, brushing it away from his face. "What's up?"

His head tilts down and his nose brushes against mine. "You want to go in the hot tub?" he rasps. "I don't know if I want you in there with them."

I smirk up at him. "Jealous?"

His eyes narrow slightly. "Tired of everyone looking at you all the time."

I shrug my shoulder. "Everyone knows how we are. No one is going to try anything anymore."

He grunts. "Archer will."

I shake my head. "He won't. I know he won't."

His fingers tighten around my waist. "It doesn't matter. I don't want anyone looking at you." They tighten around the hem of my shirt, and he steps back, ripping it over my head. He stares at me with narrowed, fiery eyes. "And if anyone does try to do anything, I can guarantee they won't be leaving this house."

I stand in front of him, chest heaving, skin flushed with need. I've missed Reign, with his growly exterior and his protective interior. I drop my hands to his chest, pressing my fingers against his pecs and digging my fingers against the fabric of his shirt.

"They won't," I whisper.

"They better not," he growls, grabbing his shirt behind his neck and tearing it over his head. His tattooed chest ripples with tension, the black ink swirling around his rib cage and up his neck. My mouth waters, and I press my thighs together as my fingers drop to the waistband of my pants. I shove them over my waist, kicking them over my ankles and shoving them aside.

Reign's eyes flare, darkening with need as they drag from my toes up to the top of my head.

"Hey, guys! Are you coming or what?" Kyler shouts from outside. The low rumble of the hot tub jets filter through the doorway, and I glance over my shoulder and out the window, seeing everyone sitting in the hot tub and waiting for us.

Reign steps toward me, his naked chest brushing against me. "Behave, baby Lake."

I press on my tiptoes, brushing my lips against his. "Always."

"Never," he whispers.

I smirk at him, dropping to my heels and skirting around him. The cold air wafts over my skin as I step outside, and I let out a shiver as my bare feet crunch into the snow. The soles of my feet burn, and I pick up my pace, hopping on the steps and swinging my leg over, slipping inside the hot tub.

The warmth instantly envelops my body, and my muscles relax as I slouch down until the water curls around my neck. Glancing over my shoulder, I watch as Reign walks out with another bottle of wine clutched in his grip.

He is much more relaxed as he walks through the snow, his briefs molding to his thighs. He's relaxed as he walks up the steps, swinging his leg over and into the water. He grips me with his free hand, pulling me out of the water and settling in behind me. He pulls me down onto his lap, and I settle onto his thighs, my blood warming as he wraps a strong arm around my waist.

He hands me the bottle of wine, and I pull the cork off, tilting the tip toward my lips and taking a pull.

The wine is sweet, curling around my tongue and sliding down my throat.

"This is so crazy," Eloise says, tilting her head back toward the starry sky. Her eyes settle closed, and her body moves every so often as the jets pelt into her body. "I wonder what Vienna is thinking right now."

"Probably watching the news and waiting for us to all get arrested," Posie chuckles.

"Missing Creed," Kyler says solemnly.

We all fall into a silence, each one of us letting out a heavy sigh.

"We should drink to him," Archer says after a moment, breaking the silence.

We all nod, and Archer lifts his bottle into the air.

"To Creed, probably the best man we'll ever know. He was the backbone to our crew, and I hope he realizes how much he'll be missed," he says, his voice turning raspy at the end.

He blinks, bringing the bottle to his lips and taking a few large swallows before passing it on.

Reign is stiff beside me, but he grabs the bottle, lifting it into the air. "To Creed."

"To Creed," we all say, and the bottles get passed around to each of us. We all take a drink, Creed on our minds and in our hearts. Both bottles get passed around until they are empty.

"Life is never going to go back to normal, is it?" Eloise asks after a while, snuggled up against Kyler.

He traces his wet finger along her collarbone, a contemplative look on his face. "No, I don't think so."

"Hellcrest Heights will never be the same," Archer murmurs, staring off into the woods. "We started the chain reaction over a year ago when we killed Zane. The dominos have been falling, piece by piece, ever since that day." He shakes his head, turning his gaze to mine. "I wouldn't take it back, not even a second of it."

"This is where we're meant to be," Reign mumbles from beside me, tightening his arm around my waist. I push against the ground, until my back molds against his front.

Settling my head against his shoulder, I glance up at him, a soft look on my face. "I agree."

The stars begin to fade as the sun starts to rise, until we're all intoxicated in the morning light. Posie starts dozing off, her arms folded under her face as she rests her head on the ledge of the hot tub. Archer's eyes are half lidded, his own drowsiness filling him.

He shakes his head, droplets of water flinging from his hair and through the air. "Come on, Pose, time to go to sleep," he grunts, leaning over and lifting Posie into the air.

She grumbles under her breath, though I don't even think she knows what she's saying.

"I'm going to sleep, too," Eloise yawns, shoving away from Kyler and stepping out of the hot tub. "Wake me up in a few hours. I want to shower before we go."

Kyler's silent as he follows her, and then it's just Reign and I.

He grabs me by the waist, spinning me around. My legs wrap around his waist, and I cinch them tightly behind him. The jets from the hot tub shoot against my shins. "We should go to sleep, too," I murmur, dropping my head to his shoulder. He tightens his arms around me, and I let out a deep, content sigh.

I don't let the worries of what's happened get to me, or our journey to come. All I think about is the right here, right now with Reign, and it's absolutely perfect.

"Not yet," he rasps, his fingers dancing along the edges of my sports bra. "I finally have you to myself since we left the cabin."

I brush my nose along his tattooed shoulder, inhaling the manly, dangerous scent of Reign. Sweat dances along the back of my neck, my body heating even further. His fingers curl beneath my bra, and he pulls it over my head. My naked breasts bounce and settle into the warm water.

Reign's eyes zero in on my breasts, and he licks his lips, his fingers grazing the plumpness before he pulls on my nipples. I arch them into his touch, loving the feel of the rough pads of his fingers grazing across my sensitive skin.

One of his hands curls around my rib cage, pressing between my shoulder blades. His head tilts down, his tongue swiping across my nipple. I let out a moan, and it echoes through the woods. He bares his teeth, and they scrape across my skin, dragging across my nipple before the warmth of his tongue envelops my breast as he sucks me into his mouth.

My hips rolls forward, and I grind myself against him, my eyes shuddering closed as I feel the hardness of him between my legs. He lets out a growl, the vibrations zinging into my breast and down between my thighs.

"Yes, baby Lake. How badly do you need me?"

My hands fly out, and I grab onto his hair, pulling on the damp strands, and his cock slides right between my folds. "So bad, Reign. So, so bad."

"Show me. Let me taste."

My cheeks brighten with a pink hue as I stop my grinding, leaning back slightly and dipping my hand into the water. My fingers dip between my panties, gliding between my folds as I sink two fingers deep inside myself. The walls of my pussy clench wildly, and I can feel my arousal drip across my fingers.

Sliding my fingers out of my panties, I lift them out of the water, knowing my arousal still clings to my skin.

Reign's mouth pops open, and I bite at my lower lip as I slide my pointer and middle fingers into his mouth. He clamps down on them, his tongue wrapping around my fingers. I can feel his teeth scrape against the sides of my fingers, and I let out a small whimper when he sucks on the tips.

My fingers fall from his mouth, dropping into the water.

"You taste like mine," he growls, his hands sinking into the water. He grasps onto the small strip of fabric between my legs, pulling them aside. Adjusting himself, he grabs his briefs and pulls his erection free. I glance under the water, seeing his cock hard and needy. I kneel above him, and he lines himself up, grabbing onto my hip with his free hand and sliding me down on top of him.

He fills me, completely, stretching my walls until I can feel him in my stomach. My mouth opens on a gasp, and I moan as he pulls my mouth down to his. He begins moving me, and I slide against him as we pick up a rhythm. The water splashes between us, the temperature making both of us slick with sweat. I can feel him grow harder, and the walls of my cunt clench around him, tighten and pull him in farther. I want all of him.

I want him to consume me, obliterate me, make it so it's only him and I in the world.

"I'll keep you safe, baby Lake. The world will never be able to take us down, not when we're together," he rasps, and I can feel my heart bloom, filling up every corner and crevice of my chest. My eyes fill with tears, and I don't blink them away as I allow them to track down my cheeks.

"We're it. We're forever," I whimper.

His jaw clenches, his fingers stiffening around me as he buries himself deep inside me. I let out a gasp as he moves me faster, until the water is lapping between us wildly. Hot flames singe my insides as a roaring pleasure rips through me. My head tilts back, and I let out a moan that echoes through the trees.

Bruises print into my sides as Reign lets out a roar, finding his own release.

Our fast movements slow to a lazy glide against each other. The water relaxes, small waves rolling between us. I loosen my grip on his hair, my fingers trailing down his neck and chest. He pulls me close, and I lean my head down, resting it on his shoulder.

"Are we going to make it to Canada?" I whisper softly.

His chest rises in a deep sigh as his fingers thread through my hair. "We'll get to Canada."

I press against his chest, raising my head to look at him. "Are you sure? What happens if something happens, like the police catch us at the border or something?"

He sighs, sliding his fingers and wrapping them around my hair. He tilts my face toward his, pulling me close until our eyes are locked on each other's.

Eyes narrowed, he utters, "The police, the FBI, the fucking Grim Reaper, none of them, baby Lake, are ever going to lay a finger on you, do you hear me? There will never come a time where you are put in harm's way. I will protect you, I will burn the world down, and I will make sure you never are injured in any way, ever again. Do you understand what I'm saying, Lakyn?"

I nod, feeling the pain as he tugs on my hair a little too tightly.

"I understand, Reign," I whisper.

"You're my diamond, baby. The rare gem I'll never let go. The piece of art people can't help but stop and stare at, wishing they could just glimpse at it for a second. But they can't, Lakyn, because you're mine. You always have been, and you always will be."

I nod, sucked into his words, into his raspy voice, into the way he holds me captive with the love in his tone.

"I love you, Reign," I whisper, leaning forward and pressing my lips against his.

"I love you, my baby Lake," he murmurs against my lips.

"Lakyn."

My eyes flutter open to the sound of Reign's voice. He stands above me, his clothes on, his hair damp, and freshly showered. Glancing up, I see my backpack already zipped and sitting at the foot of the bed.

"What's wrong?" I ask.

I turn my head toward the window, seeing the sun beginning to set.

Must be time to go.

He shakes his head. "Nothing's wrong, Lakyn. It's starting to get dark out. If you need to shower or whatever, do that now. We'll leave in about an hour."

I nod, rubbing my eyes with the heels of my hand. I can hear the movement of everybody getting up and gathering their things. Time to move it.

Time to run.

Again.

I twist the towel around my hair as I walk down the stairs. Everyone is sitting around the TV in the living room, watching the national news.

Which, of course, is focused on us. As always.

A newscaster is in front of the jail in Hellcrest Heights, tape surrounding the entire exterior. FBI, police, SWAT, and even the damn bomb squad is out front.

"This is Kelly Halloway from USA News, coming to you from Hellcrest Heights in Maine. We officially have a manhunt on our hands. Local and national authorities are teaming up to search the East Coast. Borders are closed and barriers are being set up as we search for fugitives Reign Whitmore and Lakyn Ashford. They are believed to be with Kyler Barlowe, Posie Gray, Eloise Sharpe, and Archer Santrell. If anyone has any information on any of these individuals, it is urged to please call the local police department or the FBI hotline on the number at the bottom of the screen. They were last seen in a black Ford F-150 but could be traveling on foot or in another vehicle. These individuals are dangerous and should not be approached in any form. Please stay indoors, be on the lookout, and contact us if you have any information."

Recent pictures of all of us show up on the screen, and I cringe, hating that it's a picture of me in a dress from one of my father's events.

Archer raises his arm, turning off the television. He sets the remote down on the coffee table in front of him before turning to us. "Well, we're maybe essentially fucked."

"We're not fucked," Reign says from beside me.

"So, what's the plan?" Kyler says from the front of the room. He's ready to go, his coat on, hood over his head. His eyes are narrowed, his lips pressed into a thin line.

Reign steps away from me, turning toward the kitchen. We all turn around to face him, watching as he steps behind the counter. He opens drawer after drawer until he finds whatever he's looking for. He pulls out a pen and old takeout menu, turning it over.

"Come here," he says, his fingers pressed around the pen. We all circle around him, watching him with confused eyes.

"This is us," he says, drawing an *X*, "and this…" He draws a large rectangle. "Is Canada." He starts scribbling lines and *X*'s and dots. "If we travel northeast, away from the highway and through the forests, we'll hit the border tonight. We need to skirt around the big cities and go unnoticed through the small towns. If we leave now, it shouldn't take us more than ten hours to reach the border. We could get there before the sun comes up."

Archer narrows his eyes, leaning down to look at the haphazard map Reign has constructed. He points to the middle. "There's always shit going down near the highway here. State patrol, police from all cities always hiding in the brush. We'll have to be careful. They might even have the highway blocked."

"We're not taking the highway," I say with narrowed eyes.

Archer swings his eyes to mine, looking irritated. "Obviously, baby Lake, and they will know that. So they'll probably be looking in the nearby towns. We just have to be careful when we go through here."

I nod.

"We good to go then?" Posie asks, zipping her coat up to her neck.

Reign nods.

"But what happens when we get to the border? Are we crossing with you guys?" Eloise asks. "Getting two over the border will be tough. Getting all six of us over seems impossible."

"We're not getting to Canada, El," Kyler says simply.

My eyes narrow as I look at him. "Wait, what do you mean?"

"We're not going to Canada, Lakyn," Archer says, his eyes focused on mine.

My face scrunches in confusion. "Wait, why?"

"Because we have to go home. We're not the ones that are on the run. We're just trying to help you get over the border, baby Lake."

"You guys are going to get in so much trouble for helping us," I whine.

Posie reaches out, grabbing onto my hand. "Worth every second."

"Shit might have been fucked with Creed, but he would've wanted us to do this for you guys," Kyler says.

Reign stiffens beside me, his arm snaking around my waist. "Thank you guys." Reign grabs the scribbled-on menu, scrunching it up and shoving it into his pocket. "Well, let's go, then."

With one last glance at the cabin-slash-mansion in front of us, we walk around the back, making our way deep into the forest. The air is cold tonight, bitter as it kisses the bare skin of my cheeks. My nose is already numb, and I keep my hands tucked into the pockets of my coat. We're silent, focusing on the noises around us, our eyes peeled on the forest surrounding us.

We walk for seconds, minutes, hours until our bodies are no longer cold, but numb.

"I can't feel my legs," I whimper, unable to stop them from moving, but feeling like I couldn't stop even if I wanted to.

Reign stops, turning around to look at me with worried eyes. "We're all cold, Lakyn. We can't stop now."

I stop anyway, feeling the lack of blood flowing through my limbs. I pull my hands out of my pockets, pressing my fingers against my thighs.

Nothing. I feel nothing.

"I can't feel my legs," I whisper. Posie stops beside me, pressing against her legs.

"I can't feel mine either. That's kind of freaky," she mumbles.

"We need to stop. Take a quick break and warm up. We won't make it all night in this cold," Kyler urges.

Reign shakes his head. "We stop, we won't make it before the sun gets up. We have to keep going."

"Reign, please," I beg. "Even just for, like, twenty minutes so I can get some feeling back in my body."

"Where are we going to stop, Lakyn? There's nothing around us but trees," Archer waves his hand around us, but he's right. We're in the middle of nowhere.

"There has to be someone around here. Something," Eloise whines.

Reign sighs, a lick of concern crossing his features. "Okay. Next time we see something, we'll stop. Ten minutes, though, and not a second longer."

I nod, swallowing through the fear that I won't be able to make it as long as it takes to find a place.

Everyone starts walking again, but Reign stays still, waiting for me to catch up to him.

"You okay, baby Lake?" he asks when I reach him.

I shake my head, reaching out and gripping onto him. My teeth begin to chatter, and I couldn't stop it even if I tried. "I'm just so cold."

His lips press into a thin line, and he grabs me, pulling me close. "We'll find something, Lake. Just hold on."

I nod, sniffling through my frozen nose. We continue walking, Reign keeping his arm around me. The numbness goes away and pain comes back, an almost burning roar that rolls through my limbs.

"Something's up here," Kyler says a short while later.

They speed up, the snow kicking behind their shoes as they race toward the building up ahead. I glance at the small cabin. Lights up ahead and a clearing in the trees show a small town up ahead, but this small cabin looks as if it's planted on the edge of town.

Next to the cabin is a small shed, but it doesn't look broken down in any form. If anything, it looks like it's almost in a better condition than the cabin itself.

"Let's go warm up in here," Archer says, pivoting toward the shed. We pick up our pace and make our way toward the door. Kyler grabs onto it, pulling it with all his strength. It barely budges. Archer rushes over, kicking the snow out of the way. Both of them grab onto the large handle. It takes them a few pulls, but eventually, the wooden door groans, and it begins pulling open.

It's a storage shed of sorts, with large equipment as well as a few bales of hay.

Archer's palm slams against the wall and the light flickers on.

"It's still cold in here," Eloise whimpers.

Archer chuckles. "Warmer than it is outside. Just relax a few, let's warm up, then keep moving."

I hobble over to a bale of hay and sit down, my legs thumping with unease. Posie comes up beside me, hopping up and sitting down. "It's cold as hell out there," she shivers.

"Here," Kyler says, walking over and shrugging off his backpack. He unzips the top, pulling out a bottle of wine from bottom of the bag. "Brought this to warm us up."

I let out a groan, scrunching my hands as I reach for it. "Why didn't you tell me about this miles ago!"

He shrugs. "I forgot about it until we got in here."

I shake my head, my frozen fingers pulling the cork out of the top. The wine is cold, and I tilt the bottle to my lips, tasting the sweet, smooth liquid as it slides down my throat. I drop it down to my thighs, and Posie instantly reaches for it, lifting it to her lips.

"How much longer?" Eloise says from the ground. Wet, cold dirt brushes onto her leggings, but she doesn't care, pure exhaustion covering her face.

Reign moves to the small window, glancing at the moon. "It's about one in the morning. We have about five hours left."

"Five hours?" Eloise whines, flopping onto her back. "I'm not going to make it."

"You can stay here and we can come back for you," Archer suggests.

Eloise barks out a laugh. "No, thank you. Something will happen and then I'll be stranded here forever with no idea how to get anywhere."

Posie hands the bottle off to Kyler, who takes his own sip.

Click, click.

The door bursts open, an old man in pajama pants and an oversized hat stares at us fiercely, a large shotgun in his hand.

Pointed right at Reign.

"I knew I heard my barn door open. Been watching the news all night, and the moment I heard sounds outside my house I just knew. I knew you no-good hoodrats were causing a stir. Now, the real question is, do I ask for a reward, or do I just send you all to them dead?"

The gun wobbles slightly as it moves to Archer. Archer lifts his hands in the air. "Whoa."

The tip of the gun glides across the room, stopping on every person for a second before it lands on me. "And you. The little murderer. All of you are murderers!" he slurs, his voice one of rage, absolutely livid and possibly a little intoxicated.

215

My eyes slide to Eloise's, who still lays on the ground. Her fingers dig into the dirt and she slowly shoves herself up. The old man notices, waving his gun toward her.

"Don't move!" he roars, spittle flying from his mouth.

Eloise freezes, her hands flying into the air. She lets out a small whimper, her eyes wide, her flushed cheeks quickly losing their color.

"Let us go and we won't hurt you," Reign growls.

The old man laughs, his belly shaking with the force. He turns to Reign, his finger sliding over the trigger. My entire body freezes, I think all of us do, and we stand in absolute fear as we wait for the trigger to be pulled.

"I think I'm the one holding the gun, not you," the old man spits.

Reign tilts his head to the side, not appearing to be as worried as the rest of us are. "I'm not scared of an old man with a rifle. I'll have your throat ripped from your neck before you even pull the trigger."

I gasp silently, shocked at the brutality in his tone.

Posie nudges me with her finger, and I glance over at her. She nods her head toward Archer. My eyes lift to his, and he has a knife behind his back, blade drawn, ready to be used.

My breath shakes out of my chest, but Kyler notices, because he also glances over at Archer.

A plan forms silently, as Reign and the old man are at a standoff. I have no idea if he knows what is about to happen, I don't think any of us do. All I know is something is about to go down, and someone isn't going to make it out alive.

"My wife is already inside, calling the police as we speak. Maybe I'll just hold you here until they come. Watch them all drag your asses off my property and to prison where you all belong!" He lifts the gun, and it ends up level to Reign's chest. "But one wrong move, and it'll be self-defense on my part. So I suggest you all stay where you are, and don't make any funny movements."

Reign stiffens, and that's when I realize he knows what's going on, and he's preparing for the wrath, the possible downfall.

No, I mouth.

I can't lose him. I refuse.

Reign reaches behind him, and my eyes widen when I see him pull out his mask. The old man's face twists in disgust as Reign slips the mask over his face.

My slasher.

As if on auto pilot, I reach behind me, my fingers slipping into my bag. I grab my own mask, pulling it over my face. It's still covered in blood from the two police officers we killed in the woods near the cabin. My own markings of death.

"You sick fuck. I should put a bullet right between your—"

I leap off the bale of hay, rushing toward the old man.

"Lakyn, no!" The roar comes from behind me, and it isn't just one voice, it's multiple voices, all of them telling me to back down.

"Stay the fuck away from him!" I scream.

The old man turns toward me, fear in his eyes before they narrow in anger. I watch in slow motion as his fingers tightens on the gun, the tip of his finger turning white as he pulls the trigger.

Bang.

"No!"

My body jolts to the side, but it's too late. Burning hot pain roars through my body as I fall to the ground, my head slamming against the dirt. Tears roll down my eyes as I drop my head to the side. I blink, staring as everyone rushes toward the old man. The gun goes off again, blowing a hole right through the roof.

Archer knocks him to the ground, pulling his knife around his back and shoving it straight into the man's gut. Kyler kicks the gun away, and Reign picks it up, holding it with both hands before shoving the tail straight into the old man's face. The man's head bounces off the ground, and he lets out a groan as he grows weak.

Reign hits him again with the gun, and again.

Whack, whack, whack.

It's a constant sound of flesh crunching beneath the weight and force of the gun. It's a brutal sound, one that would have me wincing if it didn't feel like my body was actively tearing in two.

The girls start hitting at him, and it feels like I'm watching back in time, when all of us ganged up on Zane, tearing him to pieces for hurting me.

These people in front of me, they are my blood. Forever.

Reign stands above him, twisting the gun until the muzzle is pointed right in front of the man's face. His breathing is labored, weakened as he stares at Reign with fearful eyes. His face is black and blue, no longer the angry man but a weak, tired, distorted image of his former self.

"Shouldn't have fucked with her. If I can find a way, I'll bring your ass back to life only to kill you again. And I'll keep doing that shit until the end of time."

Bang.

Blood flies through the air, hair and brain matter splatting across the ground, the walls, and across everyone's faces. The shotgun was powerful, to the point it wasn't a bullet to the head, but a bomb exploding inside of his skull.

He no longer has a head.

Only a mashing of what used to be one.

The gun drops to the ground, and footsteps pound as everyone rushes toward me. I'm lifted into Reign's arms, and he looks me over.

"I think I'm dying," I whisper, feeling as if the bullet was filled with flames and it's ripping through my body.

I'm tossed around as my clothes are removed, and Reign presses his finger against the bullet wound.

"Ow!" I bellow.

He lifts me up a moment before settling me back into his arms. "If you wouldn't have moved when you did, your entire chest would have exploded.

Luckily for you," he presses against the wound again, and I glare at him as I cry out, "it's off to the side, and it went straight through. You'll survive, Lakyn, but you're going to be in a shitload of pain for a while."

"It doesn't feel like it," I whimper.

"Archer, get me something to wrap it with."

I hear the unzipping of a bag and shuffling around. The sound of fabric ripping reaches my ears, before Reign tilts me to the side, wrapping around my shoulder and armpit area. Tears flow down my face, though Reign seems emotionless as he works to wrap my arm tightly.

"That'll have to do until we get to Canada, Lakyn. You'll be fine. It went through and out. We don't have any more time, though, and we have to go," Reign says, lifting me to a stand.

I wince, and Archer comes up to me. I pull shirt back over my arm and slide my coat back on. "It hurts, Archer."

He wraps his arm around me. "I know, baby Lake. But you'll survive, you always do."

"The police are already on their way! You best stay put!" a woman's voice screams from far away.

My eyes widen.

"We have to move," Archer barks, and we all rush at once, running to grab our bags and hauling them over our shoulders. We rush out of the barn and back into the cold. The wind has picked up, snow whipping across our faces as we make a dash back toward the winds. Heading north.

A fight against time. A fight for our lives.

CHAPTER SIXTEEN

REIGN

We don't talk.

None of us do.

We keep our faces buried in our coats as we trek through the snow. How long it's been, I don't know exactly. Though I do now the sun is due up in a couple of hours, and we should be able to make it to the border right when the sun is up.

Or right after.

Which isn't good news. Once there is daylight, we'll stick out like a sore thumb. In the dark, with each of us encased in the darkness of the forest, we are nearly invisible. Camouflaged into the night. We've heard sirens in the distance, looking for us endlessly for hours upon hours, but they've never come close enough to raise concern. They won't find us, at least not now.

Once the sun comes up, that's another story.

"I can't go anymore," Posie whimpers. "I've literally got no strength. I don't know how much longer I can be outside. Everything is numb. I can barely speak. I feel like I'm about to collapse," she gasps.

Archer turns around, his own face red with wind burn. He walks up and turns around once he's in front of her, crouching down. "Get on my shoulders, Posie. It'll be easier."

She whines as she grabs onto his shoulders, and he wraps his hands behind her thighs and lifts her into his arms. We keep moving, and I stare at Posie's face as her head lobs on his shoulder. She looks exhausted, her eyes falling closed quickly.

I glance around at the rest of them. Kyler looks angry, with his eyes narrowed, his lips pale, and his limbs looking like cement blocks as he can barely lift them out of the snow.

Then there's Eloise, who drags her feet, creating tracks of snow behind her. She keeps her face buried in her coat, only her eyes and red hair covered in white crystals.

Archer carries Posie, but I can see from the look in his eyes it's causing him a lot of effort.

Lakyn stands beside me, clutching her bad arm, dried tears covering her temples. Her face is also buried in her coat, and I can tell she's losing her steam, and I'll need to carry her soon.

This might be too difficult for all of us.

I'm beginning to wonder if we'll even make it.

"The sun is up," Lakyn rasps.

I glance up to the sky, seeing the sun beginning to peek over the horizon. It's a little bit warmer today. The wind has slowed down and the snow has stopped, though not before adding about another four inches. My socks are drenched, my shoes nothing more than a sponge at this point.

"How much farther?" Archer asks from the other side of me.

I open my mouth, my lips splitting from the cold. I can taste a light flavor of blood, and all that comes out is a sigh.

If I'm being honest, I don't know how much longer we have. The last town we passed was about an hour ago, and if my thoughts are correct, we should be arriving at the border shortly, but my mind is foggy and I almost don't realize where I am. Are we going in the right direction? I don't even know at this point.

"How much longer, Reign?" Kyler grunts, adjusting Posie on his back. Archer moved Posie over to Kyler about thirty minutes ago, but she's been so passed out she's like dead weight at this point.

I clear my throat, wondering if I should put a handful of snow in my mouth to wet my dry throat. "I don't know, hopefully only like thirty more minut—"

The slow sound of tires rolling over snow has us all freezing in place.

"What is that?" Lakyn croaks.

A search light comes on up ahead, flicking through the trees. It's off to the left, slowly moving toward us as the car continues to move. The lights illuminate the area a bit more, and that's when the black police car comes into view.

"Run, run, run." I clip the words out quietly and harshly, giving Lakyn a little shove in her good shoulder as we continue to move. Everyone picks up their pace, racing with such a quiet intensity that all you can hear is the snow flying up behind us. The light grows closer and I pick up my pace until we're literally bolting through the trees. I can feel the light as it gets near my shoulder, and my feet fling up.

"Get on the ground," I snap, flopping into the snow. Everyone drops, burrowing as far underneath the blanket of white as we possibly can.

I can feel the light above us, and I hold my breath as it slows in our direction. It stops, and my face scrunches in realization.

They found us.

"Run!" I roar, shoving against the snow. Kyler tears Posie off him, and she bolts to her feet. We all start running as the police lights flash on behind us.

"Stay together or split up? Stay together or split up!?" Archer barks.

I shake my head, my lungs constricting in agony.

I don't fucking know.

"Reign!" Lakyn cries, her breaths winded.

"Split up. Stay together. I don't fucking know!" I roar.

"Stay together. Fucking stay together!" Kyler barks.

We run straight, north, and I fucking pray that up ahead is the border. The border consists of a bridge, which I'm starting to think will be completely blocked off.

We are fucked.

"Stop where you are!" the officer in the car barks over a megaphone.

"Don't stop. Don't you dare stop," I growl.

Bang.

A gunshot rings out, and Eloise stops, her hands going above her head. Kyler reaches out, grabbing onto her and tearing her forward with him. "Not today, El," he snaps.

We weave through the trees, leaping over fallen branches and making our way toward the bridge. The car is stalled between trees, needing to stop and find its way through the maze of the forest. We continue going through the narrow areas, doing our best to escape the vehicle.

It doesn't go away, but we do make headway.

"Is that the bridge?" Eloise pants from in front of me.

I glance over her shoulder, seeing what looks like the bridge.

No, it *is* the bridge.

"That's it," I grunt.

Bang.

Another shot rings out, and we all duck, but keep running through the trees.

"You guys, there's something I didn't realize," I pant as we pick up the pace.

"I'm not going to like this," Archer snaps.

I shake my head, closing my eyes for a moment. "We won't be able to

223

cross the bridge. It'll be blocked, I already know it will. We're going to have to go under it."

"Under it, as in through the water? It'll be freezing!" Posie cries out.

"We have no choice."

Bang. Bang, bang.

We all duck again, leaping over an oversized stump on the ground. We rush as fast as we can, and finally, the bridge comes into view.

Blocked off. There are police officers blocking it from the United States side. Barriers and tape, police vehicles line the entrance.

We're screwed.

"Go this way," Archer says, and I see the slope down to the water is less steep, more of a slide.

I nod, and that's when I hear the shouting start up from the bridge.

We've been found.

"Run!" Archer shouts.

Lakyn lets out a cry beside me, clutching her arm as fear crosses her features.

This can't be over. This is not the end of our story.

Bang.

Bang, bang.

I glance over at Lakyn.

"Baby…"

She looks at me in fear, her blonde hair flowing into her face.

"I love you so much, and I'll see you on the other side." I shove her over the edge, and she lets out a yelp, her arms windmilling as she flies toward the water.

Posie lets out a scream as Archer pushes her, and he jumps right after. Kyler goes next, and then I run and leap.

Bang.

Eloise jumps, and I glance up at her, my eyes widening when I realize she didn't jump.

She was shot.

Blood pours from her chest as she lets out a cry, curling into herself with panic and pain.

I plummet under the water, shooting to the ground before swimming toward the surface. The water feels like glass shards, each one ripping through my clothes and across my skin. It's so painful I don't think I'd be able to take a breath if I had a choice. My chest constricts, my blood crying out in agony from the torture.

Eloise splashes beside me, and I grab at her, dragging her to the surface.

"What happened?" Archer barks.

Bang.

Bang.

Bang.

"Under. Now," I holler, quickly going under the water.

I can hear the shots echo from above the water, the bullets whizzing through turbulent waves. The panic is evident in the water. We swim underneath, the current quick enough to drag us slightly down the river. We continue to swim, only coming to the surface to take a break before we go back under the water. It's difficult to make it across when the current is consistently pulling us down the river. It's never-ending, and I know everyone else is struggling because I can barely find the strength to kick my legs any longer.

It's nearly impossible, and I don't know how much longer I can go on.

With a kick to the surface, I see the other side becoming closer. A glance over my shoulder shows a line of police officers on the other side, their guns drawn, but no more bullets are fired.

"We're almost there," Archer wheezes, his face twisted in distress.

"I can't do this anymore," Posie cries out.

"Don't stop now," Kyler shouts.

I glance over at Lakyn, who has a look of exhausted determination on her face. She kicks hard, and every movement of her arm has her eyes twitching in pain. She tries to mask it, but it's there.

Suddenly, a never-ending fire of bullets ring out, and my eyes widen.

"Get underwater!" Kyler shouts.

We all go under, swimming as close to the bottom as we can. We move farther down the stream, and my body becomes numb, almost an out-of-body experience from the cold.

Red starts to filter into the icy blue water, and my face scrunches as I glance at everyone's faces.

It's impossible to know. Everyone looks to be in intense pain, absolute agony.

I nod up, and we all start to swim toward the surface.

And right onto land.

I glance up to the other side, seeing no officers in sight. It looks as if we have turned a bend and are no longer in sight of the officers.

I grab onto shore, pulling me and Eloise up onto land. Glancing over at her, I expect her to be exhausted, wounded, and maybe angry with me.

She's none of those things.

She's dead.

My brow furrows, and I pull her fully out of the water, slamming her back against the ground. My fingers pinch her nose and chin as I open her mouth, leaning down to blow into it.

Then fold my hands together and shove my palms into her chest for compressions.

Breathe into her mouth.

Compressions.

Breathe into her mouth.

Compressions.

"Stop," Lakyn says from beside me, her voice cracking on the end. "She's not alive, Reign."

I scowl. "I just need to get the water out of her lungs."

I go back to compressions, when she pulls on my shoulder again. "Reign, stop."

"What?" I snap.

"Look at her chest."

I glance down and realize her entire shirt is red. Lifting my hands, I can see them covered in blood too.

She didn't drown.

She lost too much blood.

I sit back on my knees, taking a deep breath as I stare at another dead friend at my hands. I maybe wanted to toy with her once upon a time, thought of killing her, but not today.

Today I wanted her to live. And she didn't.

"Fucking hell," Archer growls, and I turn my head to his, seeing his side bleeding. Fuck, he was shot.

Posie starts crying, and Lakyn rushes over to her. "It's just a graze, Posie, you're fine."

"What happened?" I ask.

Lakyn steps to the side, and I see a gouge through Posie's cheek.

I glance over at Kyler, and he's already staring at me. "I'm good, I'm just fucking beat."

I shove myself to a stand, my body soaked and heavy, numb and in pain. We've been moving for hours, and we've finally made it.

Though that doesn't mean it's over. Border patrol can still get us, which means we need to move away from here quickly and find shelter.

Bending down, I lift Eloise up, tossing her over my shoulders. She lays limp and heavy, but I refuse to leave her on the edge of the border. She made it across, and we can't just leave her.

"Where do we go now? Can't we just relax a few minutes?" Posie pants, wiping at her cheek.

I shake my head. "We need to find somewhere to go. A motel or something. Somewhere to hide out until shit dies down and we figure out our next plan.

Posie turns to Archer. "When are we going home? I didn't think we were even coming to Canada."

"When they're shooting bullets at us, we don't really have a choice, Posie," Kyler says.

She nods, standing up with a wince. We all hobble up the hill and make our way into Canada.

"What are we looking for?" Lakyn asks from beside me.

"We'll find a motel outside of town. Border patrol will be prowling this area soon. We won't be able to stay here."

We all solemnly nod, knowing that we have a trek in front of us. Our journey isn't over.

It's just beginning.

"Here?" Archer says, his voice shaking from the cold.

I nod.

We can't go on any longer. All of us are wet, cold, and exhausted. The freezing temperatures have worked its way into our bones, and we're stiff, slow, and nearly immobile.

We have no more time to waste. We need to get inside and we need to get to warmth.

We buried Eloise in the woods about two miles back. Underneath the snow and as much dirt as we could get underneath. The ground was frozen, so there wasn't much we could do besides leave her. But we can't carry a dead body into town.

"It'll have to do," I mumble.

We all hobble toward the strip of rooms that look run-down. A large sign out front says *Vacancy* with half of the letters not even illuminated.

"I'll go in," Kyler grumbles, and we stop at the side of the building while Kyler hobbles toward the front entrance.

"I'm so cold," Lakyn whispers, shivering so bad she starts trembling in place. I want to go up to her and warm her up, but I'm just as cold, and I don't think my freezing limbs on hers would provide any comfort. I think any physical touch at this point would just cause us all pain.

"He needs to hurry up, I can't feel my body," Posie whimpers.

We all huddle up in a circle, our faces scouring the area until we hear footsteps from behind us.

Glancing over my shoulder, I see Kyler walking toward us with a small smirk on his face.

He lifts his hand, showing off an old-fashioned key.

He stops in front of a door, nodding his head toward us. We all shuffle toward the door, and Kyler shoves the key in with shaky fingers, turning it and opening the door.

A gust of warmth flows out of the door, and we all rush as quickly as we can inside.

"Oh my God," Lakyn cries, falling to her knees. "It's so warm in here."

"I'm going to turn on the shower," Kyler grumbles. "Posie, you can go first."

She lets out a cry and closes the door. I step up to it, slapping the Do Not Disturb sign on the outside of the door before closing it and latching the chain and dead bolt.

"I'm fucking going in with you, Posie," Archer grumbles, tearing his clothes off.

"Me too," Lakyn cries.

"The shower is small, but we can all fit," Kyler shouts from the bathroom moments before I hear the shower turn on.

Lakyn nods, shoving off the ground and tearing her clothes off. We all get to our underwear, our skin bright pink, our bodies seconds from suffering from severe hypothermia. I can feel my body near shutting down, and I know I need heat. I need it fast.

Walking into the bathroom, I let out a groan as the room begins filling with steam. Posie steps in first, Archer right behind her. Kyler steps in behind them, letting out a sigh.

I grab onto Lakyn's arm, careful to not brush her wrapped shoulder as I step in, helping her get in ahead of me.

The water is weak and thin, but the warmth hits us all the same. One by one we start dropping to the bottom of the tub, until it's the five of us, our limbs tangled and twisted as we fall to the ground. Posie turns off the shower, instead turning it into a bath. We let the warm water fill around us.

The moment the water hits my skin, it feels like prickling ice runs across me. It's painful, a burn that makes me want to leap from the tub. I can barely take it, and I grind my teeth in pain.

Lakyn starts sobbing in front of me. "It hurts so bad."

"It's okay," I mumble, my face twisted in pain as I lay my chin on her shoulder. "It's going to be painful until you warm up. Just let your blood get warm, baby Lake."

"I can't take it. This is fucking torture," she cries.

"Maybe we need to go to the hospital," Posie cries from the front of the bath. "This doesn't feel right. It's like my blood is frozen."

Archer reaches forward, his hands squeezing her calves. "You need to let the blood flow through, Posie. Just give it time."

"This shit sucks," Kyler groans, leaning his head forward in pain.

We fall into a silence, and Posie turns off the water once it's filled up to the brim, sloshing over the sides with each of our movements. The mirror is completely blurred, and the steam fills the room, thickening the air.

"We made it," Lakyn says after a while, and I know our pain is gone. My limbs no longer scream, but occasionally ache.

"We did make it," I rasp, my fingers trailing down the back of her neck. We might not be out of the woods, but I do think the worst is over. We need to find a place to go, a place to live, and figure out what the rest of their plans are, but we'll figure it out. In time, we'll figure it out.

"I'm so tired. I think I'm going to sleep for a fucking year," Posie groans from the front of the tub.

"One king-sized bed. Looks like we all have to fucking cuddle tonight," Kyler jokes quietly.

My lips flatten at the thought of anyone else snuggling beside her. But I bat the thought away, because it doesn't fucking matter anymore.

Lakyn is mine, and now she'll be mine forever.

Once the water is cold, and we've emptied and refilled the water enough times to where there is no hot water left, we all stand and use the small towels hanging on the rod to dry our bodies. The moment my skin hits the fresh air, goosebumps pop along my skin.

Lakyn sits down on the edge of the mattress, her shoulders slumping over slightly. "I'm never going to see my mom again."

I walk up to her, grabbing her chin and tilting it toward me. "Yes, you will. Once shit is settled down, you will. It might be a month, it might be a year. We'll never know. But, we have to keep moving. If you want to see your mom again, we have to."

She stares at me, her eyes glossy with tears before she gives me a simple nod.

I nod back at her. "I'm going to meet the guy, grab a rental car, and I'll come back to get you guys."

Lakyn shoots to a stand, her eyes widening in concern. "You're leaving? Can I go with you?"

I shake my head, grabbing onto her shoulders, and give her a squeeze. My eyes go over her shoulder to Archer, and he gives me a nod as he walks up to her, wrapping his arm around her waist. "No, Lakyn. You can't. You stand out like a fucking Christmas light."

She frowns at me, her lips pinching in irritation. "What the hell does that mean?"

I roll my eyes as I back up toward the door. "It means the world is looking for you, and you're too pretty not to be noticed."

A pink hue covers her cheeks as Archer pulls her toward the bed. He shoves her down, laying his head back on the pillow. He pulls her legs up, laying them over his lap as he grabs onto her bare feet.

I ignore the possessive side of me that wants to rip his hands from his wrists. "I'll be back."

"We'll be here," Archer grumbles, tightening his grip on Lakyn's feet when she attempts to yank them away.

Spinning on my feet, I walk out of the small motel room, out into the blistering cold.

Our new home.

I keep my head tilted toward the ground as I slip out of the cab, slipping the driver some money before making my way to the apartment building.

Last stop.

I was able to find a phone and called one of the family business associates. There is always a plan in place for the Whitmores, and all I needed to do was say the word, and everything falls into place.

New identity, check.

New ID, check.

New bank account, check.

I'm waiting for Lakyn's new name to be processed, a new ID to be made, and then we'll be free.

Ryker and Lyana Jarvis.

Married.

As it fucking should be.

After I stopped at the back alleyway to get my new ID and information from the weirdo who processes all the illegal shit, I hopped back in the cab to meet with the landlord.

Right on time.

I pull open the cold metal door, the scent of air fresheners and polished leather reaches my senses. I walk in, instantly finding a middle-aged man in a suit standing near the crackling fireplace as he scrolls through his phone.

The sound of my wet shoes squeaking on the tile reaches my ears, and the landlord must notice, too, because he lifts his head, appraising me quickly as he shoves his phone into his pocket.

"Mr. Jarvis?" he clips.

I nod, running my fingers through my damp hair, my other hand extending toward him. "Hey."

"You find the place okay?" He glances down at me again, and I can already tell he doesn't think I have enough money as I wear the Walmart gray sweatsuit.

How wrong he is.

"No problems at all." I glance around the lobby. "Nice place."

Everything is in a white and cream marble, from the floors to the countertops. The fireplace is a dark gray, grand in the center of the lobby. The walls have modern ceramic art placed sporadically, and in front of the fireplace is a cream-colored sofa and chair set, both of which look never used a day.

"Yeah. I rent out about five units in this building. All of which have been here for years. The latest tenant got married and were expecting a child, so they decided to upgrade to a single-family home. The unit hasn't been vacant long, so you're lucky you found it when you did. These places go quick."

I hum under my breath, not really caring for the entire story.

He rocks back and forth on his heels before clearing his throat. "Shall we go take a look?"

I dig my hand into my pockets. "Sure. I don't believe I'll be changing my mind, though. This unit looks perfect and it's just what I'm looking for."

His brow furrows slightly, and he tilts his head toward the elevator. "All right. We can still have a look and go through paperwork and such in the unit."

I nod, and follow behind him as he heads toward the elevator. It's all new, this entire place and everything in it feels almost untouched. The doors glide open silently, and a low hum of piano music filters from the speakers in the ceiling. The landlord presses floor five, and I step into the corner as the doors shut.

We glide up slowly, and I watch the doors, hating the fact that he could pop on the news and I'm sure he'd instantly find my face on the front page.

"Where you moving from?" he asks as the doors slide open.

I stick my hand into my pocket, gripping the knife I took from Kyler this morning. I hold on to it tightly, wrapping my fingers around the handle as I get ready to open the blade.

Asking about personal questions is suspicious, and I don't like it.

"Toronto," I say simply.

He nods, as if there's nothing to it. We step out of the elevator, and the landlord takes a left, heading down the quiet hallway. "And what brings you over this way? Quite a hop and a skip across the country."

I clear my throat, wishing I could slice his throat so he'd stop talking. "Work."

He nods, letting out a little hum as he stops at apartment five hundred two. Shoving the key in, he twists it and turns the nob. "What do you do for work?"

I swallow over the irritation. Enough with the fucking questions.

"I'm in finance." I guess it's legit. I do things for money. Nothing is legal, but I still work for money. Whatever.

He glances at me, a smirk on his face. "Good. A stable career. I like that in a tenant."

I nod, saying nothing.

The apartment is bright. Brighter than I particularly like, but I'm sure Lakyn would enjoy it. She likes brightness, openness. All of what this place is. An open-floor plan. Right from when I open up the front door, you can see the living room, dining, and kitchen. All elegant, light versus dark colors. Dark cabinetry against light counters. Large windows that overlook the city.

It's nice.

"I'll take it," I say from the front door.

He pauses near the kitchen, shoving his hands into his pockets as he spins on his expensive leather shoes. He turns around, barking out a chuckle. "Are you sure? You've barely had a look."

"I'm sure. It's perfect. What do I need to sign?"

Pulling up in front of the motel, my shoulders relax slightly when I see it not flooded with police officers.

I step out of the Jeep Wagoneer, stepping toward our room. Before I can even knock I can hear the chain release and the door swings open, Lakyn standing there.

She reaches out, grabbing me by the arm and pulling me inside. She slams the door closed, and as the wood rattles against the frame, she throws her arms around me, pulling me tight against her.

"Fuck, why did you take so long?" she cries out. Her arms go to my chest, and she shoves me against the door. "I thought something happened to you!" she shouts.

I slam my palm against her lips, shutting her up. "Quiet down, Lakyn," I growl. My hand goes to my pocket, and I dig out the key. My finger goes through the loop on the chain, and I let it rock back and forth in front of her eyes.

Her eyes widen slightly, and she reaches out, grabbing onto the two small keys. "You got it?"

I smile at her. "I got it."

"Does this mean we can get out of here? This place smells like burnt carpet," Posie grumbles from on top of the bed.

I glance around the small motel room, nothing more than a box the five of us have been caged in. Just another stop in our journey.

"Yeah, Posie. Time to go."

"Shut the fuck up," Posie whispers as she walks inside the new apartment. She drops her bag, toeing off her shoes as she walks toward the kitchen.

"Damn, this place is nice." Kyler doesn't even bother taking off his shoes as he walks straight inside.

"Wow," Lakyn whispers, stepping up beside me. "This place is amazing, Reign. Good pick."

I nod, taking her backpack and setting it up against the wall. My fingers slide around her jaw, and I give her a nudge until she's in front of me. Her cheeks and nose are a bit rosy, her skin cold to touch, yet I can feel the warmth in her blood. So much has happened over the course of the last few days, and she has been strong throughout all of it, never saying she can't do it anymore. Never giving up.

She's strong. Stronger than I ever realized.

"I'm proud of you, baby Lake," I whisper.

The corner of her mouth lifts slightly. "Why is that?"

"Because even if you want to give up, you never do. You've walked through snow and blood, pain, cold, sweat, and tears, and you're standing here with a fucking smile on your face, Lakyn. Remember when I called you that diamond?" She nods softly. "You're more than a diamond, baby. You're more than a fucking queen. You're more than a warrior, or a murderer. You're mine, Lakyn, and I'm going to spend the rest of my life showing you how damn amazing you are."

A tear leaks from her eye, tracking down her cheek. I lift it once it reaches her chin, swiping it away.

"Don't cry, baby Lake. This is only the beginning of our story."

Slowly, her face brightens. It brightens the entire room, and all I can see is her beauty, and the madness that brims beneath.

And I know our future will be filled with magnificence. And absolute mayhem.

CHAPTER SEVENTEEN

LAKYN

Three Months Later

"It should be on the news. Go turn it on," Reign grumbles from the kitchen, loading his plate with tacos.

I frown at him, setting my glass of wine down on the island before walking to the living room. "Did Pete say it was going to be on the five o'clock news?"

Reign drops a pile of salsa on the corner of his plate. "Yep."

I nod, anxiousness and nerves filling me as I walk to the living room. Grabbing the remote from the end table, I turn on the large flat screen attached to the wall. Flipping to the national news station, I instantly fall back on the couch when I see our old pictures, along with a picture of two people walking down the street.

It's us, but it's not us.

"A tip of the long-gone cold case of Lakyn Ashford and Reign Whitmore has been heating up. There have been multiple sightings of the couple in London. They have yet to be apprehended, though local officials are looking for them. It was once thought that they had found refuge in Canada, but they quickly went cold, almost as if they dropped off the face of the earth. This is the first sighting since they were last seen crossing the border. If anyone has any information of their whereabouts, please contact the number for the tip line at the bottom of the screen." The newscaster continues to drone on as I stare at the pictures of a couple that looks nearly identical to Reign and I. A double, is what Pete, Reign's right-hand man, set up. They are a decoy, in hopes we can finally begin living our lives here in Canada.

It's been three months, and we've done nothing but stayed holed up in this apartment. We haven't left, except for a few rare times, but we never go alone. It's either myself with Pete, or Reign with Pete.

Pete is someone who used to work for the Whitmores. He's one of the few that stayed on as the Whitmores' business was passed down to Reign. Though the Whitmores are no more, and neither is the family business—or any of the money.

It's all been transferred, secretly, into a new business, under a new name.

Ryker Jarvis.

Ryker, aka Reign, has taken over his father's business and made it flourish. He's a ten times better businessman than his father ever was. He works a lot, though all of it is from the apartment we're in.

It's been stressful, but we've made it work.

And I hope today is the day we can finally move on with our lives.

"Arch is calling me," he grumbles, lifting the phone to his ear. "Yeah. Hold on." He puts his phone on speaker, setting it on the counter.

"Lakyn!" Archer laughs through the speaker. "You're free, baby Lake!"

I laugh, walking toward the kitchen in my sweats and Reign's shirt. "I mean, I wouldn't say fully, but I guess this is a start."

"Don't be such a pessimist. You're growing grumbly holed up in your castle. Get the fuck out there and enjoy your life in Canada, and we'll see you tomorrow."

My eyes bug out. "What?" I scream.

Archer, Kyler, and Posie stayed here for an entire month before they made their way back to the United States. At first I wasn't able to get ahold of anyone, and we were—I guess *I* was—freaking out that they were apprehended or that the police were on their way to get us. Anything. My thoughts were running wild and they were all negative possibilities.

Though they never were. And it took a week for Posie to reach out to me. They were grilled and held at the police station in Hellcrest Heights for forty-eight hours before they were released, and then they were held by the FBI and border patrol were involved, and it was absolute madness.

Archer's father fixed it, as he always does. They said they didn't know where we were. That we vanished in the middle of the night staying at some place in the middle of the woods; that they haven't been able to reach us since. Archer's father went with that story, paid some people off, and the three of them were off the hook.

The focus came back on us, and we were two fugitives on the loose. I've watched from outside our large windows as the police presence grew from sporadic to constant. It's slowly died down as the weeks went on, and now it feels back to normal.

And I hope it stays that way.

I haven't been able to speak to Posie or Archer much, as they have kept their distance through this entire time, not wanting to raise any flags anywhere to alert the authorities they are still in contact with us.

Though now, Archer saying they are coming to see us? How is that possible?

"What do you mean, you'll see me tomorrow?"

He chuckles, the low rasp that I haven't heard in so long. I miss him. It doesn't matter what I have with Reign. Archer is my… Archer.

"It means we're packing up tonight and making our way to see you. We should be there in the morning."

"We?" I squeak.

"Me, Kyler, Posie, and Vienna. All of us."

My heart clenches. Vienna is coming?

"Time heals all wounds, baby Lake. Put the past to rest," he growls.

My brow furrows. "Has she?"

He takes a deep breath, crackling through the speaker of the phone. "Yes, for the most part. Yes."

My eyes water, and a small smile lifts at my lips. "I can't wait."

"Reign," Kyler barks in the background. "You watch the news?"

Reign picks up the phone, taking it off speaker. "Yeah, we did."

I can hear Kyler's goofy voice muffled as he talks to Reign. I zone them out, walking back to the living room and sitting on the coffee table as I watch them continuously post pictures of us from back in Hellcrest Heights, side by side with the pictures of the people in London. It goes on and on, for so long I lose track of time altogether.

I stand out on the balcony as the sun sets, the reddish orange glow lowering over the horizon. My black hair flows over my shoulders, a color I'm still getting used to. Reign suggested we change our looks, which is an absolute contrast from my previous light blonde hair.

Reign's longer hair has been shaved, cut close to his scalp. His cheekbones are sharper, his jawline more pronounced. He looks vicious and lethal now, most of the time with his jaw clenched and pouty lips, making me want to fall to my knees.

I run my fingers through my silky black hair as I watch the small cars below run about their lives. The vibe is different here than in the United States. Almost like it's a little freer here, people seem more at ease.

I let out a breath as the sliding glass door opens, moments before I feel arms sliding around my waist. His chin rests on my shoulder, and I can feel his chest deflate as he exhales behind me.

"You look beautiful standing out here," he rasps, his voice soft.

I smile softly, nuzzling into him. Reign isn't a soft man unless it comes to me. When he's working, it usually involves barking at people. Sometimes it involves taking a life, though he hasn't since we arrived here. As of right now, he's having other people take care of the deed, though I know he wants to get back to it. And he will.

I want to go with him.

I turn in his arms, until the base of my spine hits the railing. I arch into him, feeling his hands as they clench around my waist.

"You want blood. I can feel it in the way you hold me," I whisper.

His eyes darken, flaring with a need as his fingers bruise my skin. It's nearly painful, but it's a pain I enjoy, and I want nothing more than to allow him to bruise every inch of my skin.

"Maybe I just want yours," he growls.

His head dips down, his teeth scraping against the exposed skin on my neck.

"When are you going back out?" I ask, knowing since he came out of prison a few years back, he's regularly taken down people for odd jobs. Him being the slasher of Hellcrest Heights only accentuated his thirst.

"Whenever I feel like it," he murmurs, his lips traveling from my neck up to my jawline.

I take a deep breath. "Can I come with you?"

His lips pause, and he pulls back, looking at me with narrowed eyes. "What are you trying to say?"

I lick at my lips, staring at him a moment while I find my courage. "I want to do it with you. Whatever it is you do."

Pause.

"Why?"

My hands go out, and I trail them along his sweatshirt strings. I pull on them, bunching up his hoodie behind his neck. "Because I like killing with you."

His nostrils flare, as if he can smell the need in the air. I can taste it as the energy changes, from a smooth wine to a fiery elixir, one that causes the air to vibrate between us. His hands circle around my waist, pulling me tightly against him.

"Watching you tear someone apart is one of the most beautiful things I've ever seen," he growls in my ear.

His hands go to the waistband of my leggings, and he slowly lowers them over my hips. My eyes widen as I glance over my shoulder, worried of being seen by the world. Reign doesn't stop his motions, though, only continuing to lower them down my thighs.

"Reign…" I whisper.

He chuckles. "Let the world watch if they want to, baby Lake. Make them wish for what they'll never have."

"And what's that?" I whisper.

"You." The word floats away in the breeze as he dips his lips, securing them against mine. I whimper into his mouth as he shoves my leggings the rest of the way down my thighs. I kick them free as his fingers go to the zipper of my sweatshirt. He lowers it slowly, down my midsection until the two sides separate on each side of my rib cage. My sports bra is the only thing covering me. His hand brushes the black fabric, and I watch as my nipples peak against it.

"I want you," I whisper.

His jaw clenches, sharpening his cheekbones as he reaches down, his hands snaking behind my thighs. He lifts me into his arms, holding me tightly as he presses me back against the railing. My legs snake around his waist, cinching tightly at the base of his back. I can feel the hardness of him between the apex of my thighs, throbbing with need to burrow inside of me.

His lips go to my jaw, and he trails them along to my chin. His teeth come out, and sink into my chin, moving up my jaw, each press of his teeth against my sensitive skin making my blood turn to fire. His fingers slide down, grabbing onto my panties and pulling tightly. The tear is quick, loud as it echoes through the air. He leans over, dropping them over the edge of the balcony. My mouth opens in shock, and he chuckles, deep in his chest.

I can feel the vibrations against my own, and I press against him further, loving the warmth of him as it seeps into me.

The roughness of his fingers press into me, sliding around the curve of my ass and slipping between my folds. My eyes shutter closed as he sinks his fingers in deep. I can feel the wetness of my sex soak his fingers, wetting my inner thighs.

"You're so wet, baby Lake," he rasps.

I let out a whimper, dropping my face to his shoulder as my breath comes out in heavy pants. He lifts me higher, setting me on the ledge of the balcony. I startle, gripping onto him for dear life.

"Reign!" I shout, "Get me down!"

He chuckles, crouching down below me. "Hold on to me, baby Lake. Hold on for dear life." He bends down, his face burrowing between my thighs. His tongue swipes out, sliding between my folds. I grip onto his shoulders, wrapping my ankles around the rods of the balcony as Reign feasts below me.

He hums against me, and I jolt in his arms. His hands go to my waist, and he holds me steady as he brings his lips up to my clit, sucking and flicking his tongue against my swollen bud. It doesn't take long, as it never does when it comes to Reign. I let out a scream, and I'm pretty sure I hear my neighbor shut their outside windows.

In an instant, Reign has me off the balcony ledge, holding me tightly as he pulls his joggers down, revealing his straining erection. I begin moving to my knees, but he holds me tightly, gripping my thigh and raising it, spreading my legs.

He grabs his erection with his other hand, slapping it against my pulsing clit. His eyes drop to mine, his eyelids hooded, his eyes smoldering as he watches me. I become enraptured in his gaze, unable to blink, unable to breathe. All I can do is be suctioned into his gaze. I never want this moment to end.

He sinks in deep, and I gasp in a breath as he stretches me, pulsing against my slick walls. He grinds his hips against mine, hitting the spot inside of me that has my knees begin to quake.

"I'm going to fuck you until the world ends, Lakyn," he rasps.

I tilt my head back, staring at the stars above me, breathing in the love, in the electricity between us.

"Look at me, Lakyn," he growls, pulling out and sinking back in. My back hits the balcony, and I let out a moan as I drop my eyes to his.

"Watch me as I break you to pieces, baby Lake. Then continue watching me as I piece you together again."

He speeds up his thrusts, our eyes locked together in an unbreakable bond. Our skin slaps together, growing slick in the night air. My tongue darts out, swiping across my lower lip as I watch him with hooded eyes.

"Come here," he murmurs.

And I do, leaning forward and sinking my lips against his. His tongue slips out, sliding between my lips and gliding against my tongue. Our kiss is full of passion, electrified, and it makes my blood warm, until I'm on fire, a roar between us, unable to be extinguished.

So I burst.

Falling apart in his arms, my orgasm locks me in a hold as Reign grips me, his hips speeding up until he's pounding into me so hard a scream breaks from my throat, the balcony railing rattling behind us.

He lets out a growl, his body coiling tight as he reaches his own release, his limbs shaking as he grips me tightly.

I drop my face to his chest, inhaling him as I slowly come down, falling back to reality. Reign lifts me into his arms, holding me against him as he walks us back inside. I keep my eyes closed, my face against his chest as he maneuvers us through our apartment.

Lowering me from his arms, I can feel our soft comforter curl around me, and then the mattress dips as he lays next to me. His warm arms curl around my waist, and I snuggle into him. His fingers comb the dark hair from my face, and my eyes settle closed as his lips press against my skin.

"We're here, motherfuckers!" the voice shouts down the hall, and I bolt up until I'm sitting. Reign lets out a groan, rolling over in bed as I pull the sheets up over my naked form.

A stampede of feet rumble down the hall before our bedroom door is opened, and there they are.

My best friends.

Archer, Kyler, Posie, and Vienna all stand in the doorway, watching us with bright smiles.

"I'm not waiting until you get dressed. I don't even give a fuck," Posie chuckles, racing around Vienna and running toward the bed. She bounces on the bottom, and I jolt a bit as she crawls toward me. I open my arms, keeping the sheet under my armpits as she falls into my embrace.

"I didn't think you guys were arriving for hours," Reign grumbles into his pillow.

"Change of plans. We left sooner. Couldn't wait any longer to see my baby Lake," Archer says as he walks up to me. Posie crawls to the side, and I grip the sheets tightly as I move to my knees. Archer walks up to the side of the bed, wrapping his arms around me as he pulls me against him. His fingers go to my hair, and he messes it up as he tilts my head back "Missed you, Lakyn."

I curl forward, hugging him tightly. "Missed you too, Arch."

"Get fucking dressed, Lakyn," Reign growls, sliding out of the bed. He walks to the dresser, pulling it open and grabbing one of his shirts, tossing it against my back.

I roll my eyes as I grab the soft white fabric, pulling it on as discreetly as I can.

"Lakyn," Vienna's soft voice has me pulling back from Archer, glancing over at her.

"Hi, V," I whisper. I haven't seen her since she was so mad at me, though we have talked a few times. Water is under the bridge—for the most part, anyway—but it is still painful. To know I was a part of her lover's death.

She lifts her hand, a small box in her palm. "We saw your mom before we left. She wanted me to give you this and said she'll see you next month."

I nod, knowing of her upcoming trip. I've only talked to her twice since I left. The first time she was angry, hurt, absolutely devastated over what had happened. The second time she was much more calm, wanting to come see me on my new life adventure.

I take the small box from her, feeling the dark blue velvet against my fingers. Lifting the lid, a soft smile lifts my lips when I see a crystal-blue diamond wrapped around a delicate silver chain. Turning it over, I see a small script in the center.

Love you from afar, Mom

I blink away my oncoming tears, shutting the lid, squeezing it tightly in my palm.

I miss her.

"Lakyn," Kyler mumbles, leaning over to kiss me on top of my head. "It's different without you guys there."

I glance up at him. "You guys can always move up here."

Posie laughs. "We belong in Hellcrest Heights, Lakyn. You know this."

I nod. I know. I used to belong there, too. But not anymore.

"We only have a few days. So let's do all the shit we couldn't do last time when we were here, locked up in this jail," Kyler says.

"I'll get the drinks!" Vienna shouts, running out of the bedroom.

"Fuck, Vienna, the sun is barely fucking out yet!" Reign snaps.

She laughs, walking back with two bottles in her hand. "We have to take advantage of our time together."

I glance at Reign just as he looks over at me. I smirk at him, and he shakes his head, reaching out and grabbing onto my arm. He pulls me toward him, wrapping his arms around my shoulders. Settling his chin on top of my head, he lets out a sigh, though I know he's happy to see them.

I am. I missed them. So fucking much.

I glance at each of my friends, my heart warming. Even with us across countries from each other, these are my people. My family. The people who have killed with me, some who have died for me, and others who bleed for me.

All of them are my ride or die, and I know nothing will ever break that bond.

Nothing.

EPILOGUE
LAKYN

One Year Later

"I'm going first," I whisper.

I can feel Reign tense beside me. Glancing over at him, all I can see is his white mask, dented and dinged over the years. Our eyes connect through the small holes in our masks, and I watch his narrowed ones, glaring at me.

"This isn't your job, Lakyn. Let me handle it," he growls lowly.

My jaw clenches behind my mask. "It's always your job. It's never not going to be your job. But maybe I could sometimes take the lead? Why else am I with you? For the joy ride?"

He growls low in his throat. "You wanted to come with."

"Because I want to be a part of this!" I whisper-shout.

"You are." He leans closer to me, until our masks are almost touching. "You come with me almost every time. I let you fucking help kill the person. What else do you want from me?"

I take a deep breath. We're getting nowhere. He's hardheaded; I'm hardheaded. He wants to be in control, wanting to spoon-feed me bits while protecting me. I don't need him to protect me. I don't want him to stand in front of me.

I want him to stand beside me.

"I want to take the lead. Sometimes, not all the time, I want to take the fucking lead. You want me here? Then let me do it, just once. Maybe twice. Give me a little something to let me feel like I'm not your backup but instead your damn partner."

We stare at each other, hunched between the bushes, arguing at possibly the worst time ever. Ready to go in for a kill but instead we're quarreling about bullshit.

Sounds like us.

He's silent for many seconds until he shifts in place. "Fine. You want to take the lead? Grab your knife, baby Lake. But you make one wrong move, and you're fucking grounded from this shit."

I roll my eyes behind my mask.

Yeah. Try me.

Instead of barking at him like I want to, I lean forward, knocking my forehead against his. "I love you, Reign," I sigh.

His gloved hand reaches out, and he squeezes the back of my neck. "I love you, too, baby. Now, let's get this shit over with. We're five minutes over time."

I nod, knowing it's the truth.

His killings have been strictly work related. He doesn't kill just for the thrill, though there have been times we've slipped back in those old characters and spilt blood just for the hell of it. Though these jobs are part of his business. A hitman of sorts. Random jobs that he fills. He's the one who's at the top, yet he likes to get his hands dirty.

And so do I.

Reaching around behind my pants, I grab my knife, shifting to a stand and making my way around the bushes. The small one-story rambler in front of us is home to a man in his early forties. From what Reign said on the way over here, he works for a politician in Maine. He ended up sleeping with his wife, and it was immediately figured out.

And the call came to Reign. He doesn't ask questions, doesn't determine the morals. It's the job, and Reign delivers his part.

I walk around the back of the house, and I can hear Reign walking quietly and closely behind me. Word is that the back door is typically locked, though there's a gnome off to the side, and underneath that is a key to get inside the home. There is no security system, and apparently this guy goes to bed really early. So most likely, he's already asleep.

I smirk behind my mask when I see the gnome. Walking over to it, I lift it with my glove-covered fingers and see the dirty, damp key laying against the pavement. Lifting it up, I walk to the front door, inserting it inside the lock and turning it.

The door creaks as it opens, and the smell of garlic bread reaches my nose. We walk through the small galley kitchen, the old, tiled floor stained, chipped, and worn from years of use. The lights are off in the house, but the sound of a girl moaning can be heard from down the hall.

I let out a sigh, annoyed already that this man is a pervert. I better not walk in on him beating his meat, or I might get fucking sick all over his bed.

Walking quietly down the hall, I pass the bathroom and a small office before eventually making it to the bedroom at the end of the hall. The door is cracked open, enough where I can see the flickering lights of the TV reflecting off the walls.

I press the dip of my knife into the wooden door, slowly pushing it open. The bed comes into view, the man I'm looking for—Paul Deline—laying in his bed. The remote is still in his hand, resting on his chest. My eyes cast to the TV, seeing a big-breasted woman bouncing wildly on top of a man.

My face scrunches up in disgust. Walking into his room, I step up to the bed, walking around until I'm standing beside him.

He sleeps quietly, not making a sound. His brown hair is cropped closely to his face, and he hasn't shaved in a few days according to the scruff covering his jawline.

I raise the knife up, almost sad that this is going to be such an easy kill.

Reign stands on the other side of the bed, watching me closely, and I can feel the air begin rippling with tension.

Suddenly, Paul jolts, his free hand reaching out with a hunting knife. He jackknifes off the bed, swiping toward me.

Reign lets out a shout, leaping on the bed and ripping the knife from his hold as if there isn't a fight at all. I react quickly, clutching my knife as I lean over him.

"Sick fuck," I growl, shoving the knife down into his chest. He lets out a groan, and Reign releases him as I pull the knife out. I shove it back in, this time into his stomach area. He jolts, leaning forward, though the pain is too great and he falls back onto his back.

I pull the knife out, bringing a spray of blood with it. The man gurgles beneath me, suffering and in pain, begging for an ounce of relief. I let out a small chuckle as I bring the knife up to his neck.

"No," I growl, dragging the sharp knife from ear to ear.

Dark red crimson pours from his throat, soaking his chest and the sheets beneath him. He chokes, groaning until it becomes a whisper, and slowly, the movements stop, and I let out a breath as I pull my knife away.

The exhilaration that runs through my blood makes my limbs shake. I can feel the hum in my bones and I feel so fucking alive. It's unlike anything, the feeling of life being at your fingertips, of releasing the rage in your soul and taking the lives of those that no longer deserve to live.

Nothing is like it. Nothing is like this.

I'm ripped to the side, Reign grabbing me by the arms and pulling me to the wall. He slams me against it roughly. I stare into his brown eyes and I can see the lust there, the absolute fire in his eyes as he watches me.

"You're fucking beautiful when you take a life, Lakyn. You are so fucking magnificent." His voice changer is on, and it brings back so many memories. My legs quake, and he can tell, because he lets out a monotone chuckle.

His hand grabs my wrists, hauling them above my head. He slams them against the wall, the bloody blade clamoring against the wall.

"I could watch you kill for the rest of my life and it would never be enough. It's a high I can't walk away from."

His free hand goes to my black leggings, and he tears them over my legs. I move quickly, knowing how turned on he gets when he sees me covered in blood, when he watches the madness take over my bones.

I allow my leggings to go to my ankles, and he spins me around, his gloved hand gripping my backside. He squeezes tight, and I let out a whimper as I hear him shove his pants down behind me.

It's only a moment later that I feel the warmth of his cock nudging between my cheeks. My skin pops with goosebumps as he slips inside, and I let out a groan, tipping my head back as he fills me.

His gloved hands grip my hips as he fucks me wildly. This isn't passionate, this isn't making love.

This is angry, madness, the beast inside of him that comes out when he wears his mask, when there's blood in the air. The moans rip from my throat, my fingers gripping the knife as the blood drips down, coating my wrists and trailing down my arms.

Reign lets out a growl, and I bite my lip at the possessiveness in the way he holds me. It becomes too much, the way he brutally takes what he needs is so consuming I can barely breathe.

"Come, Lakyn," he growls, growing inside of me until I feel a pinch of pain. My wrists bruise from his strong grip, and all the warmth pools to my thighs, electricity shooting through my limbs as my orgasm rips through me. Wildly, untamed, obliterating every inch of my soul.

Reign releases my wrists, his fingers going to my chin. He turns my face to his, and my eyes connect with his through the mask, watching the array of emotions flowing through them.

"Mine, baby Lake. Forever."

Through the mayhem we've created over the years, it feels almost impossible that we're here now, but we are, and there isn't anywhere else I'd rather be.

"Yours. Forever."

ACKNOWLEDGEMENTS

Those who know what I've been through since October of last
year, I want to dedicate this book to you for keeping me on my feet
and getting me through this. I don't think I'd be here without you,
and you helped me in getting to the finish line of this book.
One day at a time, one step at a time, and here I am.
Thank you all for your support.

BOOKS BY A.R. BRECK

HELLCREST HEIGHTS

Slashers & Secrets

BLACKRIDGE PREP

Twisted Dares

Deceitful Truths

Violent Promises

GROVE HIGH SERIES

Reapers and Roses

Thorn in the Dark

THE GROVE SERIES

The Mute and the Menace

Lost in the Silence

THE SEVEN MC SERIES

Chaotic Wrath

Reckless Envy

THE FOUR NIGHTMARES OF CASTLE POINTE

Wicked Little Sins

Wicked Little Games

STANDALONES

BLISS

Where the Mountains Meet the Sea

ABOUT THE AUTHOR

A.R. Breck lives in Minnesota with her two children and two dogs. Socially introverted and slightly sarcastic, she enjoys watching horror movies and reading romance novels. When she isn't writing, she enjoys road tripping around the country. She writes primarily dark and edgy romance books with a touch of suspense. Follow her on social media to stay up to date on new and upcoming releases!

Printed in Great Britain
by Amazon

47008078R00152